L U C K

LUCK

A NOVEL

ERIC MARTIN

W. W. NORTON & COMPANY

NEW YORK • LONDON

For information about permission to reproduce selections from this book,
write to Permissions, W. W. Norton & Company, Inc.,
500 Fifth Avenue, New York, NY 10110

The text of this book is composed in Sabon
with the display set in Copperplate Gothic
Composition by Thomas Ernst
Manufacturing by Courier Companies, Inc.
Book design by JAM Design

Library of Congress Cataloging-in-Publication Data

Martin, Eric, 1969–
Luck : a novel / Eric Martin.
p.   cm.
ISBN 0-393-04912-4
1. Migrant agricultural laborers—Fiction. 2. Children of migrant laborers—
Fiction. 3. College students—Fiction. 4. North Carolina—Fiction. 5. Tobacco
farms—Fiction. 6. Violence—Fiction. I. Title.

PS3563.A72376 L84 2000
813'.6–dc21   00-035489

W. W. Norton & Company, Inc., 500 Fifth Avenue, New York, N.Y. 10110
www.wwnorton

W. W. Norton & Company Ltd., 10 Coptic Street, London WC1A 1PU

1   2   3   4   5   6   7   8   9   0

FOR JOYCE AND JOEL

ACKNOWLEDGMENTS

I would like to thank John Sterling, Jennifer Rudolph Walsh, Tabitha Griffin, and Rolando Hinojosa-Smith for all of their help with this book. And, for everything else, I give my love and thanks to Meredith McMonigle, my family, and my friends.

COTTESVILLE

THERE IS BAD luck, and then there is *bad* luck: luck so bad it borders on the riotous, luck so bad it throws its recipients into a convulsive laughter from which they cannot escape, luck so bad that words and language fail us and the breath escapes our bodies noisily and unordered. Luck that bad doesn't come around often; Harvey Dickerson would have said that when it did, "you just gotta sit back and appreciate it on its merits." In the end, when Harvey met his own piece of this dark luck, he didn't have time to sit back, appreciate, or anything. He lost consciousness very quickly and lived only a few animal moments before bleeding to death on the hot pavement in front of Michael Olive's childhood home.

There on County Route 1012, which links the dunes of the Carolina beach to a green forest stuck in the red clay soil, motorists slowed and crossed themselves or bit their lips as they went inching past the mess. Route 1012 was a country road, and drivers were used to ugly wrecks or the occasional carcass of a deer or dog, but this was something else. This was something foreign and distinct. Even the emergency road crew was amazed by the shards of charred mailbox, the pieces of teeth and skin, the jagged splinters of the car and Harvey's skull and a baseball bat thrown all across the summer blacktop. Debris had settled in the ditches and fallen on both sides of the dotted yellow line. The state workers cleaned up as quickly as they could, grumbling in the August heat, shaking their heads at one another.

There was a witness. Zebulon Hough told first the authorities and later his fellow diners at Eddie's Bar-N-Q that he had seen "the whole damn thing, from pit to patter." Eddie's was crowded and quiet; thick clouds of smoke spiraled into the ceiling fans as Zeb held court. With a full mouth he explained that yes, the mailbox had burst into flames, and no, there were no signs at all of the occult involved. No black cats. No truth to the rumor of the Olives' address as P.O. Box 666. "Six-six-six my ass," the mailman said. "The only devils involved was alcohol, my friends, alcohol and the crazy son of a bitch who sent a bomb to the Olives through the U.S. Mail." He nodded, watched the news work its way across the room. "Alcohol, a son of a bitch, and the worst luck a boy ever had." His audience agreed, and Harvey Dickerson would have agreed too. "It was three evil things that blew the fuck out of me," the dead boy would have said.

Zeb was the last one to see Harvey alive. The dead boy had been in front of him, riding shotgun in Ox's white Pinto, Ox himself driving, the both of them careless, cheerful, and drunk. They sang as they slalomed the afternoon road, Harvey singing lead, Ox filling in the choruses in his tuneless growl, both too drunk to notice the angry mailman behind them in his aging jeep, and all Zeb could do was watch and honk as the Dickerson boy leaned out the window and shouldered a time-browned thirty-six-inch Louisville Slugger. Harvey had a decent swing and the mailboxes buckled and tore and dropped like landmines into Zeb's cautious path. They passed the Hunts' and the Tates'. They hit the curve where the Olives' best land first came into sight, and the car spit up dust as the right rear slipped to the ditch for a small, wild moment. The Pinto turned sideways, and for the length of a second Harvey and Ox found themselves looking straight out over the Olives' acre after acre of tobacco. They saw the spent and yellow fields, the dry and crumbling tractor treads in the dirt, and they saw someone out there, too. It was a woman, pretty and young and Mexican, wearing a black dress and standing very still as she watched

them slide by. They watched her back until the wheel straightened out and the Pinto clawed its way back onto the road.
Harvey turned back to see her again, but she was gone.

"You *know* that was her," Harvey said. "Had to be."

They accelerated down the straightaway, and soon the
Olives' white farmhouse was rising up off the curve of the earth
in front of them. Harvey punched Ox lightly on the shoulder,
grabbed the bat, and put himself out the window one more
time. "Goddamn," Harvey said, shaking his head, "there goes
Dickerson again with a moon shot over centerfield wall!" and
Ox grunted in a low haw-haw-haw as his buddy cranked back
and swung and the Pinto blossomed into summer pyrotechnics
in front of Clayton Olive's farm.

"Well," Zeb said, late that night, "if the good Lord meant me
to save those boys, I suppose He would have given mail jeeps fuel
injection, something." Down at the far end of the bar at Eddie's
Bar-N-Q, his words were interpreted as plain malice by Harvey's
cousin Carl, who took four steps and slammed the postman's
face against the bar top, twice. That surprised everyone, because
Carl was never really a fighting Dickerson, like his older brother,
or a talker like cousin Harvey. Surprise or no, Eddie got Carl by
the hair right away, and by the time the rhubarb was over, the
Cottesville sheriff had to call up the deputies who weren't already
brawling just to keep the place standing. People said the invisible
insurance men back in Raleigh would cover the material dam-
ages, but for the Chevys and Fords driving slowly by, it was a sad
sight: familiar Eddie's in ruin, battered friends and brothers
hauled off for a night in the lockup. As a regular from Eddie's
explained it, "The night I spend behind bars instead of in one of
them, you know there's something afoot."

THERE WERE NO spaces to be had in the parking lot at
Jackson County Hospital, where Ox Bowman lay in intensive

care. Straight- and slant- and V-8s lined the banks and the
curbs and were even parked in the ditch between the hospital
and the road. Everyone, most everyone, came. They didn't necessarily come because they thought Ox was going to die. The
truth was that the end of Ox was hard for most people to imagine—even for Mr. and Mrs. Bowman, who had seen the crum-
pled side of their son's massive chest before he was rushed into
surgery. Their Jeremy had always, to everyone, seemed inde-
structible, and especially to his parents, who'd witnessed his
unlikely birth at eleven pounds, eleven ounces. He was six foot
one in the seventh grade, quickly dwarfing the stout five-ten
Mr. Bowman and his small, girlish wife, and only stopped
growing when he reached six-eight, 280 pounds. "I mean,
hopefully," said his mother quietly as she paced the aisles of Bill
Mason's Food Lion, doing her best to bring home enough food
for her enormous son. There were people who thought Ox was
a freak, or looked at his tiny parents and smelled scandal, but
Harvey always defended his large and taciturn friend. "What's
all this shit?" he said. "They got Chinamen over in China bigger than giants, and their folks so short they couldn't see over a
Dairy Queen counter." No one could argue with Harvey, once
he got going like that, and most people had long ago given up
trying, except for his dad, maybe, and Michael Olive.

In the hospital waiting room, a wash of denim and sun-red
outdoor skin shifted against aseptic white. Standing room only.
The amoebic mass of people slid and subdivided into huddles
and whispering circles, separating and recombining. On the
side of the room nearest the door, Harvey's father Brack stood
quietly with his wife, three surviving children, his brother Blue,
some in-laws, his cousins, nephews, nieces, and friends.
Although there were plenty of people who thought poorly of
the Dickersons as a clan, a steady vein of neighbors and coun-
trymen continued to file by the unlucky father and mother, paying their respects. They stood before Brackford Dickerson; they

took his hand in theirs; they told him that they were sorry. "'Sorry' can suck my dick," Brack muttered once, unconvinced by someone's profession of sympathy. By "sorry" maybe B.D. meant fate; maybe he meant bad luck; maybe it was his way of coming to terms with the inexplicable. Maybe it was his way of putting a challenge to destiny to come up with a reason why. He swore and looked past the people around him. His cheek bulged as he stared at Michael Olive.

Mike stood on the far side of the room from the Dickersons, leaning carefully against the wall, wearing bright clean jeans and a soft white button-down shirt, loosely tucked. His hair was growing out, medium long, slipping down towards his eyes, the blond fringes almost white from the summer sun. Twice he started across the room to pay his respects to the Dickersons, and twice reason stopped him halfway. He caught B.D. eying him and made sure to look away. He examined the iron stain on an old water fountain and thought about Harvey. It seemed to Mike that a grand mix-up had taken place in the order of things, that the sins of a family shouldn't be visited on the head of one son. Even the young, dead Harvey probably would have agreed with Michael this once. "I might not be the best of all samaritans," Harvey would have said, "but for fact they don't make sons of bitches like my daddy anymore."

Mike stayed on the wall, avoiding the crossfire of glances and keeping his mouth shut. Silence was expected of him, he knew that, just as he knew there were people in the room who felt this tragedy was all his fault, or at least close enough. He'd never wanted this summer to end in violence, although there wasn't any question that he'd come back to town to stir things up. "Oh, I'd say more than stir," said Eddie of Eddie's. "He and his friends brought this county to a boil. A boil," Eddie explained, "a boil turns water to steam, liquid to gas. A boil, see, messes up the very nature of the way things are."

———

IN MAY, MICHAEL Olive had showed up with fourteen class-mates from Duke University and moved into the Catholic Retreat Center east of town. His classmates drove cars with "First in Flight" plates on the back, bought their liquor with Carolina IDs, and wrote Wachovia Bank checks listing places of residence in Durham, but it was clear to Harvey that the newcomers were not from North Carolina.

"Come on, y'all," Eddie told Harvey and a couple of his friends as they got worked up about Mike and his company. "They never claimed they were Carolina Adam and Eves. If they want to pass out Band-Aids to Mexicans or baby-sit some little migrant kids all day long, what's the big deal?"

"We ain't dealing with healers and schoolteachers, Eddie." Harvey leaned in and licked his lips. "They're snooping. They're looking for trouble."

"What trouble?"

"That's a good question. All this time they spend driving around and around, and not out at that clinic, not to no class-room. They on the dirt roads, people's property. My uncle saw a gray Honda driving through his fields the other day. They didn't ask permission. They just drove."

"Uncle which?"

"Uncle Blue."

"How is ol' Blue?"

"Still a sour ol' piece a."

"Well, you tell him hey for me." Eddie rapped his knuckles on the bar, trying to get his own attention. "That Honda. Kinda new? Silver more than gray?"

"Yeah. Think."

"That's this Mexican boy's car. I met him once, came in here with Mike."

"Sorry I missed that."

"He's Duke, too."

"I know what he is."

"What was he doing out there?"

Harvey shrugged. "There was two of them. They were just, you know. I don't know. Talking to migrants."

"Might be something to do with the kids, you know, the school, or the clinic. They pick 'em up, drop 'em off, always driving those kids around who knows."

"Dunno. Dunno what the fuck it is. But they keep going back there, they never ask, it's like we ain't even there, they drive right by the house. They don't want to ask, so it makes you think. I just don't like the snooping around, know what I mean?" Harvey turned his head and pursed his lips and squinted, like he was chewing on something sour. Then his face relaxed and he was quiet for a moment. He had full lips, very red, and with his short cropped hair and quick eyes he looked like a young boy until his face drew tight again. "I'd go out there and talk to them myself if I thought it would do any good, but you know how they talk. A bunch of shit. How you get to have so many words and still can't say what you mean?" Harvey knew that in the country it was the details of things that counted—how to pop a carburetor from a '78 Impala, quick, or how deep a cedar post needs to go for a chest-high fence. The way the air feels in your lungs when it's time to plant peppers.

"And what exactly do they know?" Harvey said. "I'm sure their spelling's good, but when they start going on labor this or that. I mean, do they even know what they're trying to say?" Harvey smiled broadly and eyed his way down the bar, inviting someone to disagree with him, but no one did. He waited, to be sure, and then shook his head. "Well, I just think that's what happens, you send a kid off like that to teach him why he's better than where he's from. So he can come back wearing his college education like a funny French hat. Maybe it looks good in Paris, but you're just another asshole out here."

———

MIKE KNEW WHAT Harvey meant. He knew. "I never," he said, "I never ever thought sticking up for migrant farm workers was going to win me a popularity contest with the folks back home. I got all the strikes against me. I'm rocking the boat, we got a little money, and if that wasn't enough, there's Duke University."

Duke certainly had something to do with it. There were people, older mostly, who admired Mike for getting out, for taking on what everyone said was one of the best universities, anywhere. They admired his good fortune and his opportunity. But the younger people did not forgive or fawn.

"Duke." Harvey could make it sound like a disease, the way he said it. "Now why would you go to Duke?" Harvey asked. "Why not Carolina, if you had any kind of choice?" Harvey shook his head, and then took a shot at answering his own questions. "This is it, see, Mike's one of these persons who'll spend a lot of time trying to figure out where he ought to be. Maybe there ain't a place, I hope not, I don't know, but everyone always knew it sure as shit wasn't here. It happens all the time, people get born into the wrong place. You get your country folks trapped in the cities, city folk lost out in the country, you get a lot of problems because people can't match who they are up to where they ought to be." Harvey smiled. "People like me," he said, "we get along so well because we're lucky enough to be right where we belong. They're not many to say that. Not Mike Olive, not his crew, not any migrants, that's for sure."

What Harvey didn't say was that the difference between him and Mike had not always been so obvious, not even to Harvey. The two boys were born on the same day, and the two mothers, although not close, always had something to talk about in town while their sons roamed free. At age five, just before the real gap opened up between the Olives and Dickersons, the two boys could be seen sharing the seat of an old, rusted tractor, bouncing and holding on like jockeys as they drove at top imaginary speeds across soon-to-be-tilled fields. Up until they were ten they still fished together. They swam and they hunted. But that was it. After that, they fought: not with their fists, but in every other way there was. They fought for girls, for seats on the smokeless side of a bonfire. They fought for friends, and they always fought for the first and last word.

"When you're a kid," Mike said, "you can mix it up, wrestle, play tackle football or kill the guy with the ball, and you just fall down, bounce off each other, doesn't matter. But when you get bigger, older, you can do those same things you used to do and be sure that someone's going to get hurt. I don't know exactly what I'd do differently, but I do wish I'd seen that earlier."

THE CATHOLIC RETREAT Center was in Cottesville for ten years before Mike and his fellow students stayed there for the summer. For most of those years, the place was empty except for Father Joe, although occasional groups of Southern Catholics showed up now and then for weekend retreats. It was a strange wooden building about six miles east of town, set between watermelons on one side and tobacco on the other. Father Joe had come into the land suddenly—no one remembered how, if they ever knew. He just showed up one day in a red Dodge Ram and built the place almost by himself, slowly, with his own hands. He was a tall, wide, ruddy man, with British teeth and meaty breath, and small eyes that glinted like a full moon stuck in the depths of a well.

The Center was huge, two stories tall, set square around a large interior courtyard that was open to the sky. The courtyard was grass with a young poplar planted in the middle. Mike's father told Father Joe early on that the tree was not, in his opinion, such a good idea. "Carolina poplar will get as high as a church top," Clayton said, "rip your pipes out soon as look at them," but the tree stayed. On both the north and south sides of the building, Father Joe had built what looked like two identical front entrances to a colonial house, with columns on each side of the doorways, wide front steps, and long porches, so that both ends looked like the front of the house. It was an odd-looking place, although it was set back from the road and hard to get a good look at. Father Joe planted poinciana all along the rim of his building, and the plants sprawled and grew and flashed yellow flowers all summer long to hide his property from the puzzled world.

The Center sat a mile and a half down Route 1012 from Clayton Olive's house, but the Olives' best land, the two hundred acres everyone called the Nile, started right across the road from it. On the day ten years ago when Father Joe started construction, Clayton Olive had been out in his tractor with two Mexican migrant workers, tilling in the winter wheat. The tall grass had shot up in the cold winter rains, and while Clayton kept an eye on the activity across the way, he bantered tersely with the workers about the possibilities of a good season coming. Working together, they turned over the red soil until it showed its rich, pocked face. The hands went ahead with shovels, dislodging the outcrop and breaking up some of the bigger clumps. The soil was fine for planting, although somewhat wet for building, Clayton thought, but Father Joe across the road stayed absorbed in his construction meditations, oblivious to his new neighbor. Although Clayton put himself within earshot several times, pausing to accommodate a hollered "hey" or a quick wave, the newcomer ignored him. By the end of the week, Father Joe had leveled the land. He sat on the hood of his truck enjoying a cold beer, regarding his invisible building marked out with wood stakes and string. Clayton, unable to stand it any longer, wandered over to say a suspicious hello.

"Doesn't sound like a church," said Clayton a half hour later, after the father had described the building-to-be.

"No, it's not, exactly."

"Well, what's it for, then?"

"Tell the truth, I don't quite know." Father Joe hadn't yet fully explained the place yet, even to himself, and decided to take the talk elsewhere. "So what are they, Mexicans?"

Clayton followed Father Joe's gaze back to his own land, where the two hands, hunched brown dots in the distance, made their way down the ghostly rows of future tobacco. Clayton nodded, and said, "Yeah. These the first ones I had. Seem pretty good. They up around here early, so don't know how long they'll stay. That's the thing, you know. You finally work things out with somebody, but what about next year? Next thing you know I'll turn around and maybe there's a whole batcha new ones who don't speak English."

"'Pay up!' They know that one, huh? Aw, Mexicans are good workers, in my experience, ones I known, anyway. And good Catholics too. Catholic up and down the line. There a lot of these Mexicans up here?"

"The summer. Then there's some."

"And more a-coming. More and more every year, if it's like anywhere else."

"I wouldn't know about that."

"Well. I'd like to get them in church sometime. I doubt they have a church group, huh?"

"Far as I've seen, they got some old trucks, maybe a wife and kids along, and that's about it."

"You wouldn't mind if I asked your workers about attending a mass, would you?"

"No, I wouldn't mind at all. If that's what they want. I don't know much about them, tell the truth."

"They should want. Good Catholics, I've found, and I'll tell you what. You let me take care of their spiritual life, and you give 'em work, and we'll have their needs covered. They're gonna be happier and work harder if they get into church now and then. I'll give 'em back to you, don't you worry."

Clayton just looked at him.

"I'm serious about this. I may not look it with a Craftsman in hand, but I *am* a priest, no kidding about that. You know, Jesus was—"

"A carpenter. Yeah, we know. Got that book in our church too."

They both laughed, but the two neighbors never got much closer than that, although they saw plenty of each other over the years. They were neighbors for ten years, and amiable ones, and Father Joe didn't hesitate when Mike Olive proposed the idea of the Duke students' renting out the Center.

"Ol' Joe wasn't thinking about the Ninth or Tenth Commandments," Harvey said, "you can count on that. That kind of decision came down to simple moo-lah-lah."

"I was trying to keep together just like the any of y'all would," Father Joe said in self-defense. "What was I supposed to know? That boy's father was the first person in Jackson County I ever met. I'm supposed to turn down a sweet offer from a local boy, with a fat university check that don't bounce?"

"Someone should have told him it was a bad idea," Harvey told Eddie. "One of his people at his little church group on Sunday. What do they call it?"

"Sunday mass," Eddie said.

"Mass my ass," Harvey said. "I seen more people come out to kill a hog. I don't have anything personal against the man, but I do think a man of the cloth, whatever flavor, should have more common sense than that. See that Mike was here for one thing and one thing only. Trouble."

"Now, come on," Mike said, when Harvey's line of reasoning got back to him. "That's just killing messengers. You get to a point in history . . ." Mike stopped himself, thought for a moment in the silence he'd made. "Shit," he said finally, in a voice that sounded more like the Mike Cottesville knew.

"Someone was gonna to come out here, an Olive, a Smith, a Brown, whoever. Someone was gonna come out and look around and say: now what the hell's going on around here?"

AS THE NIGHT began on the day that Harvey died, Jackson County started to retreat into its small and separate worlds. The Bowmans sat in stasis at the hospital, praying for their son. Zeb held court at the Bar-N-Q. Carl and Eddie fought. The Duke students read or wrote or whispered in their rooms, while down the road Mike ate dinner with his parents, in silence. Brack Dickerson drank bourbon with his brother Blue on Blue's porch, staring at the empty chairs where Harvey should be, and Carl, and Blue's other boy gone in the army, down in Florida. Throughout Jackson County, people found their places and stayed there, but Harvey was everywhere that night. He hung over the pumps at the Stop N' Go as the farmers spat and pumped gas. He passed through the houses in town, over sub-dued dinner tables, through quiet sitting rooms, and then wandered out past the limits, across his father's fields and then his uncle's. He lingered there, at Blue's place, in the empty migrant camp. He drifted over the blackened patch of asphalt in front of the Olives' and waited late until Mike left his parents' house and then Harvey followed. He followed Mike on the short drive back to the Catholic Retreat Center, where Mike parked, got out of the car, and stood for a long moment in the quiet parking lot. Then the two of them, Mike and dead Harvey, turned away from the Center and crossed the still-warm black-top of County Route 1012, down and up the ditch and into the Olives' tobacco fields. The wide leaves clung at Mike's cottoned knees and rocked in his wake as he faded into the dark.

In the center of the field, Mike sank down in the onyx all around him and closed his eyes, his head tilted as if he were listening. When he finally rose his knees were damp. He walked down the rows until he reached a thin, serpentine road that swept in a long parabola through vast plots of green peppers, cucumbers, and sweet potatoes. The road tilted down a slow slant of a hill, through a breach of trees, and then dissolved into the dirt. But the tracks continued, deep ruts in the red soil beyond and between the borders of the most minutely detailed map, and as Mike followed them he saw the rectangular structures slipping out of invisibility, like shapes in a developing gray-and-white print. There was no sign of anything else there, until the breeze stirred the dry, parched leaves and with them white cotton clothes on a swaying line, strung between a tree and the trailers. In an ember glow a man smoked a cigarette in a doorway, and while the ash fell Mike saw the shadows moving in the backlit trailers. He heard women talking and children crying. Somewhere a man called out, *"Híjole,"* and another man laughed and an ageless woman in an ageless dress watched Mike from the trailer steps. He smelled roasting coffee and eggs. He closed his eyes and breathed until he felt someone take his hand and say his name. Her accent sounded stronger in the dark, and as he stepped towards her he could feel the heat coming off her smooth dark skin through the thin black summer dress. He put his arms around her and she held him as his body began to shake. Then she said his name again and pulled him into the void, stepping past the pile of trash heaped high and sculpted by child's play, the charred remains of a rock-ringed fire, sitting stumps laid out in a semicircle. A trailer door opened and the light winked brightly, once, into the clearing. Then it closed, and Mike disappeared.

HERMELINDA

I

HERMELINDA WAS TWELVE when her family left Batopilas. Her father, Francisco Contreras Salmeron, had been released from a second stint in the Chihuahua City prison after fourteen months. He returned home to meet his youngest son, the year-old Pedrito, for the first time. Arriving in town on a bus, Francisco had walked the four miles downstream to their house at La Cascada, and Hermelinda was the first to see him on the narrow road as he rounded the last bend. She was halfway up the mountain with her younger brother Alejandro, sent by their mother to see why their water had stopped. They'd followed the bed of the old waterfall, reduced to a thin, wobbly vein of water by months without rain, and found the trouble at the source. The black tubing that brought water to their house had come dislodged from its place in the shallow, trickle-fed mountain pool. Brother and sister had finished wedging the mouth of the pipe between two rocks, submerging it completely and securely, and were beginning their slow descent to check the length of the line for leaks, when Hermelinda raised her head to see the small figure below them. Staring to be sure of the familiar, lopsided step and the thin red band on the man's hat, she pinched Alejandro and pointed.

"Papá!" she yelled, waving madly, jumping from rock to rock in a lightning plummet, while her brother followed, hissing, "Shut up, Hermelinda, shut up!"—convinced that his father's sudden return was a clandestine act, an escape, an improper item for common knowledge. Catching up to her in the dirt above their house, Alejandro tackled his sister from behind, forcing a hand of silence briefly over her mouth before she wrestled him around. When Francisco arrived, his first glimpse of home was his oldest son struggling in spitting anger beneath Hermelinda, her long hair a wild net thrown over her head, as she rubbed Alejandro's face in the dirt. In three long strides Francisco closed the distance before them and lifted his daughter off his son in a swinging embrace.

"Alejandro was only scared, *mi'jita,*" her father told her later that night, as she nursed her bruises from her brother's onslaught, while Alejandro scowled on the other side of the table. They ate together for the first time as a nuclear family of eight. "Just scared that no one was supposed to know."

"Of course they know. Everyone knows everything in Batopilas."

Her father laughed. "Ah, that's very true, *princesa,* you're right, you're always right." He looked at her carefully and then tickled her without warning or mercy, reducing her to a squirming child, blotting out the canny adult brightness he saw in her eyes.

Francisco came back thin, less sturdy than when he left. The round face was compressed, and he moved more slowly. He kissed them all, too many times, round and round in a sort of chaotic receiving circle, until the little ones were running from him with genuine shrieks, and his wife shoed his lips away with an open hand and a frown. When he finally came to rest on the low stool in the roof-shaded foyer, he produced a small radio from a bundle of clothes and turned it on. He sat there examining each of his children in turn, nodding his head to the music, leaning in and squinting his eyes to search their faces for traces of a new topography, for any sign of change.

Before the evening meal he handed the radio to Alejandro and danced with Hermelinda and her younger sister Rebecca while their mother pounded out tortillas onto wax paper and pursed her lips in a silent smile. Little Camilla cried and Mani held her hand, staring seriously at his dancing father with his dark wide eyes. Alejandro, grave with responsibility, guarded the radio, extending and retracting the antenna, adjusting the controls minutely, removing and replacing the batteries over and over until his father bent over him and whispered sharply in his ear.

She wondered if Alejandro was awake later that night as her parents argued softly, as softly as they could and still disagree. The house their father had built from mud, palo leaves, and wood had only one large room where the whole family slept, and that night Hermelinda lay with her sisters on either side, her feet touching her brother's feet in the tangle of blanket spread across the children's side of the room. She remembered feeling the crowded air the eight of them shared; she remembered the heat and the sweet, acrid scent of their bodies.

"No, I don't understand. My family would have watched the children. Do you know how long that is, can you imagine that many days locked in a room with strangers, alone?"

"There was no money, Francisco, and I had the baby."

"I'd sit there thinking I'd made you up, I was a common thief like the rest of them, that I was nothing. Not a husband, father. That I was crazy. I thought I was going crazy."

"I couldn't come, Francisco, I couldn't. But every day was like today, waiting for you."

"There was someone else. When I was away."

"No. There was no one."

"All that time? How did you buy anything? Who helped you? Who?"

"Don't wake the children. I cannot prove anything to you. You have to *know*. You just have to know."

Hermelinda lay listening to her parents' voices until the wind rose with the moon and rattled through the palo-leaf roof and the knobby, crooked branches that served as rafters, whispering over the murmur of words. When the wind died she could hear her mother and father moving against each other, struggling in the still night.

They left not long after that, when the village *policía* visited her father again. The pale blue truck came jousting around the bend in a baritone rumble and a dense cloud of black smoke and dust, turned sharply onto the Salmerons' land, and braked hard in front of the house, scattering the chickens and drawing frenzied noise from the young dog, Sangre. The two men were dressed as Hermelinda always saw them in town: the same dirty brown pants, the tight T-shirts, the belt buckles big as license plates, the dusty black boots, the blue billed caps, the guns strapped to their sides. As they stepped from the car, she helped Alejandro restrain Sangre, silencing the dog with a tight clenched hand around his muzzle while he struggled and scratched in their grasp.

Their father emerged slowly from the house, greeting the men by name. They said nothing and walked past him into the room. Hermelinda could hear them moving things inside. After a few minutes they emerged, one leaning easily against the wall of the house, the other pacing slowly behind her father, staring at the back of his neck. When Francisco began to speak, they raised their voices loud against his mumble-whisper, shaking their fingers at him like sticks.

"You don't want to leave your señora alone again?" they said. "Do you want to do that, Francisco?" They looked at Hermelinda's mother for too long where she sat still and straight in the shade, with her youngest children clinging to her tight. "Tell us who was there," they said. "What color was the truck?"

"Yes, I heard the truck. There was a truck, but I didn't see."

"Yes, there was a truck, and you did see. I can almost make out the spot from here." He stood up on his tiptoes and peered through the trees, towards the small hut where the green truck had been the night before. A man Hermelinda had never seen before stepped over the fence behind their house, silencing Sangre with something he tossed from the pocket of his jacket, and spoke briefly to her father. The two of them disappeared with a bucket, and returned for more water a while later. Hermelinda's mother swore under her breath and sent the children into the house.

Hermelinda snuck outside again and met the man as he returned alone. He handed her the bucket.

"You are going to be a very beautiful woman," he said to her. "Do you know that?"

"Yes," she said, and when he laughed she saw flashes of silver and gold in his teeth. He reached into his pocket and gave her an American quarter, shiny and new. She ran her finger along the lines of the smooth bald gringo head on the coin as she watched him walk away.

"Was it green? Red? White? Blue? I'll give you some choices, Francisco." Her father shook his head. He stared at his fishing net, lying half-mended in the dirt.

"I didn't see. I heard them but I didn't want any trouble."

"Maybe they cut you in on the deal, Francisco. Maybe they're taking *mota* across your land too. Maybe you have some growing on your land."

"No, señor, nothing like that."

"You will see, when we catch them and they tell us, 'Yes, Francisco, our friend, he helped.' Your friends in prison must be missing you by now. Aren't you offended, señora," gesturing to her mother, "that he prefers his prison friends to you?" Her father stayed silent. "Is that what you want, Francisco?"

"Look around you, you idiot!" Her father paced the yard alone long after they left, shouting his speech too late to the chickens and the puzzled, whining Sangre. "We have nothing here. What do you see? A few chickens, goats, some rows of corn. Does that look like the house of a big *narcotraficante* to you? When we get hungry I can fish in the river. But we have nothing." His voice fell as he walked back towards the house, mumbling at his own toes. "Do you think I am stupid as well as poor? If I was growing *mota,* wouldn't I be rich, at least?"

"Stupid, yes, this is stupid," Hermelinda's mother whispered later that night. "Why do you take such risks? Why can't you look the *policía* in the eye, and tell them the truth? Why can't the truth be that we have nothing to do with it?"

"We're trapped, Dora. We can't say yes and we can't say no. One sends me to prison and the other to sleep with the dead."

"You can say no. You have to."

"How? They'll take their *mota* out of the mountains where they please and if I don't take the money, a few pesos to show I'm on their side, the next thing they offer me is a bullet in the head."

"And the *policía?*"

"Don't you think they know everything? They look for me because I am the weakest person, caught in the middle. They're cowards, they're afraid. If they were men they'd go after the others."

"So what will happen? You're going to go back to prison?"

"Sure, someone pays the *policía,* they all have a nice drink together and send the soldiers out to arrest me. They tell the boss they've done their job, just like the last time. I think—"

"I think that if you leave me again, for prison or anywhere else, I . . ." She shook her head. "I . . ." she said again.

"And what? What would you do? Who would marry you? Who wants an Indian girl with another man's children? Your other lover is still waiting for you, is that it?"

"Francisco, the *policía* are right about something: you can't leave us alone again."

Hermelinda held her breath, listening to the silence on her parents' side of the room.

"Say something," her mother said.

"Dorita," her father finally said, "the only thing we can do is go."

"Then let's go, Francisco, let's go."

They left as their neighbors had left, selling everything for too little and packing the rest of their lives into a fruit truck for the long drive out of the canyon. It was a terrible goodbye. Her father was from Batopilas, born and raised, and his parents and brothers all came with their families to see them off, to give them gifts and shake their heads in sorrow, or maybe shame, Hermelinda didn't know. For her mother it was worse. Dora had been a fifteen-year-old girl from the mountains when Francisco had seen her standing in the doorway of her father's house. He'd returned the following day to pay his respects to the family in a clean shirt and a new hat. Although her father barely understood Spanish and Francisco knew less than ten words of Tarahumara, the two men managed to make themselves understood while Dora's mother whispered soothing words to her daughter in the next room. Francisco married her that weekend and brought her two days' walking from the house where she'd lived in the highlands overlooking the Gran Arenal. On the night before Hermelinda and her family left Batopilas, Dora climbed the ridge above their house, and Hermelinda watched her mother standing on a promontory rock for a long time, gazing south. The daughter knew her mother could not see her home from there, that she was staring at the curve of the mountain, trying to look through it to envision the distant slope where her people lived.

The fruit truck took them up the thin road that cut back and forth into the cliff, and in a few hours they were high above everything Hermelinda had ever known. They drove through the pine forest, and then past the strange, enormous rocks of the mesa, shaped like great faces and animals, sitting on wide fields of flat land. Hermelinda had never seen so much flat land before. In five hours they were in Creel, a small town, but for Hermelinda it was a city, with a train station and buses and tourists and little hotels and restaurants and people on the streets.

They sat together near the train tracks, wrapped in blankets in the cool air of the high plateau, and felt the vibrations in the earth as the train arrived. Hermelinda stared at the people who descended to the platform. Some were belted and hatted and didn't look any different from the people she'd known, but there were others too, pale-skinned men and women swinging their bags down from the train. She'd seen gringos before in the canyon, but never so many at once, and never so close. Hermelinda sat with five-year-old Camilla on her lap, the both of them fixed on one passenger in particular, a tall woman with long, shiny yellow hair. She wore tight short pants and a tiny, truncated shirt that accentuated her breasts and exposed vast patches of the pale white skin of her stomach, arms, and nape. The pants fascinated tiny Camilla, who rose from her sister's lap as if lifted on the ends of puppet strings. She slipped out of Hermelinda's grasp and ran, grabbing at the woman's shorts, touching the shiny black material, trying to tear off a piece for herself. The woman turned to her companion and cooed at him, like a mother to a baby, and he had reached into his strange coat and offered Camilla her choice of a handful of coins. Camilla didn't even look at him. She wanted those shorts, and the woman had to pry her tiny fingers from the fabric, while Camilla cried and Hermelinda came running and the man and woman smiled and wrapped little Camilla's hand around a piece of money. Camilla dropped it and ran back to her mother, but Hermelinda stopped to pick up the silver, finding it easily on the dirty floor of the platform. The gringo couple smiled and nodded and watched her as she returned to her family and handed the five-peso coin to her father.

"What is this?" he said. He looked beyond her to find the two white, smiling faces, and Hermelinda watched his jaw stiffen. The gringos waved and then turned to follow the young man carrying their brightly colored bags to a waiting car.

"Never," her father said, staring at the coin in his hand,

turning it slowly between his finger and thumb, "never, ever do that again." He grabbed her arm suddenly, and his fingers felt like rock denting her flesh. "You understand me?" Hermelinda nodded and began to cry. "Stop it," her father said. "Now take it back."

"Please, what's the harm in her taking a few centavos from those people?" Hermelinda's mother said. "It's already gone for them, and we need it."

"You want her to learn that she owes those people something? You think that's the way for a woman to start, taking presents, being grateful to strangers. Not even strangers." He watched the gringos disappearing into the car. "Now go." He put out the coin for Hermelinda and released her arm, slowly.

"A strange time to be teaching your children pride," her mother said. She reached out with one quick hand and the coin disappeared from Francisco's fingertips, buried in the circle of her fist.

"No." His eyes burned in a cold hard stare where the gringos had been moments before. "Give me that money."

"No."

"Give it to me."

Hermelinda watched her mother's fist open, and her father reached out his hand for the coin. As soon as he touched it, the fist closed on his hand. Her mother held Francisco's hand in both of hers, pulling him in close, but Hermelinda heard her anyway.

"It's time for you to take care of us," Dora said softly. "I know you can, I know you will, but you have to start right now."

Her father swore and wrenched his hand from hers. He grabbed her by the hair, tilting her head back to expose the soft skin of her neck. Hermelinda could see a faint line of dirt there, at the top of her throat.

"Who takes care of you? Who? Who?" he hissed.

"You do, Papá, you," Hermelinda said, getting as close as she dared to her parents, squeezing Rebecca's hand, hoping she would chime in as well. She remembered looking up at her father, at the dark circles under the arms of his dark brown shirt and the pepper flakes of his coming beard on his chin, she remembered trying to find his eyes under the shadow of his red-banded sombrero. There was no sign that he had heard his daughter. Her mother and father stayed frozen in place for a long moment, like a statue or a memory.

"Okay," said Hermelinda's father finally, releasing Dora and turning quickly to consider his brood, his face puzzled as if counting the children for the first time and being amazed at their size and number. He spread his empty hands wide, stretching out his arms as if to encircle all of them at once. "Okay," he said again to the children, smiling to keep them calm, "are you all ready for this? Are you ready for the train?" He puffed out his cheeks and began to blow, "wooo, wooo," and Hermelinda and Rebecca laughed and Alejandro even smiled, and Camilla cried and little Mani, his mouth hanging open, looked back and forth between his father and the big black engine, trying to gauge the cause and effect. Her father led the way, herding the children onto the train, helping the little ones up the big iron steps to the coaches above. Hermelinda waited for her mother as she took time smoothing back her hair. Her mother breathed deeply before raising her head. She smiled. She handed Hermelinda the silver coin. "Hold this in your pocket, love," she said, and pushed her daughter gently forward onto the train for Chihuahua.

II

B<small>Y THE TIME</small> Hermelinda offered her virginity to Mr.
Dennis Clarke, she and her family had lived in Ojinaga for four
years. Every day after high school, Hermelinda walked across
the bridge over the Rio Grande to Presidio, Texas, where she
spent the afternoons baby-sitting for the Clarkes' two children,
ages six and four. Mr. Clarke was a friend of her father's boss.
His wife was an invalid who seldom left her bed, let alone the
house. In the summer, the Clarkes' house was a dark, cold cave,
with the shades all drawn and the air-conditioning breathing
heavily against the heat outside; in the winter, the rooms were
kept thickly warm and stuffy, so whatever the season, it was
not uncommon for Hermelinda to bring an extra set of clothes
suited to the separate climate of the Clarkes' small house.
Returning home in the evenings, it took her an hour to walk
back to her own house, across the bridge again and up the
uneven slope of the dirt streets that ran out from the *zócalo* and
dissolved into the desert plain. Sometimes she caught a ride
with a neighbor or friend of the family, someone familiar
returning to Ojinaga from a day labor job across the border,
but she didn't mind walking, and her mother, alone to wrestle
with her house and the young children, was too busy to object.

"In fact, I'd rather you walked," said her mother, evaluating
the sudden contours of her daughter's body. "The only men I'd
trust to give you a ride are too old to drive."

There were still men to deal with when she walked. There
were always men, men or boys who followed her after school or
cruised slowly beside her in their trucks, leaning out the windows to flatter or suggest. She could deal with that. On the
streets of Ojinaga and Chihuahua and even tiny Batopilas, she'd
watched her mother ignore the entire population of men, stepping through them as if they were no more than bramble-laden

trees obstructing a forest path. There were times she'd watched her mother turn cold, demolition glances on the men who whistled at her or called "*Ven, mamacita,*" or worse—it was a look designed to discourage, de-man, destroy. Hermelinda practiced that look in the bathroom mirror at the Clarkes', examining her own reflected face for signs of her mother's capacity for cold distance and fury. Most of the Ojinaga boys were afraid of her and called her names—beggar, *india, La Tacuache del Cobre*—although she liked some of them, and would have enjoyed their attention in moderation. Her sexual defenses were instinctive, and her public conduct was admired and praised by all the mothers and aunts of her friends. "Hermelinda will make her family proud," they said. "You can see, she pays attention to the dangers, the pitfalls of the seeming *caballero*. She's willful but in other ways she has old values, old judgment. She behaves like a young woman from our time."

They were right about her except when it came to Mr. Clarke. He was a tall Anglo, about thirty-five, with shaggy blond hair and bushy eyebrows, straight white teeth, big shoulders, outdoor arms, and an always sunburned face. He worked for the American border patrol as the agent in charge of fifty miles on either side of the Presidio crossing. He was handsome and seldom awkward, standing easily by himself in the market or on the street, in fitted jeans wrapped tight around sturdy legs, with a simple black leather belt and maybe a pale green button-down shirt hanging loose on his solid frame. He had nice breath. On winter days when she stayed at his house late enough for the sun to slip under the purple mountains to the west, he'd drive her home in his government white Chevrolet truck. She'd sit close to the middle of the wide monobench while he talked slowly to her in English and turned the radio down quiet so she could hear every word. She loved that ride, with the windows closed and the heat on low and the smell of him filling the cab.

"Are you going to your dance this weekend?" He was easy to understand, with his slow deep voice and his accent from somewhere else, somewhere more in the front of the mouth than Texas.

"If Papá lets me go," she said. She knew her father would. He was not home often enough to turn down her pleading requests.

"Yeah," and he laughed, "I guess I'll be going through that great debate with Sandy when she's your age." Mr. Clarke looked over at Hermelinda and smiled. "I'd let you go. You're more adult than most adults I know."

"Thank you, Mr. Clarke. You should tell my mother. She always worries."

"Well, I will. I'll come in sometime and tell her."

He didn't, though, and didn't linger in Ojinaga either. Hermelinda doubted if he'd ever seen the *zócalo* close up at night, with the church lit up and the men and boys driving around and around the square where Hermelinda would walk with her girlfriends, holding hands or linking arms as they talked and walked and ignored the young circling sharks without. Her friends had cousins and grandparents and uncles and aunts, all present, all accounted for as hers were not, and some nights, mingling in the finally familiar crowd, Hermelinda would imagine that she had come to Ojinaga alone, taken alone that last spur of train from Chihuahua, and that she could pick a new family to belong to: the Hidalgos, who owned the biggest store in town; the Torres clan, with their valley of onions, cantaloupe, and cattle to the east; even the family of Don Ybarra, the richest man in town, the region's most prominent exporter of all things lucrative and imaginable. Instead, each night she would return home and fall asleep a Salmeron in their cramped, rented house.

Her father was home on the weekends. He worked for Mr. Thompson on an enormous ranch in Texas, set back along a rough, jolting tangle of roads in the Chinati Mountains. It took two and a half hours by truck from Ojinaga; Francisco and their neighbor Gustavo Morales left early Monday morning and returned to their families on Friday nights. They worked partly as general ranch hands, taking care of the hundred head of cattle, fixing fences, tending the horses, and repairing the thirty-year-old water pump that spit oil and broke down once a week. Francisco wasn't an experienced ranch hand, but Mr. Thompson didn't care. He lived alone on his ten thousand acres, without family, and did not seem to rely on the business of the ranch for income. He seemed far more interested in building stone walls, of every shape, length, and configuration, than in any of the day-to-day of ranching.

"We're lucky," her father told her. "First lucky that it was so terrible in Chihuahua City that we would think about coming to the *frontera*. Lucky we came to Ojinaga and not El Paso. And then Mr. Thompson. Gustavo. Sometimes," he said, touching her hair and smiling, "I think there isn't any why, there's only luck."

Whatever it was that brought Mr. Thompson, Francisco, and Gustavo together, the result was the long days of hard work to build thousands of feet of stone walls all over Mr. Thompson's property. Francisco and Gustavo dispatched the other business of the ranch in the morning, and then the two of them drove one of Mr. Thompson's trucks along the disintegrating roads and filled the bed with rocks, selecting them carefully for shape like gem jewelers. They built walls in the old hacienda style like the ones Francisco knew from Batopilas.

"Most people use so much mortar, they don't care about the rocks," her father explained to her once, when he showed her their latest work: an enormous circle of stone, eight feet high, that enclosed a water cistern near Mr. Thompson's house. "See the way they slant in just a little, so the top is more narrow than the bottom? See how the rocks are fitted together with only a little concrete in the center, where no one can see, so that you get a perfect joint?"

"Your father has a right to be proud, honey," Mr. Clarke confirmed to Hermelinda on one of her chauffeured trips home. "You know what Cory says, don't you? He swears that as long as he's living and there's still rock on his property, he'll have your father building walls."

"Is that true, Papá?" she asked her father. "What will he have you build?"

"Who knows? Not him. Not me. As soon as we finish one thing, he brings us a paper napkin with a new drawing on it. Like he just thinks them up in that moment, little box drawings with the sizes written on the side. Sometimes he asks me, 'What do you think, Francisco? Maybe a low wall for a corral right here?' I say, okay, or maybe a shed for the horses. Then he comes back with the napkin, says, yes, he wants three sheds, one next to the other, and all the same. After that?" Her father shrugged.

"Is he a little strange, the Mr. Thompson?" Hermelinda asked Mr. Clarke the following day.

"I've known Cory a long time. If he's strange, he's good strange."

"I think so too," she said, smiling in the warmth of their agreement.

Every few months, Mr. Thompson left the ranch for a week or so, driving to El Paso and flying to New York. He never said why, and they never asked. While he was away, Francisco and Gustavo stayed on his ranch over the weekends to take care of the place, and Hermelinda's father would bring her and Alejandro with him to keep company and help. They ate steaks as thick as their father's wrist from a well-stocked freezer in the building next to Mr. Thompson's house where the men cooked and slept. During the days, Hermelinda cleaned the ranch house or cooked, waiting for the men to come home, watching her brother work on the water pump outside as he mumbled mechanical problems to himself.

Once, though, her father sent her out with her brother to look for Mr. Thompson's horses. Alejandro drove the truck up the dwindling hint of road towards the mountains while Hermelinda adjusted the radio, until the tires started spinning on the steep scree grade. They stopped the car and started walking up the narrowing ravine, negotiating the rocks that had rolled and slid across once-clear paths. They reached the water tower in thirty minutes, climbed it on either side, and looked around. Two valleys lined with steep ridges ran away from them to the west and south, a receding universe of scrub and tiny hills. Alejandro stayed put, his legs hooked around the iron girders of the tower, thrilled by the metal and the height and watching for any sign of life, while Hermelinda climbed the high ridge behind them. At the top she could see out over a long plateau. The Mexican mountains seemed larger from there, and she could make out Mr. Thompson's house and her father's maze of stone walls squatting in the distance. She traced the Rio Grande running south behind a rise, imagining her mother and sisters and baby brother at the unseen end of her thought's flight, moving around their house on the slope of the river valley. Then she turned slowly to the left and there, east along the expanse, she saw them.

"Alejandro," she shouted, pointing. "Alejandro, there!"

She waited for her brother and then the two of them started to walk quickly, one eye to the ground and one eye up to watch the twelve horses grazing without hurry in the high scrub. Most of them were brown but there was one all white and one all black. They looked good, healthier than the horses she remembered from Batopilas, maybe the healthiest things she had seen in a long time, she thought. She felt a brand of excitement that seemed new, that seemed to belong uniquely to Texas and their lives there at the juncture of the two nations. As they got closer,

Alejandro told her to walk slowly, and she imitated her brother's calm until they got close enough to coax one of the friendlier beasts to linger. Alejandro finally fumbled a rope over the horse's neck while Hermelinda talked to it soothingly, and then they led the pack, Pied Piper–style, back to the road. They left the truck and walked towards the house. Their father and Gustavo were waiting for them when the two children and their string of horses walked out of the hills like a desert caravan. The two men watched them in silence, drinking beer and talking softly between the two of them.

"Well look at you," Francisco told them when they got within earshot. He turned to his partner with a grin. "As if they tamed and broke the wildest horses in the world."

They all sat out late that night, until the cicadas stopped whining and the slim moon rose and the wind started. They watched the sky for strange lights. "People see them all the time," said Gustavo Morales, "all over the Chinati hills: colors, flashing, glowing in the distance."

"Have you seen them?" Hermelinda asked.

"One night I saw a green cloud of light there"—Gustavo pointed—"moving to the north very fast."

"It was probably a truck," Alejandro said. "Or maybe a little plane, a Cessna."

"No, there's nothing over there. No roads, no ranches, no place to put a plane. And there was no sound at all, just this dancing light. It wasn't any of that."

"Is it true, Papá?"

"Why not?" Francisco said.

"But what is it?"

"They say it might be ghosts of an old Indian looking for revenge."

"If you don't listen to your parents, right?" Alejandro said, his voice sharp and resentful with disbelief.

"Or maybe bats with glowing wings."

"Or electricity," said Francisco.

"Something."

They all sat there watching the sky, and one by one they went in until it was only Hermelinda, staring, thinking about the mysterious lights. She thought it was not impossible that the desert breathed and shined, throwing sparks in the pitch black, that it could do that simply because it was full of life. When the chill began to seep into her skin and she stood to go, she thought she saw it, a tiny orange ball of light that came off the side of a nearby mountain, sped towards her, and then dropped and disappeared. She waited for a little while longer but there was nothing else, and she went inside, massaging the muscles of her arms in the cold.

She never told anyone what she saw, and never told about the first time Dennis Clarke kissed her, next to his house in Presidio, the two of them leaning against the flank of his truck in the cool dark, her hands pulling him by his fleece-lined jacket to her warm body. She'd stayed late that night. Mrs. Clarke had been worse than usual of late, unable to deal with the children or leave her bed for a week. Mr. Clarke had dark circles under his eyes, and Hermelinda saw the sheets unevenly folded and stacked in the corner of the living room, next to the couch. The kids were taking advantage and running wild.

She knew before he did that Mr. Clarke was going to kiss her, recognizing something raw in his blue eyes, watching his desire reduce him to his simplest self, to someone who was not father or husband or border patrol or old or Anglo, but just a man, alone. He struggled with his car keys opening the passenger door while she leaned close and waited, staring at him, her back touching the cool steel of the truck, and when she reached out and touched his bare wrist he came to her without hesitation. She was sixteen and had been kissed before, once, but that was nothing like Mr. Clarke's wide hand pressing on the small of her back, or the touch of his thick, calloused fingers on her neck, or the sandpaper scrape of his cheek and chin against her face. She stood on her tiptoes, her head back and eyes half shut, half open, while he reached beneath her soft white shirt, his arm curling all the way around her body to stroke the skin between her hip and breast. She kissed him back hard and steady, feeling the rhythm of his chest and holding the backs of his thighs with her hands. How long it lasted she wasn't sure, but he suddenly straightened and pulled away, exhaling one long, loud breath, staring at her with his mouth still open as if slowly realizing the fact of his driveway, his truck, his house with wife and children behind him.

"Okay," he said to himself through clenched teeth, eyes closed and mouth tight. She kept her eyes on his face, watched it contract like he was trying to remember something. "Okay."

He drove her home and didn't look at her once. As they turned onto her street, she slid herself across the bench of the cab, took his shoulder in both her hands and lifted her face to find the curve of his jaw again with her lips.

He stopped the car and grabbed her wrists and kissed her back, roughly, once. Then he released her and looked away. "I think I have to stop driving you home," he said.

"No," she said. "You can't stop."

After he left she slipped quietly into the bed she shared with the thirteen-year-old Rebecca, turning her back on her sleeping sister and touching herself as she imagined he might. She kept her body as still as she could, and lay awake for a long time, thinking about the Clarkes' warm house, the bedroom, the bed.

It was during this time, too, she remembered, that her English began to improve, fast. She spent her evenings at home ignoring her schoolwork and plodding slowly through the books she took from the Clarke's house. Hermelinda read to the Clarke children every day, more often than they wanted, probably, but she was adamant and paid close attention when they corrected her pronunciation, their voices loud and whining and annoyed. She carried two books with her everywhere: a small black vinyl-covered Spanish-English dictionary given her by Mr. Clarke, and a notebook in which instead of writing down her thoughts she recorded all the words she'd wanted to say each day but couldn't, didn't know: raincoat, curtain, knee, bother, ditch, dangerous, mistake. Sometimes she thought that English had always been inside her, sleeping, waiting to be scooped out to the surface; sometimes she thought she was taking the language, word by word, off the lips of Mr. Clarke, sucking the English out of him when they kissed in the truck on the slow rides home. He had not stopped, and would often drive down to the river on the Texas side, hidden from the road, where they would stay as long as he thought was safe.

She was still a virgin when her father's boss shot himself in the head one Sunday, on the last day of May. It was Pedrito's sixth birthday, and the Salmerons spent the unknowing afternoon with the Morales family. The two fathers perched on their respective roofs with a rope stretched between them and set a burro-shaped piñata dancing through the air, while the children lunged after it with a crooked stick, determined, dizzy, and blind. Francisco and Gustavo pulled and yanked and laughed at the kids below until Hermelinda blindfolded Pedrito for his turn. The white-bodied, red-hooved burro hung generously still in front of the birthday boy as the undersized Pedrito hit it once and then again, but he could not crack its too sturdy sides. His swings grew increasingly wild and he was about to cry when Alejandro knelt behind him and whispered in his ear. The two brothers took the stick in their collective hands, Alejandro shut his eyes, and then they swung together, twice, savagely, first denting the belly and then ripping the piñata clean in two; the head and legs tilted to the sky one last time like a bucking bronco, and the bright-colored sweets spilled and scattered to the dirt. As the children scrambled for the candy treasure,

Pedrito stood paralyzed, still holding the stick tight in his hand and looking ready to hit something again.

For the rest of the day the families ate and drank, hovering around a long table in the yard as new dishes continued to emerge from both households. Hermelinda helped her mother in the kitchen, ferrying food and plates to the outdoors as the neighbors and friends kept arriving. Gustavo was coaxed into song, sucking on his cigarette between verses, exhaling melody with smoke while the crowd nodded and tapped. Poor Mr. Clarke, Hermelinda thought, picturing him in his hushed Presidio home with his sick, mute wife and tiny family.

It was not poor Mr. Clarke but rich, dead Mr. Thompson her father and Gustavo found on the following morning at the ranch, stretched out in his bathtub with a fist-sized hole in the back of his skull. The shotgun lay submerged in the tub beside him in the now cold, bloodied water. He'd used buckshot and pulled the beige curtain tight to the tile wall, tucked it carefully inside the basin to contain the viscous effects of the blast.

"That was his way of being considerate, I guess," Hermelinda overheard Mr. Clarke saying to someone over the phone as she supervised the children's construction of a vast wooden-block parking garage in the next room. "Keeping things as tidy as he could, making it easy to clean up." His voice was light as he could keep it, under the circumstances, but later that night Hermelinda listened to him trying to keep the waver out of his voice.

"In the shower this morning," he told her, "all I could think about was him splashing a little water up on the tile to seal the curtain, you know?" The moon wasn't out yet, Hermelinda remembered, and they sat in the unpopulated dark of his truck at their spot on the river. "That weird old son of a bitch." He held her tight against him and touched her. He laid her back and kissed her everywhere, running his lips slowly from her neck to her nipples to her belly, peeling back the rim of her jeans roughly and brushing his stubbled chin against her sex. She held his head there with both hands as he kissed her, and then he rose and she felt the sudden pressure and pain. She heard her voice that was not quite language calling out to him, but he did not understand her or did not listen or both.

She could not concentrate on her father's words later that night after Mr. Clarke had dropped her off. She arrived home late and found herself forced to sit in the front room with her parents. The pale green chair in the corner was as far away from them as the room allowed. Her father, unfazed by the hour or the reluctance of his audience, talked slowly but with no signs of pause about the ranch, Mr. Thompson, his death, and death itself. From the look on her mother's face he'd been talking for hours. Hermelinda tried to listen but could not, hearing nothing, only feeling her body, torn and sore.

"We can't know why a person does that, *mi'jita*. What he felt, or how God will look on it. We'd like to know but we cannot." Her father spoke to her as if by rote, sitting stiff and statued in his favorite chair, his eyes unfocused, his glance nowhere. "Or maybe we don't want to know." He kept on but Hermelinda could not listen, and could not watch. She was terrified that he would look at her in one piercing moment and recognize her difference, smell the sour salt on her skin all the way across the room, see Mr. Clarke dripping out of her and seeping dark into her jeans. She sat still and tried not to say a word, afraid that she might open her mouth to speak and instead cry out, that the moment would revisit her here, again. As soon as she could she went to bed, where she lay, unable to sleep, but thinking very little of her father's grief for his self-murdered boss. She did not understand that in losing Mr. Thompson, her father had lost his job as well.

The Thompson ranch was handed over to a far-off Montana brother, and Francisco and Gustavo drove out to the place one last time the following week to collect their back pay from him as executor of the estate. They took Hermelinda with them just in case he spoke no Spanish. He did not. Hermelinda's English was enough to know that there would be no bonus, no posthumous tribute to *el jefe*'s faithful workers, no plans to finish the last stone shed that was less than a month away from completion.

"My father says they would like to do it for his respects," she explained to Mr. Thompson's pale, slightly cross-eyed brother, watching his thin, tight lips press against each other in a preemptive refusal. "To finish their work here," she said. Francisco nodded as she spoke, pointing at the last uncompleted shed.

"Well, please tell your father that's very kind of him," the brother said, shaking his head. "I'm sure Cory would appreciate that." But there was really no reason, he said, and no time either. The place had already been sold to a cattle concern in El Paso; he himself would not be there for more than a few days. Hermelinda translated, and the four of them stood there in the silence that followed. They waited for the brother to say something, but instead he took a step forward and extended his right hand. It wavered without confidence in front of the men before coming to a halt at Hermelinda. She got a quick look at her father, but finding no expression there she took it. The brother's bony hand squeezed hers, hard, and they shook once, American-style. Then he shook the others' hands, quickly, nodding his head in a final way, saying nothing.

On their way back to Ojinaga they stopped the truck at the edge of Mr. Thompson's land. Francisco climbed a small hill and Hermelinda and Gustavo followed. Her father ascended slowly, stooping to gather rocks, balancing his loads in his hands. Near the top he nodded to Hermelinda, and she added more stones to his precarious pile. At the crest her father stooped and then let them drop, raising the dust into the growing wind. "*El jefe* was a man who deserved something,"

Francisco said, "and if that *cabrón* back there won't let us finish the shed, we'll remember him right here." He stamped his
foot to mark the spot and began to layer the rocks carefully in a
tight circle. Gustavo stood by, watching, bent and still. With his
hands holding his knees, hunched over like that, her father's
friend looked old. Hermelinda looked over at her father, kneel-
ing in the dirt, removing and replacing the stones, unsatisfied,
and suddenly he looked old too, an old man on his knees stack-
ing rocks for the dead. When he'd used up his stones he rose
and scanned the sides of the hill, his hand shading his eyes.

"Come on, Francisco," Gustavo said.

"One more flat one, a long flat one, that's all." Hermelinda's
father looked at his partner, but Gustavo had already started
for the truck.

"One more, Gustavo. Just one."

Gustavo did not look back. Francisco scooped up a fat,
uneven rock near his feet and held it a moment. He stooped as
if to place it on his tiny wall, and then straightened up to his
full height and raised the rock high over his head and threw it
down hard with both hands. The impact collapsed the enclo-
sure and cracked the hurled rock in two. Francisco turned his
back to his daughter and stared for a long moment north into
the desert, towards the Chinati Mountains of Texas. They
drove the rest of the way back home in silence.

In three months they left Ojinaga suddenly and for good.
They piled themselves and their belongings onto the bus for
Chihuahua, retreating the way they'd come, abandoning the
tiny house Hermelinda's mother had worked so hard to trans-
form into a living organism, an extension of themselves. "Only
to have your father ruin us again," she mumbled to Hermelinda
as they sat in the back of Gustavo's truck, waiting for their ride
to the bus station. Hermelinda didn't hear her, though, was lost
in her own feeling of ruin, the feeling of her stomach collapsing
when she'd heard what had happened, and understood that she

would never see Mr. Clarke again. She had tried, slipped from her bed and house late that last night and risked the streets between her house and the border crossing, walking briskly by the Mexican guards as they followed her trajectory, hungrily. On the American side she smiled at the familiar guard, the youngest man under Mr. Clarke's command, but he stopped her progress with one big, quick hand.

"Your papers, señorita?" He did not meet her eyes.

"David?" she said.

"I can't let you pass. I'm sorry."

"What is this? What are you saying? Please, David, I have to."

He didn't say anything, refused to say her name. When she didn't move, he turned her shoulder, not too roughly, and nudged her back towards Mexico. "Go home."

She crossed the bridge again and stood still in the middle of the river where the edges of the two nations met, looking north towards the lights of Presidio. She imagined she could see the Clarkes' house from there, but she wasn't sure. She passed through the Mexican border crossing and retraced her steps through the watchful streets, not caring who saw her or what happened to her. She felt at once inside and outside herself, a simultaneous moment of wanting to howl like the child she deserved to be, to point an accusatory finger of ruin at her older lover, to ruin his life, his job, his family, his everything she could think of. At the same time a part of her watched that bitterness from a distance, and that part of her seemed to know things she could not.

She wondered what Mr. Clarke's face had looked like that night as he arrived on the scene, with the two Mexicans handcuffed next to the confiscated truck, and the black garbage bags full of marijuana sitting in the dirt in front of them. What had he looked like when he turned them around and stared into the face of Hermelinda's father? She tried to imagine the words Mr. Clarke might have used to send the other officers driving away, and what he might have said to her father as he put them in the truck and headed south.

Mr. Clarke had driven them down to the familiar flats of the river, where he'd taken Hermelinda so many times. He stopped the truck and pulled the two men out, roughly. He uncuffed them. To the driver, Don Ybarra's man, he said, "If I ever catch you again, with drugs or anything else, I'll kill you myself. No trial, no appeals, no bribes, no help from your boss, you understand?" He pointed and the man began his unhurried traverse of the river, stepping carefully through the shallows.

"To me," her father explained, "he couldn't say anything for a long time, only stared at me like he was waiting for me to disappear into the air. I wasn't going to move until he said so. He looked like he might like to shoot me. Finally all he said was, 'I wish you and your family had never come here.' I knew he was going to release me then, so I stayed quiet. 'I can never see you again,' he said. 'Do you understand?' I nodded. 'Then get your family and go. Don't come back.' And I went as fast as I could. But it took me a while to cross the river. I fell a couple times. When I got to the other side, though, he was still there. His head down, like a dog. Just walking little circles in the dirt."

"You were lucky for Mr. Thompson, that they were such good friends. And Hermelinda," her mother said, jerking her daughter from her reverie, "taking care of his children. Do you think he did it for you? Because you're such a good person? No, you're lucky he had some reason for mercy." Her mother glared at Francisco, but he was looking at Hermelinda, hard, and she was looking across the river in her head, watching Mr. Clarke pace slow circles in the dirt. The river rushed deep and fast and wide behind her closed eyes.

They left Ojinaga by bus, climbing slowly into the mountains that waited south of Ojinaga.

"And now?" her mother said as they began their ascent. "Back to Chihuahua?" Her voice was unsteady, unbelieving, as she thought of the newly planted flowers she'd left behind and the concrete city ahead. Hermelinda heard her mother from far away as she stared out at the plains below, and at the Mexican river cutting out of a steep canyon to join the Rio Grande.

"What, Francisco, what will we do in Chihuahua?"

Her father shook his head and turned to his wife, taking hold of her arm and shaking her gently from the past until her glance moved from the windows to his face. He nodded then and unfolded a piece of paper on which Gustavo had scribbled a name and a phone number. He handed her the paper. She looked at him without comprehension, and he pointed again at the paper.

"Not Chihuahua," he said. "Laredo."

III

A<small>T SEVEN O'CLOCK</small> in the morning, Hermelinda would meet Lupita Mendes on the Mexico side of the Guerrero Street bridge and they'd cross together, briskly, walking past the stalled traffic backed up behind the border crossing into Laredo, Texas. Sometimes it seemed to Hermelinda that all of Nuevo Laredo gathered on that bridge each weekday morning, the cars packed in tight, wrapping one another in their exhausts, while men and boys navigated the narrow alleys of stopped traffic hawking newspapers, cigarettes, and gum. One of the boys who lived on her street was out there every morning, washing car windows, charming or bullying his way past wagging fingers and words of protest, and sometimes he'd wave to Hermelinda as she passed with her backpack full of books. Animated on the bridge, he was reptilian at home, forever perched on the stoop of his parents' house, half asleep, rousing himself only, it seemed, for this early-morning commerce, and perhaps again at night to slouch with his friends in the doorway of the neighborhood pool hall. That's how Nuevo Laredo seemed to Hermelinda in general, like a kind of lizard in reverse, afraid of the day, living and active in the spaces between the light, the early mornings and the late nights. It was the largest place she'd ever lived, a real city, but during the day it felt more deserted and more impermanent than all of the places she'd known. The population shifted, quickly and constantly, familiar faces could not be depended upon, abandoned buildings filled and emptied by the week, it seemed. Returning from Laredo, Texas, to its Mexican counterpart every afternoon, Hermelinda would walk carefully through the squares and avenues in search of any reason to stay away from the small, crumbling room where her family lived. Sometimes she left the busy main vein of Calle Guerrero and moved through quiet streets wondering who could possibly live in all of these buildings. She looked in the corners and cracks and alleys of Nuevo Laredo and wondered where everyone was.

She did not wander in Laredo. Laredo, for her, was a strict series of streets, a narrow route between the bridge and Nixon High near the airport. She had walked this once, more than forty blocks, on her first day of school, taking her time weaving through the wobbly grid of the city. She stopped on North Jarvis Street to examine the house where she was supposedly living, matching the address printed on her matriculation sheet to the number on the squat gray building, examining the doors and windows as if she might be expected to describe them to the principal upon her arrival at school. "North Jarvis," she said aloud, in English, practicing. "I live with my aunt on North Jarvis."

"No one cares," Lupita would tell her later. "They know the half of us live in *el otro lado*, they don't give a shit. As long as you have a Laredo address for the school to send grades, you could live in Nicaragua for all they care."

María Guadalupe Mendes, Lupita to everyone but her angry mother, lived in the south part of Nuevo Laredo; when Hermelinda first met her she traveled to school by bus. She took one to the border from her house, quickly driven and stopping often, and another from Jarvis Plaza on the American side to the corner of Meadow and Plum. The trip took almost two hours each way, but Lupita would usually run into friends as she crossed the border, and the last hour went quickly. She'd been crossing the bridge with friends when she saw Hermelinda that first day. Hermelinda passed them briskly, her scuffed black flats slapping on the metal walkway, and their conversation had stopped for a moment to notice her. Lupita registered the threat of beauty and recorded Hermelinda's dark skin and cheap shoes in a quick glance. That girl, Lupita thought then and again when she stood in the front hall of Nixon High, two hours later, watching Hermelinda enter the building for the first time. The new girl hesitated in the doorway, her face damp, her dress darkened with sweat from the long walk and unrelenting heat.

"You're late," Lupita had said, not kindly, in English. She hadn't meant to say anything, but she was too curious, too eager to see how this tattered beauty was going to behave.

"It's a long walk," Hermelinda said, in Spanish.

"It's a stupid walk, is what it is."

"It *is* a stupid walk," Hermelinda said. She pursed her lips in a tight, shameless smile and stepped close to Lupita, grabbing her by the sleeve. "But now I know Laredo, and I know you, and I know I'll never have to do it again. Come on, show me where to go." And Lupita, despite herself, smiled back and showed her.

From the beginning, she had Lupita, and she had the boys who bought her burgers and drove her from the border to the school. She was careful with them, and brought Lupita with her always, but she was too poor to turn them down. She had nothing. She knew the boys and what they wanted, and suspected that they were drawn to her by her powerlessness and poverty and by the lingering hints of sex that seemed to stay with her after Mr. Clarke. Sometimes she felt she was walking a step behind herself, observing, noticing her difference from her peers—she moved differently, not like a *coqueta* or a tease, but with a physical, expectant walk and a way of looking at men that they did not seem accustomed to.

Her new home was the most predatory place she had known yet, dirtier and meaner than Ojinaga or Batopilas. It was more violent, too. People were shot, someone every month or so, their bloody faces spread out in pixels on the front pages of the dailies. Still, she felt at home in Nuevo Laredo. She liked the size and activity and growth and wondered if there hadn't always been a city girl waiting to emerge from under the layers of her small-town, familial self. She liked the hectic main strip, where she was forbidden to linger but which really was the safest place to be. She liked the tourist bric-a-brac and fake doctors and liquor stores and overpriced *taquerias,* and she liked watching the hustlers and the drunks and drug dealers dance with tourists and police in a complicated series of steps through the alleys and bars and concrete hotels. She never had any money, of course, but on the weekends she'd go to the dance club near the border on the Mexican side. There were mostly Laredo kids there, crossing the bridge in their parents' cars to crowd the American-style bar with its neon lights and tightly packed dance floor. They came to *el otro lado* to drink, have sex, buy drugs. They did not flinch at the prices listed in dollars and pesos on the painted wall above the bar. The boys hit on rich Mexican girls, who cared more, dressed better, and seemed to come in more appealing shapes and sizes, seemed to ripen more quickly south of the Rio Grande. The girls moved in groups through this swamp of adolescent want, weighing each prospective partner with their eyes, evaluating their silent or stated offers.

Hermelinda stood outside the bar on Friday nights with Lupita and waited for someone she knew to take them in. She had one outfit, a hand-me-down black dress from a family Lupita's mother cooked for. Sometimes she even saw the girl the dress had once belonged to, driving with her father in an enormous blue Mercedes. It was Hermelinda's dancing dress, her party dress, her social dress, the only thing she had, really. The dress was a subject of ridicule for the girls at the club and at Nixon High during the week. Her "wicked witch outfit," they called it. Her *poncho de puta.* She wore it anyway, and took special care. There were occasions when she cut her nights short, hurrying home to immediately attend to a stain on the sleeve or body.

Hermelinda was beautiful in that dress. It was as if the fabric had been cut with the geography of her body in mind, hugging the contours of her torso to her slim waist, gently, before flowering down in a short layered skirt that moved weightless across her brown, shifting thighs. The dress was blackest with her long hair down when she stood in the outside light, but it could turn dark green if she tied her hair up with a green ribbon to expose her nape, or look navy blue with a suggestion of borrowed eyeliner. There were some boys, in fact, who didn't notice that it was always the same dress as they watched her move through the crowd, elegant among the tight jeans and blouses of the Laredo girls.

Her mother was afraid to talk to her when she came home at night, afraid of what she was doing, afraid of Nuevo Laredo. Their new home was smaller than any they'd known before. Dora was nervous when she went out, reading the frantic commerce of the streets, watching Laredo growing before her eyes across the river, knowing anything that grew so fast must be feeding on something, and knowing that the something was Nuevo Laredo, was Mexico. She hated the concrete and noise and streetlights, had not ever realized she hated those things until leaving the high walls of the Copper Canyon behind her for what she suspected was forever. Trading the quick, tumbling river that had flowed by her childhood home in El Arenal for the thin, muddy crawl of the Rio Grande was no trade at all, she thought, only a loss. Their proximity to the United States did not thrill her. In Laredo Dora saw displays of wealth she had never seen before, and watched the wide eyes of her children expand in the exposure to luxury, to unlimited material possibility. She had never been one to think of the United States as the promised land, despite the Batopilas tales from returning heroes with dollars in their pockets and the names of strange cities on their tongues.

"It is United States that is corrupt," Dora said. "The radio is always talking about corruption in Mexico but it is them."

"You're being stubborn," Francisco said, "stubborn and

blind. Can't you see what a good education Hermelinda is getting? How good her English is? Don't you ever think about
their possibilities? Who knows, just think, maybe a television
journalist. You know? With the right education." Dora snorted
and whipped the dirty dishes in front of her with a wet cloth,
but Francisco pressed closer. "And next year Rebecca will be at
the Nixon, too, such a better school than anything in
Chihuahua. Could you ever have imagined, our children with
an American education? Science, Rebecca likes science. In the
United States, they have women engineers, scientists, they have
women everything. Don't you think about how good this is for
them? Think about what we knew, what they know? How can
you not want things to be better for them?"

The men supported the family, but only barely. Alejandro,
who had never been very interested in school, had stopped going
when the Salmerons arrived in Nuevo Laredo. He left the house
early every morning and returned late at night. Hermelinda saw
him more often on the streets upriver from the bridge, where he
worked for an old man named Mauricio Trujillo, than she did at
home. They worked there every day of the week, repairing cars.
It was a poor neighborhood, but safe and abandoned during the
day. People from Laredo would cross the bridge and leave their
cars for Trujillo, and Alejandro and the old man would work on
them on one of the empty dead-end streets near the river.
Sometimes the people from Laredo would bring Trujillo an esti-
mate from a licensed shop, or a complicated explanation of
what was wrong; sometimes they would only tell him they
wanted it fixed for a certain amount. On rare occasions, they
might send a maid or someone to pick up Trujillo and Alejandro
and bring them to their car. In any case, the two of them kept
busy. The old man was arthritic and would often stand back
with his wrinkled, bald head cocked, listening to the discordant
tune of a suspect engine and shouting orders to Alejandro.
Trujillo still supported a family from his streetside business, and

he kept Alejandro there working long hours, working as long as there were cars and daylight. Everyone knew Trujillo, and they were rarely without work. He had been there forever; the cops didn't bother him and people seemed to trust him, at least with their cars.

Sometimes, in the empty afternoons after school, Hermelinda would visit her brother while he worked. She'd stand quiet against the wall and watch him reaching his hands into the innards of engines. He seldom spoke to her, here or elsewhere, but she felt he was glad for her presence. She didn't like Trujillo. He grinned at her and stared at her breasts, but he didn't say anything to her anymore, not after the first time she'd come, when Alejandro, holding an enormous wrench in one hand, had slid from underneath the oily bottom of an old Chevy, sat up, and stared the old man into silence.

Trujillo did not pay Alejandro well—twelve dollars a day, never more, and less if they only worked on a few cars. According to Lupita's father, Alejandro was just another in a series of young hands to do the hard, mechanical work, while the old man profited. That was the way of things, Hermelinda's father said.

"That's how you have to learn—from selfish old men who know everything about something. It's a good living, a mechanic. You can do it anywhere. You will make more money when you have your own tools, your own shop."

More money: that was always a problem, a problem no one was allowed to talk about. Although Francisco was able to envision the clear, impending careers of his children, and would boast about his stable of future mechanics, journalists, and engineers to anyone willing to listen, his own occupation was never steady or sure. He was a farmer, had grown up in the dirt of the Copper Canyon coaxing corn and onions out of the ground. He knew how to take care of trees and ward off pests. He knew which mushrooms you could eat and which it was best to leave

be. He was a passable fisherman, and good at finding wild peppers and fragrant leaves for tea. But for all his enthusiasm, he
was not a man for the city. The city distracted him. His mind,
his instincts, it seemed to Hermelinda, simply worked too
slowly. For a full year he scrambled for work, day after day,
week after week, steering clear of the border's enormous unofficial market which moved just under the surface, like a hot, com-
bustible flow of lava inches beneath a fragile skin of rock. There
was money there, but Dora would not have it.

"How long could we last," she said to Francisco, "if we lost
you here? Who would help us, without family, without friends?
There must be something you can do that isn't dangerous."

"Yes," he would answer, "there must be," but what that
something was he didn't know. He sold newspapers; he watched
cars in a hotel parking lot. He trimmed trees for a wealthy family on the edge of town. Nothing seemed to stick. Each engage-
ment quickly dwindled instead of flowering, and he started over,
time and time again. Alejandro's money kept the family afloat,
and it made Francisco crazy. Hermelinda fended for herself, and
attended school in the summer too, to stay away from home.
She worked hard to improve her English, her writing and reading. She sat in shady squares writing compositions in a faded red
notebook, scrambling after the fluency she knew she needed to
help herself. Afternoons she often spent alone in the tourist section of Laredo, where she knew she would not run into her
peers. Visiting the museum and art gallery near the river again
and again, she started conversations with older gringos from
Texas and other places too, paying attention to her accent, trying to evict the heavy traces of Mexican street talk from her
speech. In the museum Hermelinda was not so interested in the
Anglo relics from the near past, but she enjoyed the impressive
air-conditioning and the absence of commerce, and there were
long inscriptions in English and Spanish for her to compare.
Other afternoons she went with the neighborhood boy to the

pool hall down the street, where she persuaded the owner to turn the television to American shows. She watched and listened, understanding the lovers and cops and millionaires on the screen better with each passing day.

In the winter Alejandro had a shouting fight with Trujillo and would not go back to work. He refused to tell Hermelinda, or anyone else, what the argument had been about, refused to say anything at all, in fact. He sat in a chair in the back room all day long, listening to the radio, unresponsive to any attempts by his mother or siblings to deliver him from himself. On the weekends, he was waiting for Hermelinda when she came home, sitting outside on the street, smoking. He wouldn't speak but looked at her with something that seemed like hate. One night when she made to leave, he stood in the doorway, blocking her path. She knew better than to try to slip past him, and did not go out at night after that.

The family managed for several months on Francisco's income, and then, suddenly, they left. Their neighbors, a pair of brothers from Monterrey who worked as bus drivers for *Estrella de Oro*, returned home one night to find the door to the Salmerons' room ajar. The place was abandoned. The floor was littered with clothes, a few toys, an accumulation of school papers, broken pencils, single shoes. A cheap poster of the Black Virgin of Esquipulas was the only thing worth taking.

"They left," one of the brothers told a confused Lupita, who came looking for her friend on the following afternoon. It was only a few months before they were to graduate from Nixon High School. Lupita couldn't believe it. "Things were bad for them," said the brother. "Maybe they went home." But no one, not the brothers or Trujillo or Hermelinda's teachers or the window-cleaning boy down the street, knew where they had gone. No one knew.

LOVERS

1

Mike drove back to Cottesville in his father's yellow truck on the first Saturday in May. The other students followed behind, fourteen of them in eight cars. They took the highway out of Durham and past Raleigh, driving single-file, like a military caravan, until they hit the trees and open fields of the east. Then Mike turned off and they were out on the country roads in Jackson County.

They crossed the Achee River in the early afternoon, passing the metal signs waiting for them at the town limits. Cottesville, 8,861. Jackson County seat. 4-H Club. Once, when Mike was young, there'd been another sign up there with the rest, those simple three K's with the circle and cross, and the chapter number underneath. He remembered the summer when the two state trucks from Raleigh came to take the sign down. Two men coned off a lane and managed the slowed traffic and one man watched and two men unbolted the aging sign from the frame, and finally it was gone. Mike hit the horn as he led his friends into Cottesville for the first time, knowing their eyes were passing quickly over and through the real and phantom signs behind him. He was ashamed. He never told them what they could not see.

They were in Cottesville for three weeks before Mike saw her. The heat was already starting to thicken like a slow-stirred roux, and the fields filled up with workers, farmers, migrants from near and far. Mike was out all day and up late at night, presiding over stacks of memos, letters, copies, releases, schedules, applications, forms. The small office of the Catholic Retreat Center, with its brand-new wall unit and enormous desk, had become *his* office, and he was in there on Friday night when George showed up with the pictures.

While the others were working at the health clinic, collecting data in the camps, or volunteering in the schools, George Whipkey was taking pictures. They were the kind of pictures Mike never could have found on his own, although he felt he'd seen them before, or thought them, or imagined them. Familiar and foreign at once. He blamed it, or credited it, to George's distance, to his advantage of neutrality—the advantage of not quite giving a damn, of believing more in art and women and pork and beer than anything else. George wanted pictures. The rest didn't seem to matter to him. But the pictures agreed with Mike, even if George did not.

"Don't pull that country-boy stuff on me," Mike would say. "You know what's going on out here as well as I do."

"Hey, I'm doing my part," George said. His Tennessee drawl stretched the words out slow as he raised a cigarette to his lips and took a long pull. "I'm smoking fast as I can to pay your workers, put you through school. I'm fighting the good fight."

"They're really pretty damn good," Mike said. He was looking at one of the prints. Two small boys no shoes no shirts built a house from a pile of scattered trash. One boy had a raw red rash and open sore on his leg, sharply focused. Mike looked. Was that his father's camp? The trees in the background weren't right.

"How can you take a shot like this and not think about what it means?"

George looked at the picture. "It just, uh. Doesn't feel like my place."

Mike watched him trying and stayed silent, refusing to help him out.

"We're just different," George said.

"The camera's eye," Mike said. "The innocent bystander."

"Hey, now, Mike."

"All right. I just . . . you got more sense than anyone else out here. Be nice to have you watching my back, is all."

"You know I always got your back."

Mike nodded, looked at the picture again. "George," he said, "just because they're good ol' boys doesn't mean they're *good* ol' boys."

"I've seen a lot worse, you know," George said. "There places in Appalachia make that look like Disney World."

"Appalachia? That's a consolation, Appalachia?" They could talk like that all night and sometimes did, arguing and jawing over the contact sheets and the prints, while the others watched TV or read or wrote in journals or coupled in quiet corners of the Center, out of sight.

There were three pictures so far that Mike liked best. One was of an old rotten-toothed Mexican wearing brown pants and a baseball cap. The cap had "Horny as Hell" written in big flaming letters across a beet-red Satan with a forked tongue dangling from his mouth. The old man's arm was a blur of motion as he slapped another domino towards a maze of others resting in focus on the hood of a dead Plymouth. The second picture was of a huge tattooed black man coughing up something dark into the dirt, and the third showed a young big-eyed girl with tangled dark hair running down the rows of tobacco, her head tilted back over her shoulder at the camera, as if someone familiar had just called her name.

"Everyone always said you were a talented bastard, but I thought they were just trying to make a Tennessee hick feel at home." Without looking up he watched George smile, shift his feet uncomfortably in the warmth of praise.

"Sheeet. If an orangutan took as many pictures as I do, there'd bound to be a few keepers."

George left for the fields early every morning. He skipped

the shower and fumbled into dirty jeans to get to the Olives' land in time, but no matter how early he dragged himself out of bed, it was easy to arrive too late, to pull into the semicircle of trailers after the men had already left for the day. He didn't dare take pictures with the men gone. The women stayed indoors and waited for him to leave. He'd drive to the fields to find the men already working with Clayton Olive in the tobacco, or standing around the truck, getting ready. They worked quickly in the morning, trying to beat the heat. George made some small conversation with Clayton Olive and then took pictures. He followed them down the rows or found a good angle near the truck. After two days, though, somehow Mr. Olive made George feel like a shade of a man, standing on the sidelines with his camera. Olive didn't say anything, just looked at him sometimes with his mouth shifted over on one side. George took his pictures but couldn't endure that kind of silent judgment for long before he put down his camera, without thinking, and rolled back his sleeves. A breeze came and the leaves rippled down the row in front of him, rocking in place like a swaying sea of elephant ears. Then George waded into the green thickened field, bent, and took one leathery leaf in his hands, and when he looked up, Clayton was handing him a small, curved knife. He took it, and cut the leaf at the stem, cut another, and kept going.

"Somebody had to be the good son he almost had."

"I'm trying to appreciate that but my goddamn back hurts too much."

"What kind of mountain man are you, anyway?"

"The smoking, drinking, lazy kind. I hope."

"Oh, you love it. You couldn't be happier."

George lay down on the carpet, stretched his arms back. "Your dad told me tell you if you could come out there and give a hand, next week. Monday, Tuesday."

Mike made a small noise without opening his mouth. No. If

George saw the geometry of rows, or the composition of a man leaning against the side of a truck, Mike saw only expectations, old ones, everywhere he looked in the fields. "Yeah," Mike said, "well. I'll give him a call."

George had his eyes shut now. The skin on his face looked loose, uninvolved.

"If you don't want to get out there, don't," Mike said. "Just don't. Although I think it's probably good for you."

George didn't work as much for Clayton after that, but Mike was right, he realized. It was good for him. You had to have a way of stepping into that middle space where you weren't an insider, but you weren't an outsider either. Unless you were a really lucky bastard, nothing was going to happen until you found that middle space. So George worked. He blacked his hands with the tobacco tar beside the migrant workers, and they tried to talk to each other. He loaded the stacks with them and threw back tiny cups of water from the same coolers. The men pantomimed the camera when they saw him, and said "click-click," and he suspected that was their name for him. Click-Click. They treated him like the retarded cousin or the class clown. They laughed at him.

"Fondly, I'd have to say they're laughing at me fondly. But goddamn. I think I've taken a picture of every last inch of your tobacco fields," George said.

"There some good ones though."

"Yeah, there are. The boys don't even flinch in front of ol' Click-Click anymore. But I'm ready for something."

"Y'all barely started on the Nile. You just getting going."

"Shit. What are you running out here, a fiefdom?"

"It's a lot of land," Mike said quietly.

"Well. I'm full up on the workingman for a while. I'm ready to get them with their families."

"You will, you will."

Usually, George waited until the weekend to develop his

film. He'd drive back to Durham early, develop, and then bring everything over to Ninth Street to sit at the bakery, where he settled with his equipment at a wide wooden table and checked out the healthy tan summer girls in their tight white T-shirts and cutoff jeans. He looked over his contact sheets, first scanning, quickly, so that the miniature shot-after-shot blurred into a jerky movie playing out behind his eyes. Saturday night he'd meet some friends and go out drinking beer. So it was usually Sunday night when he'd hang out with Mike, show off his pictures, shoot the shit.

George was relaxed those Sunday nights, but he wasn't relaxed on Friday when he came pulling in from Durham and marched into the office and threw a stack of pictures onto the desk.

"I took these this morning," George said.

"Whatya got?" Mike was distracted, checking the time, waiting for Sarah and Raúl to come back from an outreach trip to one of the migrant camps on the east edge of Jackson County. He knew the farmer and wondered about the conditions and the crewleader. "It's only Friday," Mike said absently.

"This couldn't wait," George said.

He'd been sitting on the hood of his car, he told Mike, early morning, 5:15 a.m., waiting for the trailer doors to open to the hum of Clayton Olive's big truck pulling in to take everyone to work. He wanted to take a few shots of the men sitting on their stoops, but still didn't dare, yet. He felt aware of the violation that might constitute, crossing the lines between work to family and home. That morning, with the truck late, the men emerged still on schedule, talking to one another in quiet morning tones as they milled around the trailers, rubbing their hands together to keep warm, and one of the men who'd worked alongside George the day before appeared near his car. He pointed and said something with a big smile. The man was short, friendly, medium-dark-skinned, wearing an old Texas-style hat. He was a smiler, with a very expressive face, but he and George had no language in common. The man pantomimed a camera, pointed, smiled. George nodded, to say, Yep, that's me, I'm the crazy white dude that takes pictures. The smiling man nodded back, turned his head, and shouted towards a trailer. On his second shout a girl, about fourteen, flopped through the trailer door and ran towards them. She stopped beside her father, her eyebrows raised in question. He put his hand on her shoulder and spoke to her.

"He says you can take some pictures if you want," the girl said in fluid if accented English.

"Sure," George said. "I'd really like that." He turned to the smiling man and nodded again, moving quickly to the car to get his camera and lenses. A little boy had joined them now and stood close by, staring at the equipment, and George handed him an empty camera case to hold. "Here you go, little guy. Just tell him to hold on to that, okay?" he said to the girl. She told him while George checked his light meter. Then he was ready, fast. He took a step back and snapped two quick shots of the girl and her father before they both started talking to him at once. "What?" he said. "What's the matter?"

"Not us," the girl said, pointing at the trailer.

"I'm sorry," George apologized, congratulating himself on another mistake, wondering what insult he had committed now, but the smiling man smiled and took him by the elbow and pulled him towards the trailer, shouting. The man raised one finger and arched his eyebrows as if to say, "See?" and then pointed at the trailer. George tried to put an enthusiastic look on his face. He was confused. There wasn't anything wrong with the trailer, but it didn't seem like something to be too proud of, not in a photographic sense.

"All the men in the camp crowded around us now," George told Mike, "all waiting to see what's gonna happen. I see faces of moms and kids in all the other doorways, you can smell the breakfast, you know, everyone's been up a while. There kids outside, too, running up behind me to check me out. Like I've been invisible before, and then suddenly, there I am. So I'm standing there, looking at all the possible pictures I could take, and Mr. Smiles just keeps pointing at the trailer and pulling me forward like a crazy man. I gotta say I'm thinking pretty quick for so early in the morning, because I change my lens right then, put on the eighteen-millimeter, that way if I have to take pictures of the goddamn trailer, maybe I can still get in some of this madness around the edges. I'm starting to think that's gonna be a pretty good shot, all these people watching me take a picture of a trailer.

"'Are you ready?' the little girl says. Looks me right in the eye, very seriously, and says, 'My dad says you're going to make her famous.' She sounds kind of doubtful, like she knows her dad's a total nutter. And I'm doubtful cause I'm looking at the trailer and I don't know *what* she's talking about. I say something like 'Sure, hon, I'll do my best,' and I ask her if after I can take a picture of her, too."

"Making a deal on the side, huh?" Mike said.

"Trying. But she says no, 'I'm too ugly, I'm going to be a scientist.' What? At this point I'm starting to feel like a genuine *Twilight Zone* when Mr. Smiles grabs my shoulder and yells, 'He sto!' 'Hee-stow'?"

"Probably '*Listo*,'" Mike said. "Like, 'Ready.'"

"Right, '*Listo!*' Well, there it is."

George separated the contact sheet and the six pictures he'd printed and laid them all out neatly on the desk. They were wide-angle shots, as he'd said, taken from slightly to the side, and framed a crowd of men in work clothes and boots standing around one of the trailers. The morning mist hung over the other trailers in the background, rendering them ghostly, vague, suspended in space. Closest to the camera, in sharp and undeniable focus, a young woman in a slightly wrinkled short black dress stood on the steps of the trailer. Her hair was long and dark and painstakingly combed, hanging shining and curled in waves to the base of her neck. She was dark-skinned and full-bodied. She was beautiful. She stood straight and elegant on the trailer steps as if it were a coronation balcony high above a madding throng. On the contact sheet, Mike could trace the pictures chronologically: he saw her initial protest to being paraded out in the morning like this; the annoyed look; the self-conscious desire to be somewhere, anywhere, else. But by the fifth shot the self-consciousness was gone. She laughed. The eyes of the people crowded in a half-circle below her stayed fixed on the woman, but she herself turned to the camera and smiled, not in self-deprecation or embarrassment, but with something else.

Mike looked, all heat and blood.

"Her father thought I was a newspaperman or something. I don't know. I don't know what he thought, I don't really know what the hell was going on, he thought that I could make her famous." George tapped the desk beside him, where the woman continued to gaze out at George and Mike. "Look at her. Best picture I've ever taken. The goddamn queen of Mexico, living on your dad's land."

"I think," Mike said, but that was as far as he got. He picked up one of the pictures and carried it over to a standing lamp.

"Maybe I'll go out there," Mike said.

"Maybe, huh?" George said, smiling, but Mike did not seem to hear him or notice or care.

SHE MET HIM first on the front steps of the trailer, where he stood wrestling Spanish from his full lips and running a hand through his yellow hair. He was terrible. He stood relaxed when he'd finished, not budging in the face of what she knew was her mother's best unfriendly stare. He glanced quickly at Hermelinda, where she sat propped at the window, watching, then turned his eyes back to her mother to try again.

Her mother did not want to understand him. She set her face in stone, but still he stayed.

"*Qué dice?*" her mother called back finally to Hermelinda, who was smiling, watching the transaction.

"He says that he's the repairman," Hermelinda told her mother, translating the Spanish to Spanish and deciding not to laugh.

"Repairman? Look at his hands, he's never repaired anything in his life. You know who he is, the *dueño*'s boy, come to spy on us for his father, no?" They talked very fast so that there wasn't any chance of Mike's understanding.

Mike spoke again, repeated his practiced phrase, and then they all broke down, Hermelinda and her younger sisters bursting into laughter behind her mother, who hushed them. Mike laughed too, spreading his arms wide, bowing his head in mock defeat.

"What was so funny?" he'd ask her later. "What did I say?"

"To translate? You said: 'I am the son of the big chief, and I want to help the house.'"

"That's not too far off, is it? That's nearly perfect in caveman Spanish."

"Caveman?"

"Now see, you're not so perfect either." She made him explain and recorded it carefully in her notebook.

There was nothing funny about this son of the big chief to Hermelinda's mother. *"Cállense!"* she yelled at the children behind her, and then Hermelinda moved from the window and put her head over her mother's shoulder.

"Hello," she said.

"Hello."

"What do you want?"

"I thought I'd come out to fix some things in the trailers. My father owns the land."

"Yes, I know. And he sent you to fix some things in the trailers?"

"We did a few repairs before you got here, but I thought I'd come back and see if there was anything else."

"Qué dice?"

"Nada, mamá. He's not saying anything, just chirping like a bird." To Mike: "What else?"

"I don't know."

"Well, how are you going to fix anything if you don't know?"

"You can tell me. Translate for me to the other families." He looked over his shoulder at the rest of the camp. "There must be something."

She didn't answer him. She watched him. They waited for him to leave, but he didn't leave. He relaxed, instead, his stance shifting slightly as if to better prepare himself for a long wait. He looked at the ground, looked around at the other trailers.

They all stood and waited, and when Hermelinda could tell her mother was about to do something, shout or hiss or break into tears, she told her, *"Está bién, mamá.* I'll get rid of him," and walked down the stairs and past Mike while he watched her.

"Come on," she said.

"Gracias, señora," Mike said to her mother, but Dora was already inside with the children, ignoring him but somehow still watching them both warily out through the open trailer door.

"*Cómo te llamas?*" he asked, his accent very flat and ugly. He had to walk quickly to catch up with Hermelinda as she moved as fast as she could in front of him without running.

She didn't answer. They arrived at the Gomez trailer and she knocked on the door. Señora Gomez appeared, her frightened eyes barely visible in the gloom within.

"Don't be worried, señora," Hermelinda said. "I have this gringo here we can't get rid of who thinks he wants to fix your trailer. Is there anything you want him to do?"

"Really?"

"Probably not. But we'll find out."

The two women looked at Mike. He smiled, stood his ground.

"It's okay, tell him everything's fine. We don't need anything." Señora Gomez glanced nervously at Mike.

"She says the door do not close," Hermelinda announced, pointing. "The windows too so the bugs get in. And we need two new mattresses and the light is not working, and what else? Oh yes, there some holes in the wall you should close and they need a new pipe under the sink."

"Oh," Mike said. He looked at the trailer and squinted, not noticing when Hermelinda winked at Señora Gomez. "She said all that, huh?"

"Yes, Spanish is a very fast language."

"I can see that," Mike said.

"He doesn't know, anymore," Hermelinda told Señora Gomez. "He's going to leave now." The señora said nothing, looking down at the ground.

"Well, sounds like a good start," Mike said. "I'm going to get some more tools, I'll be back. *Tú puedes esperar?*" he asked the señora. "*Yo traer más cosas.*"

"It's more proper if you say *usted* with the older woman," Hermelinda told him. "Not *tú*."

"That's right," he said. "Thank you. I forgot."

"You have to be more careful the way you talk to people. In Spanish."

"I guess so," he said slowly. His eyes hit her for the first time, and she looked away from that moment of soft, cool blue. "Well," he said again, "is there a proper way to tell her 'It was good to meet you'?"

"*Mucho gusto.* But you shouldn't shake their hands," she said, as he extended his towards the señora and then withdrew it, glancing back and forth between the two women.

"*Mucho gusto,*" he repeated. He kept his hands at his side, bowed his head slightly. He pointed to himself. "Miguel. Michael. Please tell her I'll be back in an hour or so, if that's convenient."

"It's better you say '*Mucho gusto, señora,*'" she said as he turned to go, lowering her voice an octave and giving a slight, solemn nod with her head. "For respect, you know."

"I'll remember that. Next time," he said.

"*Eres terrible, Hermelinda.*" Señora Gomez was a little horrified but finally allowed herself to laugh when the boy had returned to his truck and driven away.

"I know," she said. "But he won't come back so soon, maybe." She knew as she spoke, though, that it wasn't true.

He was back in the afternoon. She stayed out of his path, eyeing him from the window when she was sure he wouldn't notice. She shouldn't have talked to him like that. It was boredom, perhaps. He was pretty. He was something she did not know. He worked until the early evening, finishing with new hinges for the trailer door, which didn't seem very complicated, but he was there for hours before he decided it was done. He left just as the men were coming back from the camps, the busiest time of day, with all the kitchens humming and exhausted husbands and fathers calling for their children or their dinner, depending on their mood. He waved to them as he drove past carefully on the narrow road, and they all watched him go.

"What was he doing here?" her father asked the women as he stepped into the trailer. He removed his baseball cap and peeled off his filthy shirt, filling the small space with a sour mix of sweat, dirt, and hair.

"He was fixing some things at the Gomez house."

"Do you know who that is?"

"Is he a movie star, Papá?" Hermelinda asked, her eyes wide.

"No, he's not a . . . ah, you already know. Smart-ass." He threw his disgusting shirt at her and she yelped, batting it to the floor. "Well, Nacho won't like it. That's the son who made them change things around. How they pay, when to pay, how much, same money for every person. Nacho said for the father it didn't matter, but it was him." Francisco pointed a swollen finger at the world outside.

"Isn't that better?"

"Fuck no," Alejandro said, mumbling from the doorway, where he stood smoking a cigarette.

"Alejandro," her mother said, tilting her head in warning.

He ignored her. "It means you get slow old men and little boys getting the same as me," he told Hermelinda. "And if someone's lazy?"

"The boys aren't getting the same," her father corrected. "Otherwise we'd have Pedrito out there, tomorrow. I don't know." He shrugged. "Sometimes it seems like you can work hard and not get so much reward. Nacho doesn't like it, but that's because he has less control. Less money for him maybe. But everyone says this is one of the best farmers to work for."

"Because he's rich," Alejandro said.

"That doesn't matter. Sometimes the rich ones are the worst," her father answered.

"Why doesn't the son work in the fields?" But her father just shrugged and shook his head.

When Mike came again the following day, Hermelinda stayed inside. She watched him trying to put Señora Gomez at ease when she came to the door, but he couldn't know how wrong he was to be there, how his presence disturbed people. Even a dumb gringo boy had to know it a little, the way people looked at him, the way the children were too quiet. He must want to be there very badly, she thought. He worked steadily through the morning, his shirt darkening in the heat, the lines of his body becoming visible through the wet cotton.

She went outside in the afternoon, to take some trash to the dumpster, and he was up on the Gomezes' roof. He waved as she passed. On her way back, he called out to her.

"Hey," he said. "Would you do me a favor?"

She kept walking. Inside the trailer again, she watched him climb down off the roof, pick up a tool she did not recognize, and then climb back up. She did not go outside again until he left.

He was on the roof the next day again. When he called out to her this time, she walked quickly over to the trailer and stood beneath him.

"Listen, you are not being polite," she said, in a hushed voice.

"I'm sorry?"

"Leave me alone."

"I'm sorry."

She meant to go then, but instead she said, "Why don't you work in the fields with your father?"

"Why?" he said, crouching, looking at her closely now.

"Yes," she said. "It's curious, no?"

"I guess it is."

"Well?" She glanced back to her own trailer, but her mother was still out of sight.

"My father would like to know the same thing. I'll tell you what I told him, see if you take it any better." He reached down as he spoke to her, exploring a crack between the roof and walls with his fingers. "I don't think I'm a farmer. Would you hand me that caulk? The white tube."

She passed it up over her head, feeling her shirt shift to expose her as she raised her arm. She caught him then, saw the effort expended in trying not to look at her. She felt something, a pleasant nervousness, a quickening, as he concentrated on the caulk.

"Well, what are you?" She was very conscious of her body as she lowered her arm. She stayed where she was. "You're not a person who fixes roofs, I don't think."

"What am I," he said. "Now there's a question." He put the new tube in the caulking gun, screwed it tight. "What do you say to that."

"You must be something."

"I must be. How 'bout you?"

I'm a poor girl living on a rich man's land, she thought, but said nothing.

He waited for a moment, and then looked away, as if he'd heard her anyway. "I'm a student," he said. "I guess that's what you'd say."

"Oh," she said. "You look old."

He laughed. "College," he said. "University."

"You fix roofs at the university?" The words kept coming out of her before she could stop them, and she knew that this was not right, to be standing here playing *coqueta* with a stranger on a roof. She should walk away, right now.

"No. I helped my dad fix a few out here, though."

"And at the university?"

"Law," he said. "The law."

"Are you smart?"

"I'm a little bit smart. Can't you tell?"

"Not so much. Not yet. Why do you want to be a lawyer?"

He stopped caulking for a moment, raised his head, and looked right at her. She met his eyes this time and they stayed like that for a short pause before he answered her.

"I don't really care so much about the law," he said. "But

there is a whole lot of law in this country, and it seems to me if you want to do anything you need to know it."

"Like fixing roofs."

"I don't guess it helps too much in fixing roofs. But other things."

"What things?"

"Well, for one, making sure you don't get pushed around. Maybe even pushing some other people around, people who you think need to get pushed. Maybe that's the honest answer. To learn how to be a kind of bully, sometimes."

"And who do you bully?" she asked, then lowered her voice. "Maybe Señor Blanco?"

He didn't hear her at first, or didn't understand and stooped on the roof with his lips pressed tight, trying to make sense of the sounds. "Ignacio, you mean? You mean about things here?"

"Yes."

"We worked something out with the pay, with the money."

"Yes, the money," she said. They were almost whispering now. He was as low as he could be to the roof without lying down, while she stood up very straight, bracing herself on the side of the trailer.

"We thought the crewleader took too much," he said. "It was supposed to make things better."

"Better for who?"

"Better for you," he said. He looked worried now. "For your family. For . . . the people who work. It's not better?" There was a softness in his eyes now, a weakness that was more like a boy than a man. She felt that all it would take from her was a single syllable one way or another to change him, and she held that moment without speaking because he kept looking at her, waiting for her verdict as if it meant something.

"Hermelinda!" Her mother was yelling from the trailer steps, holding little Pedro by the collar. *"Vente!"* Hermelinda turned then, and ran for the trailer without looking back.

The next day he was there only for the morning, and the day after that in the afternoon. He'd moved on to the Hidalgo trailer by now. She stayed out of his way, feeling the weight of her mother's surveillance whenever she stepped outside. But she could also feel him watching. He did it carefully, so that she maybe would not have noticed if she wasn't waiting.

She spoke to him again when she went out to look for her little brother Pedro, later that afternoon, but only because Pedro was hiding in the cab of his yellow truck. She pulled her brother roughly from inside, dragging him out of the seat by one arm, while he watched.

"I'm sorry," she said, not looking at him, hissing at her brother under her breath.

"I don't care," he said. "I really don't. Is that your brother?"

"Yes."

"Oh. I guess you like trucks, huh," he said to Pedro.

She took a step back, started to turn to leave.

"I didn't want to sound stupid the other day," he said.

She wanted to say something, but she was under control now. She looked at him dully, she hoped.

"Listen," he said again. "If I'm doing the wrong thing some-one has to tell me. I thought fixing up the trailers, and getting more pay for . . . I thought it would be better for *me* if I was the one who lived here and worked for Ignacio and my dad. But I don't, so the fact is, I don't know. If I'm being stupid, some-one's got to tell me."

All she had to say was yes, she thought. Or walk with her brother back to the trailer. "I don't know," she said.

"Okay," he said.

Pedro was inching away from her already, headed back towards the huge yellow truck, but Hermelinda had forgotten about him. She waited for Mike.

"Maybe we could talk about it sometime," he said. "Maybe we could talk." I need to be gone, she thought. But he was still looking at her and she had to say something. She wanted to.

"To make it better," she said, "it's mostly more money." She knew that the way she was talking to him was terrible, dangerous, wrong. But what if he listened? He was listening, she could see it. What if she could help her family, could help them through him?

"I think the money is more," he said calmly, "now than before. Maybe for the best guys, who work the fastest and the hardest, it doesn't seem like more than they made before, because we split it up in equal shares. But I bet that as a family it's more. And this way the incentive is for the group, and that must make . . ." He moved his hands together as if he were squeezing a ball. "A better environment?" His voice rose in question as Hermelinda heard the screen door of the trailer slam and she knew she'd stayed too long.

"I have to go," she said. "Pedro!" She collected her brother swiftly and turned for the house. He was saying something else behind her but she couldn't understand, and although she wanted to turn and hear him, she did not.

On Friday he did not come. She watched for him, expecting at any moment to see the morning or afternoon dust rise and the yellow truck slide into the clearing. When her father and brothers came home that day they were in a good mood. They had dollars. Hermelinda's father withdrew to count it again in the bedroom, alone. When he came out, he kissed Hermelinda's mother and handed her the small plastic bag with the money, whispering in her ear.

Outside, in the middle of the camp, Ignacio Blanco was distributing paper bags full of food. Hermelinda went to collect the Salmerons' share of chickens, peppers, cheese, corn, eggs, meal, flour, and rice. There was even a rectangular brick of sausage. "Eat," he said. "Fatten up. Don't matter to me."

Her father laughed at the sight of the food-filled bags, tossing peppers to his daughters, pretending to throw eggs at his sons. "Nacho's angry with the farmer," her father said. "I think he's trying to spend as much on food as he can, to prove this new way doesn't work."

"If he's so unhappy, Papá, does that mean he was stealing money before?"

"Was making more, for sure. But I don't worry about him."

"We should worry," her brother said. "He'll figure out a way to get it anyway."

"Or leave, take us somewhere else, maybe," Hermelinda said, "if he doesn't like it here?"

"Worry, worry, why do you two do all this worrying? That's what me and your mother are supposed to do," Francisco said cheerfully. He picked up one of the chickens and squeezed it, nodding his head in approval. "Still frozen. That's my biggest worry right now because I'm hungry. Very very hungry." He made snarling noises at Pedro and tried to devour the screaming boy, chasing him around the tiny trailer until he finally caught him and kissed him on the head.

It rained the next day, and there was no work. The men stayed in bed all day, sleeping. The younger children snuck outside to play in the rain. Hermelinda read an English book she'd brought from Laredo, a story about a young soldier in the United States civil war. She'd read it before, but it was a good book, and she liked the practice. She spoke English less now than she had for years, and she felt it slipping from her grasp, word by word. In the late afternoon the rain stopped and she went for a walk with Camilla through the woods. They did not go too far, unsure of the farmer's property and the terrain and the possibility of meeting someone they did not want to meet. She walked quickly, trying to fight the fatigue which seemed to accompany the long days of nothing to do, and nothing imminent.

He drove into the camp that night when there was just an impression of the finished sunset in the sky, an orange-black outline which ringed the trees beyond their trailer. She watched him hesitate as he stepped out of the truck. The men had come out onto their doorsteps when they heard the engine, and they watched him. He walked to the Hidalgo trailer with an electric drill in his hand, had a short conversation with Señor Hidalgo, and then left the tool with him. Then he turned and headed for the Salmerons'.

Her father met him outside, buttoning up his shirt with one hand and shaking Mike's with the other, inviting and pulling him inside at the same time. Mike ducked his head in the low doorway and then sat at the table. The family had finished eating, but her father barked commands at the children and Hermelinda's mother. Camilla warmed beans over the stove and heated chicken pieces in an oily pan. Her mother began making tortillas again; Rebecca squeezed a fresh lime to mix with water and sugar in a tall, cracked glass.

"No, por favor, ya yo como," Mike said. He pantomimed a full stomach, shook his head politely. No one paid him any mind. A full plate of food was placed in front of him, piled high and steaming, and he thanked everyone before picking at it obligingly. Hermelinda watched from the small bedroom as he ate and struggled with the Spanish.

"I," he said, and pointed at Pedro. "There is a school."

Hermelinda's parents waited politely for him to make some sense.

"School for little children like son," he said. He pointed at Pedro. "How old?"

"He's seven years old, señor."

"Yes?" Mike said, feigning surprise. "Seven years?"

Pedro was hiding behind his father, refusing to play the gringo's game.

"Yes, seven is good," Mike said to Hermelinda's parents, nodding first at her father and then her mother. "There is a school." Hermelinda could see that her little brother did not understand the *güero's* mangled words, but Pedro did understand that a decision was impending that would affect him. He had emerged from his cover and looked imploringly up at his father, shaking his head. He frowned.

"When I am little, I don't like school," Mike said. "I wanted," he said, and he paused, moving his arms, pretending to drive.

"Yes, to drive," Hermelinda's father said. He moved his arms too, smiling. "To drive."

"To drive. I don't want school," Mike said, nodding. "I only want to drive. The truck. I was like you," he told Pedro. "But school is more important. The most important of all."

"Yes, yes, señor," her father said. "I agree, I always agree that education is the most important of everything. My children have very good educations, American schools, they will not be like me. Much more intelligent."

"What kind of school is this?" Hermelinda's mother asked. Everyone looked at her now. She examined Mike closely, and her mouth was straight and hard.

"For children migrants," he said. "To study in the summer."

Her mother stepped towards the kitchen stove and pulled a big manila envelope from a shelf. "I have his school papers here," she said. "All the papers for all of them, I keep here." She stood on the other side of the table from Mike and handed him pieces of paper one by one. "This is Pedro. And this is Pedro too. That's Camilla and Rebecca and that's Manuel." She stood there, her hands outstretched, waiting for him to hand the papers back, but he put them on the table and examined them, one by one.

"Yes," Mike said, looking at the papers. "Good."

"When is the school?" her mother asked.

"Monday," Mike said. "Monday, Tuesday, Wednesday, Thursday, and Friday."

"Yes," her mother said, "but what hours? Where is it?"

"In the town. There's a van to take him at eight in the morning. And three in the afternoon."

"Okay," her mother said. "I will go and talk to the teacher on Monday. I want to see the teacher and the school."

He didn't understand her this time and glanced at Hermelinda in the bedroom, hoping for help, but she leaned back on the bed out of his sight, and she heard him asking for the mother to say it once again. Then he understood and they agreed. When she peeked again her mother was putting the papers back into the manila envelope and her father was gesturing urgently at the uneaten beans. Her mother put the envelope back in its place and came into the bedroom, where she began to pull clothes out of a plastic bag. Pedro followed her, sensing disaster.

"*No mamá,*" little Pedro said, starting to whine.

"*Oye, vas a ir.*" She looked at Hermelinda. "He doesn't have anything to wear, nothing. Sew up these old pants of Mani's." She raised a pair of brown pants with a rip in the crotch. She held them out. "Now," she said, when Hermelinda did not move. She held the pants out in front of her.

"Tank you," her father was saying to Mike in the next room, with an accent that made Hermelinda cringe. "Tank you tank you."

"I'll do it in a minute," Hermelinda said.

"Now," her mother said. She tossed the pants at Hermelinda, not gently, and left the room.

Hermelinda held the pants in her hand and probed the rip with her fingers. It was big, wide, and awkward. It would take a patch. She wondered if they had anything else that brown. It was an ugly color.

The farmer boy didn't leave. She could hear him still in the next room, explaining something. A health clinic for migrant workers. "It's a little far, but even if you have no money, people can go there."

"Ah, we are not sick, señor, thank you, thank you very much. We are all very healthy, thanks to God. I had three teeth pulled in Laredo, you know, I feel very good now, but before they hurt very much, I would go to this clinic for that but the problem is already finished." Her father opened his mouth wide, gestured at the gaps inside, towards the back.

"Yes," Mike said, unsure of himself. "I work at the clinic."

"Very good," her father said. "The clinic is very good."

"Yes," Mike said again. "Many people come there every day, but they don't have enough people who speak Spanish."

"Yes, yes," her father said, "it's important to speak English here. My girls speak English very well. Rebecca, Camilla, Hermelinda."

"Yes," Mike said. "I know. Hermelinda speaks very good."

She heard her name in his clumsy voice for the first time and had to stop herself from rising and going into the room. She bent her head to hear what came next.

"The clinic wants a person to translate," Mike said. "It's seven dollars the hour. Hermelinda wants to work?"

She felt a quick rush of anger as he said her name again. She was angry at him and at herself that she could have let him think he could do this. He turned when he saw her standing in the doorway. "I thought maybe—"

"*Sí, ella es muy lista, no?*" Francisco said, delighted and bragging. "*Muy bonita, muy lista, la joya de los Salmerones. Hermelinda? Ven, ven acá!*" She did not budge, but instead slipped into the inoperative bathroom and latched the door. "*Ella está un poco tímida,*" her father said, and her mother snorted. Hermelinda came out of the bathroom then, entered the room, and glared at everyone.

"I apologize," Mike said to her. "I didn't mean to say anything inappropriate. The clinic told me they needed someone yesterday and I just thought maybe—"

"Thank you, we'll have to talk it over. Goodbye," she said definitively.

He rose. "Forty hours a week," he said. "Seven dollars an hour."

"Yes, we heard you," Hermelinda said.

"*Sí, señor Michael, sí,* tank you, tank you *para todo.*" Her father followed Michael to the door, all but bowing and scraping as he went. He walked him out to his truck, thanking him all the way. He rushed back to the house, where everyone waited for his return, and the argument they sensed would follow.

"No, Papá," Hermelinda said. "Don't you see, he's trying to buy us with all these things. It will be bad for us here in the camp, I know it will. Everyone will hate us. Maybe he's trying to make things worse in the camp, I don't know why. Or I don't know why but he's trying to buy us."

"You're wrong, *mi'jita,* he's a good man, his father is a good man. I know a good man when I see one."

"Like the men you knew in—"

"Hermelinda," he growled.

"Remember, Papá, you taught us not to let anyone buy us like this."

"This is different. This is a real chance. You could become a doctor!"

"*Mamá!*" But her mother shook her head.

"If your father says you should work, you work."

"But he doesn't listen, he doesn't think about——"

Her mother was already gone, off to look for more clothes for Pedro.

She squeezed by her father, who was still in one of his fantasies, dreaming, perhaps, of more money, or his daughter the imminent surgeon. Outside she found her brother sitting on the steps. He was smoking and staring off across the dark fields towards the road. She sat down beside him, one step down, so his smoke drifted over her head and away.

"What do you think?" she asked him, looking up at him over her shoulder.

Alejandro shrugged.

"I don't like it," she said. She wasn't sure if that was true, but it made her angry, she knew that. "I can't believe Papá would just let me do that." She spoke quietly, not knowing if she was talking to her brother or herself.

"We need money," her brother said finally. His voice was very even, very matter-of-fact. "To get out of here."

It was quiet outside, and dark. They looked around at the night together. There were stars out but when she looked at them it seemed to Hermelinda that her brother was right, that they were the wrong stars. There wasn't anything about this world to champion or defend. They were nowhere. They were here for work, to get as much money as they could, and to return to someplace where they belonged. She was just being scared. She was just acting like the precious little girl she'd never been, and never wanted to be.

"I want to," she said to her brother. "I want to go back."

"I know."

"I'm going to do it."

"Yes," he said. "Good."

ON MONDAY, HER mother went with Pedro to the school and came back satisfied, even optimistic. Hermelinda could hear her talking to her father about the possibility of having Camilla go, maybe Rebecca too. If there was room. There must be room, her father said, Señor Michael would find them room. He was sure of that.

On Tuesday, Mike came to take Hermelinda to the clinic. She didn't talk to him at all on the drive. They listened to the radio as she stared out the truck window at the endless same-ness of the countryside, the blocks of trees and fields that were not different from the trees and fields around her trailer. It was a twenty-minute drive. There was a little country store and a restaurant. There was an old gas station, with cracking asphalt for a parking lot, and two weathered red pumps in front. It looked closed. Mike drove in silence, relaxed, it seemed to her. He waved small finger waves at the few other trucks driving by, dangling his arm out the window in the cool sluicing early-morning air.

"This too cold for you?" he asked.

She shook her head no although it was and he nodded at her and then rolled the window up anyway.

At the clinic she didn't understand anything at first, only that there were too many people and not enough doctors and that her job, as far as she could tell, was to explain this over and over to the people who didn't understand English. She liked the doctor, though. He was a short man who spoke very quickly and through his nose, joked with her and answered her questions about the forms and procedures and anything else. "Don't ever leave us," he told her at the end of the first day. "We'll have you doing heart surgery by the end of next week." She thought of her fantastical father and laughed.

She was not so crazy about Raúl, who went to school with Mike. His Spanish was different, very fast, and he talked too much. As he drove her home at the end of the day, he explained that he was working at the clinic all the time, driving out through the countryside to find migrant camps, make referrals, make sure people who needed medical help got help. He told her this and plenty more, talking to her nonstop in Spanish for each of the twenty minutes between the clinic and her temporary home.

"It's great that you're at the clinic. You're somebody they can really trust, you understand exactly what they're going through. And someone who can really talk to them, that's rare. Mike doesn't really understand what it's like out here for migrants. He understands enough to know that it's hard, but he doesn't have to deal with the whites like we do. Of course, they're all racists, all these farmers, it's impossible to do any-thing, even Michael's father, even Mike, you know, they don't know what it's like for us," he said, as if the two of them were equals, this clean boy with a foreign car and the penniless girl from the border. "He puts all this emphasis on the crewleader, you know, and the ignorance of the farmers, but he won't really come to grips with the active part his people play in all this. Not enough, at least. You haven't seen the town yet, right? You can really feel it there. You think you have the devil sitting on your shoulder the way they look at you. How are you treated at the Olives' farm? Just because it is his farm does not mean you can't tell me what's wrong. You shouldn't think that. Are they really paying what they said they'd pay? Are your parents getting all their money? Is anyone ever threatened or anything?" She did not remember answering any of his questions but that didn't seem to stop him.

She was disappointed when Raúl picked her up the next day, and for a week it was the same. She got used to him a little. It was strange to her the way he talked about her and her family as migrants; she didn't think of herself like that. She didn't think of the families that came to the clinic as being like her family, although many of them were Mexican, and some were even from Laredo. She helped them checking in and out, assisted them in completing forms and questionnaires, entertained the whining children, and relieved women of their crying babies so they could see the doctor or use the bathroom. There were some people in terrible shape. Many were visibly damaged, with sores or gaping wounds or limbs angled the wrong way. Others looked like they were rotting away inside, their skin intact but pale, withered. Sometimes you could hear the sickness in their voice or throat or lungs. There were children who did nothing but cry, or worse, the ones who barely moved and made no noise at all. There were people who looked fine but had diseases and conditions she'd never heard of, never known existed. Many of the men stared at her, of course, long and hard and all the time.

Back with her family she could not think of the specific things she'd done during the day but felt exhausted nonetheless. Sometimes Mike was at the clinic, and he'd wave to her but did not seem to pay her much mind. He moved as if he was busy. He'd drop off people from the camps, pick them up, talk to them at length in the dirt parking lot around the clinic's trailers. People called for him on the phone, often. She did not understand the relationship between the confident young man at the clinic, who seemed to be in charge, or close to it, and the tentative boy who'd repaired roofs for her neighbors at the camp. There were little things she recognized. He'd get that soft look in his eye sometimes when he was talking to patients waiting to be seen by the doctor, or trying to make people feel at ease when they were coming to the cramped, busy clinic for the first time.

On Friday, Raúl was elsewhere, and when Hermelinda stepped out of the clinic trailers, Mike was waiting to take her home.

They'd driven for a few minutes when she said, "You should have asked me first." It was the first time either of them had spoken to the other directly since Mike had driven her to the clinic, that first time. "If I wanted to work."

"I've missed you," Mike said.

There was only the engine then, low and regular, and the tires' waltzing rhythm against the cracked ribs of the road. She pretended to herself that he hadn't spoken at all.

"And I'm sorry I didn't ask you first." He glanced over at her, but she kept her eyes straight ahead. "Christ," he said, "I feel so awkward, I feel so damn stupid."

He stopped the car, pulled over to the side of the road. "Would you like to drive?" he said. She was poised, as he spoke, ready to become all elbows, nails, and knees if she had to. "I thought maybe you'd like to drive. It's a pretty good car, I know all the cops in the county. I just want to do something with you. I thought maybe you could drive." He scratched his head, rubbed the back of his neck. She didn't answer. "Okay," he said. "Could you just please forget I ever said any of that?"

"I don't know how to drive," she said. "I never did it."

"Never?"

"No."

He opened his door, stepped outside. "Please," he said. "Would you please drive me home?"

She looked at the steering wheel, the pedals, the dashboard. She did not want to want to drive. But she wanted to drive.

She leaned over towards the driver's side and listened to him explain, and then slid over and took the wheel in her hands. She pressed down on the gas and listened to the engine crest and then fall. She took the shift on the steering column and pulled it down to "D." The car began to roll forward.

"Brake," he said, jogging alongside her, but she hit the other pedal and the car jumped forward, and she turned the wheel to get back on the road, and then she was cruising down the road, there was a thud behind her, she was yelling "Michael, Michael," and then somehow he was talking to her from the back of the truck. He slid the little window aside and explained everything again, slowly, as she drove, and they went all the way home like that, as if it were the most normal arrangement in the world. After a little while he was silent except for telling her directions, and after that he sat down in the bed of the truck so that only the top and the back of his head were visible to her when she looked behind. She forgot about him sometimes as she held the wheel tight, trying to understand the dimensions of the vehicle, trying not to hit trees and mailboxes and the other troubles of the road.

When they got near home he was there in the window again.

"Do you want me to—"

She shook her head fiercely, the long hair falling down over one side of her face, where it stayed, since she would not remove either hand from the wheel to brush it back.

She bumped them up the road to the camp. When they reached the clearing she hit the gas instead of the brake, again, and then the brake double hard so that they skidded to a noisy halt into the center of the camp, bringing all the women and children out of their trailers to find Hermelinda stepping out of the cab and Mike jumping out of the back in the funnel cloud of dust.

"You made me nervous," she said. "On my shoulder."

But he didn't look mad at all but very happy, his eyes wrinkling up on the sides, and he didn't say anything but put his hand out, and she took it, and they shook hands twice. He seemed about to say something then but instead he began to run. Behind her, the truck, still in gear, had started to wander out of the clearing towards the fields, and now Mike caught up to it, fast, his yellow hair a golden blur through the air, but just as he reached it the truck bucked up and then crashed down into the ditch between the camp and the pepper field, and Mike stood there with his hands on his hips, and the kids ran eagerly towards the disaster, shrieking, and the women laughed behind them, and it was all anyone could talk about that night. When the men got home Hermelinda had to tell the story again and again, and she did, but she did not tell them about the feeling she'd had when she sat behind the wheel alone and imagined herself alone like this in a truck heading for anywhere, driving out on the roads of the world to all the places that must exist and all the places she could know. Does everyone know about this? she wondered. And if so, why was it more people didn't just disappear?

Mike had a long walk back to the center. He returned later that night with George to pull the truck out of the ditch. The men crowded around and watched, calling out advice and encouragement. They wanted to hear the story from him. Tell us, they said. Stay and tell us. They nudged George with complicity and pointed at Mike, smiling. Mike struggled with the words, but it didn't matter. The crowd helped him. They knew the story. Hermelinda listened, but stayed in the trailer, out of sight.

Come back, the men said, as the two gringos left.

They were there the next night, sitting around the fire, eating spicy green chicken that made Mike cough, at first. He had to tell his story again, but mostly he was silent, trying to listen to the stories traded in return.

On Monday, when he drove Hermelinda home from the clinic, Mike brought a ham. After that, he stayed most nights. At first George came with him, but after a while it was just Mike. He always brought something with him: bacon, a roast, a case of beer, strawberries or blueberries or maybe a watermelon. When he was there for dinner the men would always eat first—Mike, her father, Alejandro—and then sit outside on stumps. Inside Hermelinda helped her mother feed the others and then ate her own dinner, watching out the window as her father talked with Mike, while Alejandro sat by and smoked, absent and quiet. When Hermelinda finished her dinner she'd come outside with her brothers and sisters, who would hang around for a few minutes before disappearing somewhere into the night. Hermelinda sat next to her father, holding his hand sometimes, laughing at his stories, reminding him of other ones, asking him to tell them again. In between, in the silences of those nights, she sat with her father and this American Mike and watched the difference in the stars as they breathed in the hot vegetable air. She liked that he could sit there without saying anything, too, and she knew it was partly because maybe the things he wanted to say were for her and her alone.

They were never alone until one night after dinner her father rose early after eating, excusing himself.

"I'm going inside," her father said. "Will you please look for your sisters?"

"What's he saying?" Mike asked Hermelinda.

She tried to keep the embarrassed smile off her face, that

expression that only a parent could coax out of his grown child. She told him.

"Oh," Mike said, looking at the father, who was waving his hands and clucking at them as if he were shooing barnyard chickens. "Did they run away from home?" he said.

"They're probably in bed."

"Something's getting lost in translation."

"It only means we're supposed to take a walk."

"You and me."

"Yes."

"Really," Mike said, sounding genuinely surprised and pleased. "Lucky me."

"Yes."

Mike rose and followed her and they walked through the camp in silence. She led him to the Blancos' trailer, where a rooster was caged outside. The bird strutted and jerked, flew at the side of the cage as they approached. Mike bent down to look at him carefully.

"He fights," Hermelinda said. "Señor Blanco wins a lot of money with him. They say."

"I had no idea. I wouldn't want to fight him." Mike tapped on the cage and the rooster recoiled, then attacked the place where his finger had been. "I've never seen a cockfight. When do they fight?"

"On Sunday. Sometimes."

"Have you seen them?"

She shrugged. "Yes. It doesn't interest me."

They both watched the rooster, who stood in the middle of his cage, his head turned perpendicular to them but looking at Mike's fingers, ready.

"Do you know," Mike said, "I think you do, but do you know that you interest me more than anyone I've met in a long, long time?"

She did not flinch, did not move from his side, and did not

look at him either. She thought she could feel the heat coming off his body in the slowly cooling night.

"Maybe you don't meet very interesting people," she said.

"Maybe." He laughed quietly. "I don't know. I don't think that's it." He was looking at her now, and it was not the look she was accustomed to seeing from men. It was something soft and hot at once, like the blue-black middle of a flame. "Hermelinda," he said, and there was more but she stopped him there.

"You've been very nice to me and my family." She tried for a courteous voice, courteous in what she hoped was a final way. "Thank you for that." She intended to go but noticed that she had not moved.

He leaned towards her. *"Quiero besarte,"* he said, quietly, and his accent was very good this time, which made her want to smile.

She did not smile. "My father likes you," she said, not look-ing at him, but thinking about his lips anyway, their real full-ness, their texture. "My mother says she doesn't know, but my father says you are a good person."

"He's a kind man."

"He's foolish. You can go kiss him if you want. He's foolish and I think you're a coward."

"Why?"

"Because you wanted all the time *besarme*. Pretending all these reason, pretending the jobs."

"Well, it wasn't *just* pretending. But you've got a point there."

"Yes, I have a point."

"Even the first time I came out here to see you."

"I know."

"I saw a picture of you," he said. "It was just a picture, and I was curious. I wanted to see you. I thought it was only because, you know, you were beautiful. But you turned out to be a lot more than that."

She was going to go. "You were afraid of me."

"Maybe a little. But not as much as I should have been."

"Too afraid to say what you wanted."

"Yes."

"If you were not a coward you would come and tell me right away."

"Would you have kissed me?"

"Of course not. I'm not going to kiss you now."

"Yes you are." He leaned in and took the back of her head with one hand cupped behind and beneath her ear, and he kissed her.

She pushed him away lightly, but not right away, and they looked at each other while the rooster hissed beside them and she thought: Maybe. She wasn't sure but she suspected that they would have to kiss again, soon.

"I don't trust you," she said. She stooped to eye level with the rooster in his cage. The rooster made a low growling sound but did not move.

"I'm sorry," he said, too loud, and she hushed him. He whispered, "I'm crazy about you." He was waiting but she would not get up.

"Now you go home," she said. The rooster was looking at her, head tilted slightly, as if trying to understand her better. She didn't look up until she heard the engine whir and fade into the night.

They kissed again on Sunday, when he came to watch the cockfight and bet ten dollars on the loser. Everyone seemed very happy with his loss. The fight was over quickly and it was obvious Mike did not know quite what had happened. He seemed overwhelmed by the excitement and feathers in the air, the hours of buildup and drinking and talk with the men who tested him, probed him, tried to get him drunk, teased him. He survived it fine. She wondered if Mike realized, perhaps the last one in the camp to realize, that he was courting her, officially and publicly, that he was being sized up, that there were those who thought he was a rich *patrón* looking for some fun with a Mexican girl and others, only a few, who took him seriously, more seriously than he could know. The older men snickered at him; Alejandro watched him carefully; her father plied him with drinks and food, gave him impassioned and confusing advice about betting on birds.

Just before he left she followed him behind a trailer and kissed him again, slowly, for a long time, putting her hands on his firm warm body beneath his light cotton shirt. There was no reason why more than at the end of that day, at that moment, she wanted to.

III

SHE FOUND A message written on a pink message slip when Raúl dropped her off at the clinic that Monday. The time was 8:04 a.m. and the urgent box was checked. I want to take you on a date, it said.

She found him alone at the end of the day. "I want to see a movie," she said.

"Yes?"

"And popcorn, and an ice cream in a soda with two straws."

"The whole thing."

"And a very fast car with no roof, and—"

"Let me make an offer, quickly," he said.

They went on Wednesday. Acton was the nearest theater. There was no convertible, and the movie was not very good, but they did not care. Hermelinda wore a long green dress, torn and sewn a little at the bottom at the back. People stared at her, then at him, then at her again. They were out of place there, and in fact they were not sure what kind of place they would not feel that way in together. Mike didn't run into anyone he knew. He worried that someone was going to make trouble for them, and it distracted him, a little, trying to predict where trouble might come from. How it would look, what he would do. Hermelinda seemed immune to this kind of inspection. She was either far cooler than he was or naive about the South or simply and unfortunately used to it. She was quiet during the movie, staring at the screen, not seeming to notice his hand on her arm, talking to him only to negotiate the exchange of drink and popcorn. But in the car on the ride home she seemed happy.

"Is there a bigger city we can go to?" she asked.

"Raleigh," he said. "Chapel Hill."

"Raleigh." She tried the city on her tongue. "Is it far?"

"It's a little far."

"Are there more different people there? Are there more Mexicans?"

"Yes and no. Not really Mexicans. But more, that's for sure. And more different, I guess. Black people. It's a real city, kind of."

"I only know two cities. Chihuahua City, and Laredo. Chihuahua City is a big city. There's a big church, and a market, you can get anything. They have an old street where no cars can go, people only walk up and down."

"That sounds nice. I'd like to go there."

"There are ten stores for shoes on that street."

"Ten."

"Maybe more, I can't remember."

"Ten seems like plenty."

"Shoes are much more important in Mexico. You have to have nice shoes."

"You do have nice shoes," Mike said. "I've noticed that."

"No, I, no I don't at all."

"I like them."

"These are just any shoes. They are too old."

"Well. I'll tell you what. I don't think Raleigh's going to be as exciting as Chihuahua City, especially shoe-wise."

"I want to go."

"We'll go, definitely. We'll go buy us both some shoes, while we're there. You can help me out."

"Yes, I think you need some help."

"Well, all right."

"Mike."

"Yes."

"Let's go tomorrow."

"Too far for tomorrow."

"Then let's go back there again."

"To Acton?"

She nodded. "To the movies."

"But we've already seen it."

"I don't care."

"Did you really like it?"

"I liked the feeling of it." She didn't know if she could explain the feeling to him, how she felt normal for that hour and a half for the first time since her family left Mexico. He was quiet, agreeing with his head. Maybe he understood.

They went back to Acton the next night. She held his hand on the street, lacing her fingers through his and walking lightly beside him, telling him about the first movie she'd ever seen, projected on a white wall outside in summertime Ojinaga. She remembered shooting. Men with mustaches who rarely spoke. The sound crackled and popped, like an ancient radio. Lots of desert and horses and guns.

They sat in the back row at the theater. He put his arm around her and she leaned back against him, and they stayed that way through most of the movie until she put her head against his shoulder and rubbed her hand on his chest. She felt his hand on her leg and when she tilted her head up he kissed her, and they kept kissing like that, oblivious to the awkward position of their bodies, until finally they were aware of people moving around them, the house lights coming up.

They saw the movie a few more times over the next two weeks. Her parents were always waiting for them when they came home, and he had to go inside and talk to them so that they could examine the look on his face and assure themselves that he was honorable. He felt like a teenager again, and maybe it should have bothered him but it didn't; even as he felt the want building up inside him, he was grateful to have time alone with her. There were times when he felt he did not deserve it, did not deserve the way she looked at him, the way she let him stare at her, kiss her neck, her lips. One night on the way back from Acton she closed her eyes and he listened to her breath fall into a slow steady pattern, and he could not think straight the following day, remembering the feeling of watching her sleep.

He lived his other life distracted. He made more trips than he needed to the clinic, to see her, to watch her hurrying between the clinic's trailers, working. He let the other students do the evening outreach trips, spending his nights sitting outside the Salmerons' trailer. He skipped a meeting in Durham to take her and Pedro and her sisters fishing one day, although there wasn't as much fishing as splashing around in the water. Alejandro came too, but did not fish or splash, just sat on the banks smoking cigarettes, dozing in the shade of a poplar tree.

The clinic was beginning to occupy Hermelinda, both the days and now sometimes the nights when she would sit on the trailer steps and think about the parade of sick men and women and girls and boys—she didn't like it, and she worried sometimes that she would get sick from one of them, and that her family would get sick, her father and brother, and then where would they be? But she kept working. They gave her a check every week which Mike cashed for her, about $230. She gave her delighted father $200 and saved the rest.

Sometimes a woman at the clinic would see Mike talking to her and ask her, afterwards, *"Es tu novio?"* and Hermelinda always meant to deny it but she'd say *"Sí"* to see them smile knowingly and compliment his looks or his character. He'd brought them to the clinic, maybe. He'd enrolled their child in school. Sometimes he'd just helped them, a vague claim that was never explained or specified. She meant to ask Mike about some of these people, but never did. She never told him he was her *novio,* either.

The Fourth of July was a Saturday, and everyone worked, her father, her brothers, Mike, and Hermelinda too, but on the fifth, Mike showed up at the Salmerons' in the early afternoon with five chickens, a twenty-pound pork butt, a cooler full of beer, and a bag of South Carolina fireworks. His friend George came too, the big boy with a camera never far from his hand, and took pictures of Hermelinda's father rubbing the pork in salt and pepper. Mike and George stood around a makeshift smoker with the men, drinking beer and tequila and talking deep into the afternoon, listening to the meat pop. At the end of each bottle they'd lift the cover and pour the remnants of the liquor onto the meat. Mike could see Hermelinda in the crowded kitchen of the trailer, her hair tied up on her head, her hands at work or held out awkwardly in front of her, caked with flour or tomatoes or something, but she did not emerge until late afternoon, when she and her sisters began to bring bowls and dishes to lay on the table outside. On cue, several of the other trailers began to spit food from their doors, until soon the table was covered with high stacks of fresh corn tortillas; spicy *pico de gallo* served in old coffee tins; pinto beans creamier and more silky than any Mike had eaten before ("Lard," Hermelinda's mother explained to him, "no secret, only lard"); twisted cords of fried flour and sugar; peppers stuffed with he was not sure what; a sort of spicy corn soup. The roast emerged charred and massive from the smoker and Hermelinda's mother quickly hacked it and the chickens to pieces at one end of the table and then stepped back. There was one static beat before the table was consumed, swarmed by men and hydra-handed children. Mike spotted Hermelinda's little brother Pedro walking away holding a steaming piece of meat bigger than a baseball, juggling it back and forth expertly between his hands. Mike turned to George to tell him to take a picture, but found his friend with bulging cheeks, holding half a chicken in his hand.

"Brrrhm," George said, pointing to the food with his chicken. "Ufgrrrd."

Hermelinda came into view then, standing behind the crowd, observing the commotion, and they smiled at each other. He winked, slowly, in an exaggerated way, and she laughed and shook her head. He felt giddy, young, and he stood up on a stump and flicked his beer can with one finger.

"Yes, the foolish American would like to make a toast,"

Mike said in English, "to all of you." Most of them didn't understand him, but they stopped talking and pretended to listen anyhow. "This is the best meal I've ever had to celebrate American independence, or anything, for that matter." He stopped for a moment to make sure he didn't fall off the stump. People laughed, and Mike grinned. "Here's to the Fourth of July," he said, "here's to pork, to you, to fireworks," he raised a cluster of fireworks in his hand, "to any excuse to celebrate, good harvest, all that, all of you. *Buena gente,*" he said, pointing to his audience and drawing some laughs and appreciative calls from the crowd. *"Buena honda."*

They liked that. They shouted back their approval. As they raised their beers and proclaimed brief toasts of their own, Mike looked for Hermelinda. She was talking to another woman near the table, the woman leaning to whisper in her ear, the both of them looking at him appraisingly. He waved. Someone grabbed his arm and pulled him in for a shot of something very clear and very, very strong.

"Arriba, abajo, al centro, para adentro." They drank.

It wasn't long before the explosions started, George having armed the children with an alarming number of fireworks, and as the heads around them tilted to the sky, Mike took Hermelinda's hand and they slipped off into the shadowing woods, moving through the ferns. They walked in silence until they reached the old machinery shed. They went in and he pressed her back against the door.

"Hermelinda," he said, "I don't think I'll ever be more happy than right now."

"Oh, but you're only a boy," she said, and he laughed.

"A boy?" he said, putting his hands around her and pulling her to him.

"Well. *Un joven.*"

"Sí, muy joven. Mucho amor."

"English," she said.

"Porqué?"

"My English is so much better. And look." She moved away from him, leaning her elbows on a dirty windowsill and pointing to the world outside. "This is America, man." She exaggerated her words, trying to mimic the country Carolina accent, turning her lilt into something crazy, hilarious. He laughed. The eyes wrinkled up and for a moment he looked older. The sound of his laugh was deep, always deeper than she expected.

"You have a very nice laugh," she said. "You make me like you when you laugh."

He moved up behind her, putting his hands on her hips. His hands stayed there but she felt the touch traveling over her body. She brushed his hands off gently and moved across the wooden floor of the shed, and he followed, as if they were dancing. What would it be like for them to dance, to descend on a crowded hall, the one in Ojinaga, the trucks, the black dress and shoes, the hat and belt and boots. His face a little red at first because he did not know, but she'd teach him, he would try hard, to dance, to please her. Why when he could be anywhere doing anything with anyone did he want so badly to be with her?

He kissed her. She held him back, his head in her hands at arms' length, and looked at him. Flushed by the day of sun and drink, his face a little red, he squinted at her. He was a beautiful boy. "You're very pretty, Michael Olive," she said, and she felt a little dizzy as she put her hand under his shirt, touched his cool skin. They began to unbutton each other's clothes, then, taking them off. They stood naked in the shed, and she saw his body in the evening light, almost a boy's width at the waist and hips but his shoulders broad. The muscles in his arms pulled his skin tight. The blond hair on his legs puffed out in the slight evening chill. Diagonal lines sloped down the bones from his flat stomach, past his hips, to his sex.

She lay down on their pile of clothes on the floor, and he followed her. He kissed her wrist. He moved across her body, slowly. She was still at first but then began to move beneath him, rolling her hips into his.

Afterwards she stretched away from him and he draped one hand over her middle and they lay there like that for a while.

"When we drove here from Laredo," she said, "the driver got lost on the way. We were in some mountains, in a different state, I think. It was so green, I never saw anything so green with rivers and just trees, only trees, everywhere. It was so beautiful. The roads were smooth and curvy and there were no cars anywhere. No fields. And I asked one of the men, had he been here before, are there other places this beautiful, and he told me he saw the beach one time, when he was working with fish, and that was the most beautiful."

"Here?"

"In North Carolina, he said. You don't have any beaches?"

"No, we have them. I didn't know there were migrants there."

"Are they beautiful?"

"Yes. Very."

"I've never seen the beach."

"Never?"

"Only on a river. Not the ocean. Only pictures. Aren't you going to take me?"

"Of course I'll take you. I can't believe you never . . . I forget sometimes. You know?"

"No."

"Right now I want out of the world," he said. "Just take you. Everywhere we could find."

"We should run away?"

"Yes. Pack up a little bag on the end of a stick, just start walking."

"No, we'll drive. You'll get money and a car and we'll run away."

"You would do it?"

"Don't ask me that."

It was quiet, inside and out.

"You would want to? I mean, if."

"I want to see the beach. I want to go to an American city and see it from very high up, in a building, over everything. At night with all the lights."

"I want that too. I want to take you. You deserve everything," Mike said.

She rolled over and looked at him, kissed him. She touched him and thought, Yes, this is my real secret: that I want everything and deserve it too.

HARVEY AND MIKE

SEVEN

THE FIRST GUN Mike ever shot belonged to Harvey's father. Mike was seven years old and the gun was a .30-30 rifle. It was bigger than the gun Mike had watched Harvey use out behind the house. Harvey's uncle, Blue, had handed down an old cut-down lever-action .22, and Harvey wouldn't let Mike hold it or fire it or even touch it. For days Mike just sat there and watched as Harvey tried to assassinate every bird that passed his way.

"Let me have a go."

"You don't know how."

"You don't either."

"Watch me."

"Yeah," Mike said. "Your daddy teach you?"

Harvey made a wet sound with his tongue against his teeth. "I already shoot better than he does."

"Oh," Mike said. "I bet you could teach me good, huh."

"No thank you," Harvey said, grinning. He knew Mike better than to fall for that.

Mike watched for a while more and then got up as if he were going to leave. He passed behind Harvey and then reached over and put both hands on the barrel of the gun. He pulled, hard, but the smaller boy surprised him by holding on tight and whipping his upper body like a snake to wrench free. Harvey retreated and stood frowning at a distance, pointing the gun at Mike. "Don't even."

"You couldn't hit me."

"Ha."

"You scared I'll shoot better than you."

"Ha," Harvey said again, turning his attention to a rock and taking careful aim.

Mike started back through the woods towards his own house. He listened to Harvey shooting. When he'd got out of sight he circled back around and went up to the Dickerson house. Harvey's dad was out somewhere, and his mom was in the kitchen, cooking. There was something about Mrs. Dickerson's cooking that never smelled right to Mike. He'd never eaten there, though. Harvey didn't eat at Mike's house, either. That was just how it worked.

Mike slipped in the screen door and let it shut softly behind him. He went to the closet in the hallway where Brack Dickerson kept his guns, and picked up a rifle that looked like Harvey's, only bigger. Then he walked out the way he'd come and went to find Harvey.

Harvey was still back in the woods. He wasn't shooting anymore, just sitting up against a tree, talking to himself. He saw Mike coming and smiled like a skeleton until he saw what the other boy had in his hands. He shook his head, slowly, as if he didn't even realize he was shaking it.

"This here's a real gun," Mike said, hefting it to his shoulder and pointing it off into the woods.

Harvey kept on shaking his head.

"Come on, what, you scared?"

"He find that gone he gonna kill you and me both."

"Well, we better hurry up, then."

Mike stooped and brushed his way through the thick spring firs, and Harvey followed. Ten minutes into the woods, the land dipped and the trees thinned to a clearing ringed by rocks. It was a good place to come if you didn't want any witnesses.

Mike put the gun on the ground, squatted down, and looked

at it. Harvey stood behind him, and then came up beside him and started pointing. "That's the safety," he said. "You cock it just like mine."

"You ever shoot this?"

Harvey shook his head. "It take a bird all the way apart. Bring down a deer, a big buck." Mike looked at the gun and nodded. "Well," Harvey said. "You gonna shoot it?"

"Yeah."

"Come on."

"All right."

Mike picked up the rifle and put it to his shoulder.

"What you shooting at?"

"Low branch on that tree."

"That one?"

"Yeah."

"Your feet too close together. Get your elbow out."

"Shut up."

Mike got his elbow out but the gun shook, like a thin branch in the wind. He pulled the trigger, but it did not give. He propped the barrel on the ground and worked the lever. It took all his strength. Then he heaved the gun back up and before he'd even come to a stop he fired. The gun jerked and crashed and Mike was lying on the ground, with the gun on top of him. His ears were whining.

"Mike?"

"Yeah."

Harvey picked up the gun off Mike's chest and pointed it across the clearing.

"It's heavy, huh," Mike said.

Harvey had a hard time cocking the gun but somehow he did. He raised it and pulled the trigger, and the gun cracked again, jerking his whole torso back, but he kept his feet. "Goddamn," Harvey said.

"Let me try one more."

Harvey shook his head. He cocked the gun and fired again and the recoil almost dropped him this time.

"I'm gonna hit it," Mike said.

Harvey didn't hand him the gun but Mike took it. He cocked it and then brought the stock up against his cheek, trying to look down the barrel. He could barely get his finger on the trigger. He put the pin between the sights and held everything stiff. The gun knocked him back, and when he put his hand to his cheek he brought back blood. Harvey started laughing.

"You gonna have a black eye."

"I think I hit it."

Mike got up and the two of them went over to the tree.

"Look at the branch, I think I hit it."

"No," Harvey said.

"I did, look there."

"That ain't nothing."

They argued and pointed, talking fast. Mike gave the gun back to Harvey, who put a dangerous scowl on his face and looked off menacingly into the woods, sighting up real or imaginary targets.

"We gonna come get you!" Mike yelled out into the woods.

Harvey kept up the pose for a full minute, then put the gun down and looked at it. "I can't believe you took it," he said. His face went slack then, as it sank in, and he looked more like an old man than a seven-year-old boy.

"It's ours now," Mike said. "We'll keep it out here, hidden."

"Yeah," Harvey said. "I can't never go back, now."

"We could share it. I mean, it'd be yours but we'd have a partnership."

"Yeah," Harvey said again. He sat down on the ground. "I'm gonna have to live out in the woods." He looked around like he was lost.

"We can do it. We can hunt."

"You don't have to."

"I'll do it."

"I don't want you." Harvey was disappearing, there, as he sat, going someplace Mike didn't know or understand.

"I'll bring it back."

"It's too late now."

"Give it here, Harvey."

"I need it. He's gonna come after me."

"Here." Mike took the gun away from him with one sharp and sudden yank. He put his head down and ran back towards the house. Harvey followed, yelling. Mike hit the house and ran in the back door without looking. He could hear the screen snapping behind him as he put the gun back in the closet, struggling to put it back in its wooden slot. When he shut the closet door, Brack Dickerson was standing there, with the afternoon light behind him blurring his edges. Mike heard Harvey breathing behind him, and heard his own dull heart kicking in his chest. He stared at the black spikes of hairs on Mr. Dickerson's chin, then forced himself to continue up to the small blue eyes beyond the wrinkles and squint.

"It was my fault, sir," Mike said. "I stole your gun, I shot it. I didn't hurt nobody."

"You what?" Brack just looked.

"I used your gun, sir. In the woods. I took four shots. I didn't hit nothing, and I'm sorry."

"Didn't hit nothing," Brack repeated. "I'll be fucked." He shook his head, the same way Harvey always did before something happened, and then reached out and grabbed Mike's skin and shirt. His one thin hand felt like five pairs of pliers. The other hand started for Harvey.

"He tried to stop me, sir, he did," Mike said, his voice slipping up too high, despite himself. "He even tried punching me in the eye. See. But I had that gun, wasn't nothing he could do. Sir."

Brack lifted Mike slightly off the ground and looked at his face. All those sirs seemed to slow him down a bit. "You did that?" he said to Harvey.

"Yessir," Harvey said. "I knocked him back, but he wave that gun around, I thought I was gonna die."

"Well," Brack said. He looked closely at Mike's bruised eye. "That's a start." He grinned. "Ain't that something. You lucky either of you alive, if you shoot anything like your old man."

"Yessir," Mike said.

"Shut up," Brack said. "You just shut your hole. I ain't done with you, Harvey, don't believe it, but I'm gonna take this little boy home to his poppa. Clayton's gonna have to change his mind about a whupping, because you got one coming. I'm either watching or I'm whupping."

Brack led the way out to the truck, dragging Mike behind, and Mike snuck one last look back at Harvey. The boy was smiling a big smile, with his nose wrinkled up like a weasel, trying not to laugh, and for some reason, despite his own dark future, just down the road, Mike found he had to bite his lip and bury something like laughter, too.

TEN

Even on the longest days of the year, four-thirty in the morning was dark. There were different degrees of dark at that hour. Sometimes the moon could seem as bright as the sun until the sun came out and reminded you what bright was all about. There might be mist coming off the fields, or more likely hovering over the resevoirs and ponds, sucking up light like small, terrestrial black holes. It was too early to be awake, Mike thought, a time when the world wanted to be alone with itself. Even at ten years old, there was a part of Mike that knew, every morning, that he was not a farmer—no one who had as hard a time as he did in the mornings could be any kind of farmer. He was sure to run someone over in a tractor, one day, if he kept it up, or break his leg stumbling into an irrigation ditch. He'd waked up before sunrise almost every day he could remember and hadn't felt right about it once.

His father's voice penetrated his resting mind slowly, grafting itself into dreams, repeating and repeating until the sound dragged Mike from sleep. Mike. Mike. Mike. Mike. Clayton stood down at the bottom of the staircase, chanting like a morning monk, and at the first tiny moment when Mike opened his eyes to the tolling of his name, he hated his father. How could you do anything but hate the person who bullied you out of sleep? There were mornings when he would come stumbling down the stairs in his underwear without even realizing it, and his mother would turn him around gently and send him upstairs to dress. She'd be in the kitchen, cooking, with a whole huge breakfast waiting and ready. Mike couldn't even imagine when she got up. He'd never been awake before her in his whole life.

"Eat a biscuit, Michael," she said, and his arms and hands and mouth obeyed, while his small brain fizzled and popped and his eyes blinked and fogged. He kept eating until someone told him to do something else. "All right," his father would say, putting a thick hand on Mike's little shoulder. "Let's go, got to beat that heat."

Mike followed Clayton to the truck, his head down, his eyes half shut. On the bumpy ride to the fields, he often fantasized about collapsing from exhaustion, dying from fatigue. That would show 'em. That would make them think again.

He did not complain or put his head down once they got to the fields. He knew better. It wasn't only that he was the boss's son, and therefore suspect as favored and spoiled and soft—it was mostly about Harvey. Harvey, really, was the thing that kept him awake in the end. If he let his guard down for a second, Harvey was bound to peg him in the head with whatever was handy—an ear of corn, a sweet potato, a small rock. Those were the rules. The weak survived, but they got hit in the head, a lot.

In those days there weren't as many of them out there: B.D. and Harvey, Clayton and Mike, Manuel Riesgo with his two brothers and their sons. The youngest of the sons was the same age as Harvey and Mike, a small boy named Pedro. "Pedro," Harvey used to say to Mike. "That's like being a nigger named Sambo."

"Pedro's just Peter. In Spanish."

"Peter," Harvey repeated, drawing the two syllables out. He could make anything sound obscene, when he tried. "Well, that ain't much better, is it?"

"He's all right."

"I didn't say he wasn't. He do got a stupid name."

Pedro had as good an arm and aim as either of them, and they all three had to look out for one another that morning in the cucumbers. Boys and men alike fanned out through the field, flashing their arms like ditch-digging terriers as they crabbed quickly down the long rows. Out of the sight of their fathers' watchful eyes, the boys started their private work with the overripe cucumbers, throwing at one another hard from the shoulder, without mercy. It was a trade-off between how good a shot you could get off and the risk of getting caught. None of them wanted to get caught. Pedro and Harvey could expect a beating when they got home for goofing off in the fields. Not Mike—he tried to keep it a secret, but everyone knew his father never laid a hand on him but once. He'd get a talking-to, have his rifle taken away for a while, maybe his bat and glove. But nothing worse than that.

"You gonna turn out soft," Harvey said.

"Not my fault he don't hit me regular."

"Like a little girl."

"Ain't done you no good. Still can't take me."

"They ain't a word for what I can do to you."

"You got damaged brain from B.D. beating on your head. No way no how."

By midmorning, Harvey and Pedro and Mike would all have dried seeds and other mess clinging to their work shirts. They weren't throwing or talking anymore. It was hot and they were too tired to be bored. The sun had long since worked its way up over the trees to start its steady, brutal work. The men and boys braced themselves for the row after row, filling their pails over the brim before hefting them to the truck, where Clayton caught them and emptied their load. In return they got a little fairground ticket, with the word "Olive" printed in all caps. Every ticket was worth fifty cents, and it was a matter of pride among the men and boys who turned in the most tickets. Pedro's older brother Memo always had the most, and Harvey always had the least.

"I get one goddamn son," was Brack Dickerson's loud and public refrain, "and he turns out lazier than a bunch of Pedros." Chastened Harvey sat and bore it. He knew the truth, as did the other boys—that before turning over the balance of his tickets to his father, Harvey had already sold some of them to Memo at thirty-five cents a pop. He tried to get Mike in on the deal, too.

"You know where your poppa keeps those tickets?"

"Maybe."

"I'll pay you thirty-five for them. Each."

"No you won't."

"Come on, momma boy."

"Forty-five."

"Forty-five! Thirty-eight."

"Forty-three."

"Forty." Harvey crossed his arms and watched Mike shrug. "All right, forty-one. But you're gypping me."

"Aw, come on, Harvey. I don't even know where those things are, anyway," Mike said, although he did. "I had you going, though."

"We could find them," Harvey said, not willing to let it drop, but Mike refused to start the bidding up again.

It was a big summer in Jackson County, a record year for the tobacco harvest. It was also the year the Olives started crossing that line between whatever they'd been and something closer to rich. Clayton's two hundred acres of tobacco land, the piece everyone had always called the Nile, was planted all the way. The land was so thick with crop it looked like a tobacco jungle. It was the most productive piece of land in Jackson County, and a big one too—bigger than the thirty- or forty-acre average most farmers had for tobacco allotments. At the end of every week, when Clayton doled out the wages to the migrants and the Dickersons and the other men he hired on for tobacco, you could see the silent arithmetic in the pickers' eyes as they matched the dollars in their pocket to the futures browning in the Olives' drying sheds. The men were hauling well over a ton of tobacco off every acre of the Nile. When all the multiplication was done, the Olives' tobacco from that one year was worth almost half a million dollars.

It was also the last year Harvey and Mike worked together, the last year the Dickersons worked for the Olives. Brack Dickerson had worked on that land with Mike's father long before it was Olive land, all back through the years when it was still part of the once Worten plantation. Mike's and Harvey's fathers were both day laborers then, both of them poor in cash and land and most of the other kinds of poor there were. There were pictures with the two of them, standing in front of an old Chevy truck next to other men like themselves, with old man Worten in the truck bed behind them, frowning what everyone always said was his uniform frown. Mike couldn't remember any of it any better than he could remember Worten himself, this fabled and cranky ancient man who'd never sired, never married. Worten had outlived most of his kin, and disregarded the rest, until he finally died and left the Olives a fortune for no reason anyone could adequately explain. The land, the drying sheds, the tractors, all of it. Mike tried to remember but he couldn't. He was five when it happened, he felt he should know something important, but when he sat sorting through the thin catalog of snips and scenes in his head, he found nothing, good or bad. He didn't have answers to the questions and black rumors Harvey helped to circulate his way.

"Why you think you get all this land, Mike? What you think you did for it?"

"I don't know."

"You did something for it, though, you know that, don't you? My daddy says nothing happens for nothing."

"Worten, he was just a crazy old man. He loved his dog more than anything else in the world. He would have given it to his dog if they let him."

"His dog," Harvey said, his mouth hanging open, the doubt and spite painted there for everyone, for Mike, to see.

"I don't know. Momma said I was always getting on his land, making trouble. He liked that, I don't know. Kind of like he adopted me."

"He did something to you." There was nothing gentle in Harvey's words. "Too bad you don't remember."

Mike remembered Worten's dog, a brown furball that bit everyone but him. He played with it sometimes under a porch. Whether it was the porch at the Worten house or at his old childhood house, he didn't know. His mother told him the dog followed him around like a duckling, even into the Olives' house, and that she'd once been bitten by the bitch after speaking sharply to her own boy.

"I was friends with his dog, and he gives us land?"

"Ed Worten was an unpredictable, crazy old man," Clayton said. "I worked for him half my life and never understood him for a second."

"Was he a bad man?"

"No." His answer sounded almost like a question.

"Was he Harvey's granddaddy?"

"No." Clayton sounded more sure, now. "Harvey tell you that?"

"No. I just heard it."

"Yeah, well, way this county talks, you can hear anything you want, you listen long enough."

"But Harvey's grandma and grandpa were living on Mr. Worten's land, weren't they then?"

"Yes indeed they were."

"And I heard—"

"Mike, now we had chickens on our land, before *you* were born, don't mean a chicken snuck in the house one night . . . " Clayton stopped himself there, smiling at his own self. "Doesn't mean a chicken born you," he said.

The day the Dickersons quit the Olive land, they were all out in the sweet potatoes, late afternoon. Mike was in the row next to Harvey, the two of them going as slowly as they could. The heat was taking over everything—their bodies, their minds, everything they touched or saw. On the other side of Harvey, Manuel Riesgo, Sr., was moving slowly, too. He was a big man, on the fat side, and he cast a slight shadow into Harvey's row. It wasn't much, but there was room for a ten-year-old boy to get some shielding from the sun. Mike crossed into Harvey's row and the other boy got ready to attack until he saw what Mike was doing. He nodded and got in close beside him, and the two of them crawled and jockeyed in Señor Riesgo's shadow, matching his movements, forgetting to pick.

Neither of them saw Harvey's father coming. It took a few moments for Mike to understand what was happening, for him to make sense of the sudden frenzy of dust and dirt and noise around him.

"You lazy son of a bitch, goddammit!" Brack was yelling. He kicked Harvey down the row like a dirt clod, with Harvey all rolled up and quiet. It didn't last long. Harvey's father was looking down at his dirt-dredged son and talking to himself under his breath. He looked back at Mike. "Life's nice and easy for the little cocksuckers of the world, isn't that right, boy," Brack said. "It's a big game, isn't it?" Mike could see his own father moving their way, quickly, from his new truck, and the Mexicans staring and listening.

"You ain't better than anybody," Brack said to Mike. "You don't deserve nothing." Brack took a step towards Mike and raised his hand, and Mike just stood there, feeling like a dumb animal looking down the throat of a gun, but then Brack was walking away. "Come on, Harvey," he said, without turning around. "Get your tickets and come on."

Harvey uncurled himself slowly, like a grub, squinting and breathing hard through his nose. He brushed off the top of his pants and put his hand in his pocket, pulling out a small yellow handful of the tickets he'd got for each pail of sweet potatoes that day. He stared at them for a moment, as if he was counting them. Then he stood up, brushed off the back of his pants, and looked at Mike.

"Give me your tickets," he said in a whisper that was both soft and hard at once.

Mike stared at him and then took his own small handful of tickets out of his pocket and handed them to Harvey. The smaller boy wrapped his hand around then and pressed them into a tight ball. One ticket slipped out from under his thumb and seesawed towards the ground, but Harvey didn't seem to notice. He kept his fist shut tight and followed his father's trail, slowly, back towards the trucks.

FIFTEEN

MIKE WASN'T PITCHING that day; he was playing second
base. There was nothing extraordinary about the game. Mike
got two hits, drove in two runs. He usually did something
decent, most games. He was a good baseball player, better at
basketball. He would have played football, too, but Harvey
and his people pretty much owned that team, and Mike decided
to take the fall season off. He didn't love football, anyway, and
he certainly didn't need that kind of trouble.

Cottesville won the game 14–10. Acton didn't have much of
a squad that year, but they were a big rival, and a win was a
win. It was a beautiful spring night, warm and sweet, with
enough people in the stands to make you feel you were doing
something worthwhile. There were plenty of Acton folks there,
too. Acton was close. They had a movie theater and a couple of
restaurants and a main street that people walked and drove
down on weekend nights. Everyone in Cottesville had been
over there at one time or another. The Cottesville–Acton football game was the big deal, but the baseball games weren't bad,
either.

Harvey was there in the stands that night. Mike noticed him
in the third inning, leaning over a blond trio of Acton girls in
the bleachers, chatting them up. Mike watched him from his
post at second base, checking Harvey's progress between
pitches. The girls were laughing; he was doing fine. Harvey
was good at that. With a face like that, Mike thought, you'd
have to be. One of Harvey's girls caught Mike looking their
way, and she smiled at him across the diamond. Thinks I'm
checking her out, he realized, and smiled back, winked. He
could see her talking to Harvey now, asking about him. Who's
that good-looking boy out at second? Good. Piss Harvey off,
that might, although he could almost hear Harvey talking his

way through it. By the time Harvey got done, Mike might be a pervert, a half-wit, or maybe a cousin, a best friend. Whatever Harvey saw fit. He could and did talk his way in and out of anything. He made people who knew him nervous because sometimes he had that Dickerson mean streak, bad. There'd been a time in sixth grade when Mike had an eyelid that twitched sometimes, and Harvey would sit next to him in class and mimic him in a grotesque pantomime from bell to bell. It was a long time ago, now, but Harvey still did it, sometimes, in the hallway, jerking his head to one side and batting his eyes in a sort of simulated epileptic fit. Sometimes Mike just had to laugh. It was a shame, he thought, that the two of them were always officially at odds, because the truth of the matter was that Harvey was one of the only guys in Cottesville that seemed more than ordinary to Mike.

He spotted his mom in the stands, too, sitting next to the Hunts. His girlfriend, Cordelia Potts, was a few rows behind her. Later in the game, in the seventh inning, Harvey did his old trick of going over to talk to Cordelia just when Mike was going up to bat, but Mike was used to it by now and he managed to work the pitcher to a walk anyway. It was hard to believe, but Cordelia and Harvey had gone out when they were all freshmen, although Cordelia couldn't quite explain why. "He just," she'd say, when Mike asked, but that was as far as she'd get. She shook her head and smiled her big pretty smile. "I don't know. He's just Harvey."

After the game, Mike hung out for a while with Cordelia and the Hunts and his mom, talking about the next game, the season, sneaking an indecent squeeze on Cordelia when the adults stopped paying attention. By the time he got back to the locker room, the rest of the team was gone. He slipped out of his spikes and uniform and took a shower. There were nights he'd go home right after a game, but it was Friday and he was supposed to hang out with Dale and Josh and a bunch of them.

Dale's older brother was organizing a fire or something out near the quarry. Cordelia said she'd try to get out there, but Mike had his doubts. He put on his jeans and a white long-sleeve cotton shirt and went outside.

It was later than he'd thought. The parking lot was mostly cleared out and the diamond lights were down. There were three guys from Acton he didn't know sitting on the hood of their car, three guys who shouldn't be there anymore. Mike kept his eye on them as he looked around for a sign of Dale. He went around back just in case his buddy was out in the football field smoking cigarettes, but there were only a couple of freshmen there.

When he got back to the parking lot, something was going on. The three guys who shouldn't be there had got up off their hood and were crowding around a couple of girls. Lilli Hollister, it looked like, and her younger cousin Sally, barely twelve. Lilli's voice was loud and high and shrill. It was always loud, but the high and shrill made Mike pick up the pace a little bit, starting towards the congregation at a half-jog.

"You all right over there, Lilli?" he called out, and the three unfamiliar Acton heads swiveled his way like hungry owls.

"Oh, she's all right," one of the Acton boys said, as Mike continued their way, cautiously.

"Mike!" Lilli said, breathy, a little too dramatic for his liking. "They won't let us go!"

An Acton boy tugged on her arm. "Come on, sweetheart, where you want to go?"

"Mike!" Lilli said again, in the same uninterrupted key. "They were talking disgusting to me and Sally."

"Good disgusting or bad disgusting?" This was Harvey. He came out of the shadows of the main building, walking his walk with his hips forward, his shoulders back. A strut if ever there was one. "Come on, Lilli, I'm sure it nothing you ain't heard before." He winked at her and then at the heads from Acton.

"Oh, but Sally, Harvey!" Cousin Sally didn't speak or move,

... either the disgusting talk or the ensuing chaos had cast her frightened face in stone.

"Oh, that's right. Sally. What do you say, Mike, you think her tender ears and years will survive?"

Mike was almost up on the Acton boys now. "Well," he said to Lilli. "Get on out of here."

"Mike, they wouldn't let us."

"They let you now."

Sally took Lilli's hand, practically dragging her cousin from the scene.

"I know a slut when I see one," the biggest Acton boy said, watching them go, then looking back at Mike defiantly.

"A slut?" Harvey said. He was almost there too but taking his time. "Mike ain't no slut. He'd like to be, I'm sure. But I do have more of a way with the ladies. Come on, Mike, tell the truth."

"You do all right, Harvey," Mike said. He was not relaxed. His right hand was balling up on its own, and he made an effort to release it. He watched the Acton boys trying to decide what to do.

"Better than these boys," Harvey said, coming to a halt next to Mike. "Ga-damn. You got to talk nice to girls. Even Mikey here knows that. Y'all don't learn that, you ain't gonna get none. Just gonna be you and your little woodrow and some lonely nights."

"I'll talk how I want to the white trash pussy you got around here."

"My god goodness gracious," Harvey said. "You do got yourself a serious potty mouth, don't you."

"What you gonna do about it?"

"I'm going back with you boys, that's what. I never realized those poor Acton girls might be so ripe for the taking."

"You wouldn't last a day in Acton. You and pretty boy both."

Mike was ready now. He was ready for whatever was coming.

"Oh, you'd be surprised. Mikey here, he does have the stupid hair and all, but he got that good swing, and quick as a cat."

"Yeah?" The Acton guy liked the sound of that. Here was something he understood.

"And me, well, I always get by," Harvey said. There was the sound of a car behind them, and Harvey nodded, happily. "Most everyone likes me, except maybe Mike, and a few misguided youths like yourselves. I got lots of friends."

There were two cars there, pulling in, Ox and Carl and Jimmy in Ox's Pinto, Dale and Josh in Dale's truck, with two more in the back. The Acton boys stepped back. Josh jumped down quick and Ox pried himself out of the driver's seat of his car. "What's going on?" someone said, ready for menace.

"We just having a little postgame with these boys from Acton. So long, boys," Harvey said, waving the foreigners into their cars. "You tell your sisters and your girlfriends not to fret, we'll be over to visit soon."

Mike watched Harvey laugh and lean in and wave at the Acton boys as they pulled out of the lot, fast. "They didn't want none," Harvey said softly.

"Uh-uh."

"We still Cottesville, ain't we."

"That's right. They didn't want none," Mike said, smiling.

"That right." Harvey took a few steps towards the Pinto and then called over his shoulder loud, this time. "Next time maybe you help me out a little there. The cat get your tongue?"

"I was saving my strength for the dirty work, Harvey," Mike yelled back in his own public key. "There was just that small one for you, which stuck me with the other two."

They jawed at each other as they went to the two waiting vehicles, hurrying to indoctrinate their friends. Then the truck and the car pulled out of the parking lot in tandem, with the two groups still shouting at each other as they forked their separate ways into the night.

TWENTY-ONE

ONE TIME THAT summer, Mike and Harvey found themselves in the same place at the same time, alone. It was out at the quarry, late night, July. Mike saw the little campfire as he walked up through the woods to the water. He didn't know who else was out there but he didn't want anything to do with them. He walked around to the far side of the quarry, slipped out of his clothes, and dropped quietly into the water. The quarry water was black and heavy at night. You had to work a little bit to keep yourself afloat, and Mike always had that quarry feeling of odd things sitting on the bottom, hundreds of feet down. The fire played its light through the trees. Mike expected to hear a bunch of people over there, whooping it up, but it was quiet. He swam out to the middle of the water and put himself on his back. There wasn't any moon. He stared up at the sky and floated and thought about Hermelinda.

Someone swore and a stick broke on the opposite bank, and Mike splashed himself upright. He could make out one figure working his way down towards the quarry's edge. The figure squatted down and peered out over the water.

"Who we got out there?"

Mike could hear it was Harvey. He stayed quiet, smiling to himself, swimming gently towards the sides where he knew he'd be harder to see.

"All right," Harvey said, "who is it? I'm gonna start target practice someone don't tell me something." Mike could see him picking up some skipping rocks off the bank. He stayed quiet and still. Harvey called out again a few times. He threw a few rocks and then lost interest and went back up to his fire.

Mike got out and sat back naked and dripping on the rocks. He could see Harvey sitting over there propped back against a tree, tossing little sticks into the fire. He thought about going over there and scaring the wits out of Harvey, or not, or just sitting down at the fire for a little while, if Harvey could handle that. But in the end Mike decided that he didn't feel like talking, and that Harvey was probably here because he felt the same. Mike wondered how long it had been since he'd seen Harvey by himself. He was used to thinking of Harvey only in motion, in crowds, with his crew, but Harvey seemed pretty content over there by himself with his fire and his sticks.

Mike stayed there sitting on his own bank, watching Harvey feed his fire, watching the light caught up in the trees and reflecting off the still water between them. The two of them stayed there for a long time, until Mike felt his eyelids closing down. Then he got up and worked his way around the quarry and back through the woods towards his car. He could hear Harvey singing something to himself, a low song Mike didn't recognize, fading away.

AUGUST

1 ST

UNTIL NOW, HOT has been only a word, a form of polite-
ness traded between strangers when there's nothing else to say,
a mild complaint. A single syllable. Ts'hot. Hot has been a term
of relativity, but there's nothing relative about it now. In the
Catholic Retreat Center, late at night, students can be found
lying on the floors of uncarpeted rooms with their shirts off,
breathing deliberately, their skins sticking to the dark stained
wood. Outside, George Whipkey has taken up serious smoking
again and lingers on the east steps far into the night, sucking
gently on cigarette after cigarette, drawing them out. He tilts a
glowing butt to the still sky, letting the ashes stack high like a
leaning tower until his hand shakes and they flake away. He
waits for the moon to rise. He stares at the shed and the fields
beyond and the smooth strip of County Route 1012 retreating
through the trees out of sight.

In the shed beside the Center, Father Joseph Cavanaugh lies
naked in a narrow cot, his head propped on a windowsill, nose
almost touching the screen, as he tries for air. The nights, he
thinks, are even hotter than the days now. The quiet makes
them hotter, the dark too. He is aware, as he lies there, that
every inch of his flesh has a real and inarguable weight. His
stomach sags sideways into the cot. His lids feel thick and
swollen, his feet and hands like stupid meat. He wants the students to be gone. He wants the Center to be empty so he can
clear off the huge desk in the air-conditioned office, roll out a
blanket, and sleep. He wants to put on a pair of old shorts and

sit barefoot in the grass in the inner courtyard, with everything quiet around him, with no parade of toilets flushing, no youthful chatter, no phones ringing, no cars starting outside, no doors opening, closing. He wants to take a week and visit the family house near Charleston, where the breezes come in off the water and slide the length of his mother's long, perpendicular house, with his sister and her kids downstairs muffled by the sound of the ocean. He remembers the feeling of waking in his bed at the shore house, year after year since he was a child, and the sense of immense space when he'd step onto the porch and look out over the water, squinting into the morning sun. Even after ten years in landlocked Cottesville, by the end of every summer he feels constricted and cramped.

On the other side of County Route 1012, behind the picked and spent pepper fields, Francisco Salmeron snores in a trailer, his mouth gaping open and undulating like a sea anemone. His wife lies half on top of him in the narrow bottom bunk. The floor is a huge spread of blankets, piled one on top of another, where the sisters Rebecca and Camilla sleep on their sides under a thin sheet. Their heat radiates in the slight space between their mutually turned backs and funnels up like a chimney towards the top bunk, where Pedrito is curled up against Hermelinda as she sleeps on her stomach. Her skin sticks to the gray T-shirt she wears to bed, and she dreams of sitting naked in the clear cold of the Rio Urique back in Batopilas, wading in the shallows, obscured, watching the boys on the bank walking with their poles and buckets to a favorite fishing hole. She sinks down up to her neck and a fish zags around her, sniffs her arm, bites her. In the main part of the Salmerons' trailer, fourteen-year-old Manuel does not dream or stir but only sleeps, like the dead, on a blanket near the door. His older brother, Alejandro, sits propped in the doorjamb, one leg in, one out, knowing that in a handful of hours he will be back in the fields again with his father and

brother. He is exhausted but too bored to sleep. He finds himself wishing that the next morning the *patrón*'s truck will pull
into the camp and cough, sputter, let out one huge puff of
smoke, and shudder and die. Alejandro steps forward, direct-
ing the men to push the truck under the shade of a nearby tree.
He takes off his shirt and crawls under the chassis, lying with
his back bare against the cool, packed dirt. He puts his hands
up into the car and touches it, reaches, pulls, twists, squints. A
toolbox drops onto the dirt near his legs, and the others' footsteps fade and die. He works. He cleans and disconnects,
removes and replaces. When the men return at night the engine
hangs suspended by a coarse chain to a thick branch overhead.
They stand around and watch. The next day the truck coughs
again and comes back to life like oil bubbling from the
ground, and the *patrón* smiles and counts off the bills, one,
two, three, four, five, six. Seven. More money than all of them
make stooping through long days in the fields in the sun. He
fixes tractors and cars and trucks and when he has fixed one
after the other it is time to leave. He packs the tight stacked
green bills into a sturdy shoebox and they begin the return to
Mexico, where there are streets and cars and girls to look at.
Alejandro thinks about his sister Hermelinda changing her
clothes in the cramped trailer, the smooth arc of her breasts,
the dark irises of her nipples, the knob of her hip, her thighs.
He closes his eyes and tries to sleep.

Across the fields to the west, out of sight, Clayton and
Dolores Olive are spaced evenly apart on their queen-sized bed,
stretched straight between the curly scripted ironwork at the
head and foot. They sleep peacefully as the central air hums on
low. Down the hall, in a room still postered with adolescence,
Mike's head has fallen and rests on the top of his childhood
desk. He is fully clothed in khaki pants and a short-sleeve light
green oxford. His face is pressed against a yellow legal pad list
of things to do this week. *Call Coe. Call W. Meeting with Gr?*

Raúl—Blue. Conrad. Dinner at house with H. A continuing string of names and letters and symbols. Each entry is a demand he has made of himself, and the accumulation of all these demands, and especially the last, has so exhausted him that he has fallen asleep in this awkward position.

On the side of the road in front of their house, the Olives' mailbox is empty and dark. The stuffy air inside has cooled a little from the afternoon when the door opened and the hand of Zebulon Hough loaded a bolt of bills and circulars inside. Zeb is still opening doors as he sleeps, first of mailboxes and then refrigerators, pushing aside quart containers of milk and softening melons as he searches for pie. He finds a misshapen piece wrapped in tinfoil squatting in a dark corner of the fridge. The pecan pie, left over from Eddie's buffet, causes the mailman's mouth to twitch as he sleeps, while across town in his living room, Eddie himself is sitting up watching television, thinking about making a new dessert for the week to come. He has seen the program he is watching before but does not even realize it, only half-watching as he thinks of replacing the pie with pudding and then about Monday's order—potatoes, chickens, Tabasco, salt. It's hot in his house, but he is used to running around the restaurant all night, sweating, and he hardly notices anymore.

Throughout Jackson County, the farmers sleep and sweat— Hunt, Dickerson, Bowman, Tate. This night does not seem different from summer nights their whole lives long. Many of them have moved only a matter of rooms through a single house over their forty or fifty years, down the hall, upstairs, downstairs, putting their kids to bed in the rooms they themselves once slept in as children. Harvey Dickerson is asleep in one of these childhood rooms. Even sleeping, his mouth is not still as he mumbles pieces and parts of words and speeches. His father, Brack, snores brutally in the master bedroom, disturbing his own sleep with the tremendous bursts of sound, as Mrs.

Dickerson, trained by habit and medication, lies oblivious beside him. The incredible sound winds through the house and out and across the fields and comes close to reaching Harvey's Uncle Blue a few farms over, whose whole body jerks in his sleep like an old dog. Blue's boy Carl is in the next room over, snoring in the bed his older brother has left behind. A few miles beyond that, Ox Bowman rests diagonally and curled on a bed too small for his six-foot-eight-inch frame. His sheets are salty and damp with sweat, partly from his nightmare, partly from his size. The heat is hard on Ox, who always gets the worst work in his father's fields, is always asked to lift the heaviest objects, move the most difficult and tedious loads.

There are ghosts, too, moving through the hot, still night, bodiless impressions of the living and the dead collecting as they pass through the present from the future or the past. No one sees them commingling on the shoulder of Route 1012 or in the Olives' tobacco fields or at the Retreat Center or Eddie's or the health clinic. They take their positions while the people sleep.

3RD

W*here once,* MIKE Olive writes, clicking his fingers quickly across the keyboard, *African-Americans were the general rule, today the majority of migrant workers in Jackson County are Latinos.* He stares at the words and then, letter by letter, deletes them, watching them wink off the dull screen. He walks a slow lap around the room, then seats himself again, gripping the rests of the wooden chair tight, the tendons rippling the back of his hands. "Shit," he says, to no one.

He's typing again when George, knocking the door open with

two hard raps, appears outside the office in the hallway. "Hurry up," he says. "I'm having some drooling issues already." He bangs a conga rhythm out on the doorjamb, rocks on his toes.

"One sec. I've got to make a phone call before it gets too late."

"Screw the phone call." Mike is already dialing the number. "Cornhole. They better not run out of fried chicken."

Mike listens to George go lumbering down the hall. "Come on, pick up," he says to the phone. He reaches over and types a note to himself at the end of the page while he waits for the machine to finish its message. *Origins,* he writes, *blacks: s, deep s, n, Haiti, Jam. Mex: national, immigrant, cit., border. Other?*

"Hi, Professor Grimes, it's Mike. I'm putting together this draft for D.C., hoping you can take a look at it this week. Whenever's a good time, I really appreciate it. Uh, well, hope you're enjoying the heat. Don't forget this swimming hole out here I been telling you about. I'm gonna go eat some pig right now, be back in a bit. Talk to you, thanks, bye."

He finds George in the parking lot, sitting in his car, with the engine running, the music loud.

"Sarah coming?"

"For what? The coleslaw? The vegetarian chicken-fried steak?"

"Raúl? Cynthia?"

"Will you get in here already?" George smacks the empty seat beside him with one big hand. "Just you and me, kid, and your meat-loving people. God bless them."

They pull out of the Retreat Center parking lot and accelerate quickly down the road towards town. Mike looks for his mother's car as they pass his parents' house but finds it missing.

George notices him looking. "They already down there?"

"Probably."

"See?" George curses playfully to himself, mumbling about pork.

They slow down as 1012 turns into Main, and roll gently by

the Stop N' Go and the low institutional face of Cottesville
Elementary. The First Baptist Church, the Food Lion. Mike
glances at his watch as the yellow sign of Eddie's Bar-N-Q
comes into sight.

"What?" George says. "What?"

"Lot might be full. Turn down Christie."

They park on the street in front of the Joyners' house, cut
through the Bar-N-Q lot, and open the door. The air-conditioned air gasps past them into the world outside, surrounding
them in a cold, dense perfume of food. George advances on the
buffet table like a deer dog as Mike closes the door behind him.
By the time he reaches the table, his friend is holding a heavy
plate in his hands, biceps drawn tight from the sudden pounds
of chicken, ribs, and shredded barbecue.

"Sorry, Eddie, I brought George back to bankrupt you
again," Mike says, as the proprietor appears with a fresh batch
of mashed potatoes in an enormous metal bin.

"Hey, Mike, haven't seen you for a spell."

"I know it. I had so much last time, this the first time I'll eat
since."

"Help yourself to some potatoes, young man," Eddie is saying to George, holding out his offering.

"Thanks, I think I'm gonna start out with an all-meat
course. I'll be back."

"I know you will." Eddie puts the potatoes down on the buffet table, checks on Mike's progress down the line. "You call
that eating?" Eddie points at Mike's modest collection of meat,
Brunswick stew, green beans, sweet potatoes, and cornbread.

"I'll be back, too."

"If your friend leaves you anything. Better hurry."

"He's been behaving himself pretty good."

"Oh, he gets along."

At the edge of the main room, George is waiting for Mike.
"Figured I'd let you seat us," George says low and quiet,

"being the native guide." Mike scans the room and sees the town collected. They nod at him and he nods back. The way the faces lift from the plates and look at him, he feels he could be ten years old, that ten years has not changed the place or the people a bit apart from a few hairdos, a few new young faces in the mix. The young kids seem to Mike like replacements or reinforcements, no different from what he once was or Harvey was or any of them. How long can that go on? he wonders. One day Eddie will die, Mike thinks, my mother and father will die and everyone in this room dead and gone but time goes stubbornly on, and the fact is this place will change, will have to. But when will it have to? What will make it happen?

An unfamiliar couple are sitting in the corner where his parents should be, talking to the Evans family. They look plump and pasty, foreign. Guests. Mr. Evans catches his inquisitive eye, and the older man nods almost apologetically, pointing with his head towards the back of the room, and there Mike finds his mother and father sitting at a long table with a few other farmers and their wives and children. The two new arrivals make their way across the room, slowly, with Mike pausing to pay his respects to Mr. and Mrs. Hollister, to Ricky Cox and his wife Sally, to Zeb Hough, just getting up to leave.

They sit at the end of the table, with Mike at the head, looking down at the twelve faces tilted his way. He feels like a factotum crashing the board meeting, sitting accidentally in the executive chair.

"Hello, everybody," he says.

"Tea, Michael?" Eddie's wife, Elma, appears at his shoulder with a pitcher, and he turns, grateful for the interruption.

"Yes, ma'am. Thank you."

She pours for Mike and then for George, who begins to drink immediately, inhaling most of the glass at once. The cup rattles back onto the table as he puts it down.

"I like your shirt," George tells the Hunts' kid sitting across the table. Travis Hunt looks down at his shirt, black with big gold letters across it, reading, "Tobacco is not a drug, stupid!" He contracts slightly, like a turtle, as George smiles at him.

"It's nice to see you, Mike," Mrs. Hunt says, warmly. She's always been nice to him, and he's glad she hasn't decided to stop now. "We were just talking about you." She nods at his parents.

"Awful things, I'm sure."

"Oh yes, awful. We were remembering the pond you wanted to build, that time, hot summer like this."

"Oh no."

"His father," she says to George, "was recollecting the time when Mike was eleven, was that it?"

"Eleven," Clayton says.

"This was the last summer near as hot as this one. Michael managed to take their tractor and even got started digging up the ground before his daddy here caught him up."

George looks at Mike.

"He said he was gonna dig himself down to water, have his own private swimming quarry," Mrs. Hunt says. "Isn't that right." Clayton nods and the table laughs. "That was the last summer hot as this one."

"They say that every summer," Mike says, "just so they can tell that story again, I think."

"No, that was. You'd look out at the fields and it was just yellow, and not just tobacco."

"Looking like that to me now."

George excuses himself and heads back to the buffet table for another round.

"He's got an appetite, that one," Mrs. Hunt says.

"Doesn't he though."

"Eats like a farmer," Clayton says. "Make one too, he wanted."

"Got the gut for it," Mike says.

"He working for you some, what I hear?" Mr. Hunt asks.

"Here and there, not regular. It's fine. He's a." Clayton glances over at Mike. "A photographer, isn't that right?"

"Yes," Mike says. "He's a good one."

"You make a living at that?"

"Not much, I doubt."

"I don't know, these young people, seems like there's a bunch of ways to make a living," Mrs. Olive says.

"We'll see about that," Clayton says. "How long before he's home asking for his old room back?" The farmers laugh and look at Mike.

"It is a nice room," Mike says, smiling.

"Michael." Mr. Tate, sitting down at the far end of the table, raises his voice a little so that he can be heard. "I've got a question for you."

"Yes sir."

"What," Mr. Tate says. "What, there was a few of your friends out on our road the other day. A boy and a girl?"

"Yes sir?"

"Do you know what they were doing out there?"

Mr. Hunt says something under his breath, but Mike can't hear, and Mrs. Hunt silences her husband, quickly.

"Well, sir, I don't know exactly, but I can tell you close. We've been doing basically three things out in the migrant camps, all over the county." As he begins, he finds himself counting the people in the room who have already heard his speech, and wonders if they can hear him now. If he's using the same phrases. How the approach has changed, minutely. "The first thing is, there's that Head Start program and another K-through-eight deal for their kids. So we try to get them organized on that. Set up transportation." He speaks slowly, beating out a subtle rhythm with his fork. "Most of the kids have a tough time keeping up in school, because they do move around quite a bit. So whatever they can get in the summer's pretty good. We do some tutoring, sometimes, too, we have the time."

They're all listening to him, every word, even young Travis, whose face is set against him in trained disgust. Mike doesn't blame him. He takes a break to let their attention wander while he eats a bite of sweet potatoes, chewing without hurry. He takes a sip of tea. He does not dare look at his father before starting again.

"We've been doing some work for the health clinic, too, out there near Creech Corner. They got two trailers, and they got a doctor and a couple of assistants, just for the season."

"Oh, I seen that out there," Mr. Tate says.

"I was wondering, who sponsors that, Michael?" Mrs. Hunt says.

"It's federal money. The people that come in, you know, the migrants, are supposed to pay whatever they can afford, they have a sort of sliding scale. But the clinic will take in anyone, if their facilities have the means to help them. They're not equipped for brain surgery, but they can help most folks."

"A little brain surgery might be a good idea out there," Mr. Hunt says. Everyone laughs. Mike smiles, obliging. He wonders, briefly, what Mr. Hunt would look like with a bloody lip, a broken nose. He spots George heading back to the table with a full plate that looks heavier than his last one.

"What we do," Mike says, talking a little faster now, "is do some initial screening out in the camps, see who needs to go to the clinic, what kind of attention they need. We do some, uh, presentations at night for them on hygiene and health, we take their blood pressure—"

"He tried to take my blood pressure once," George says, sitting back down at the table, "but I wouldn't let him."

"They don't make gauges big enough for you, George."

"You go out there, too, on those, uh, presentations?" Clayton asks. He's looking at George.

Doesn't trust me, Mike thinks. Scared I'm making it up.

"Sure, I been out there," George says, wiping a dot of potato off his chin. "We got soaps and Band-Aids and towels and little stuff. Diapers, thermometers, you name it. We're like little drugstore Santas out there."

"Part-time taxi service, too," Mike says. "If they don't have a way to get to the clinic."

"That's what those two were doing?"

Mike nods. "Yes sir. Some one of those things."

"What's the third thing? You said three, right?"

"I did," Mike says. "The third thing is a project we're doing on tobacco and migrants. Collecting research, looking at the different aspects of it. Economics, sociology, history, like that."

"A school project, huh?"

"They give me credit to come home for the summer, I'm not gonna say no."

"So, what, then you go back and tell those university people how things go out here? Tell them a little truth."

"Little give and take, you know. Fitting Cottesville into the big picture. Farming's changing everywhere, but people don't always look at tobacco and North Carolina."

"What do you mean by that?"

Mike can feel his pulse going a bit. He's forgetting to eat. He tries another mouthful but does not taste it. He wonders how much he's going to say. His father watches him, close.

"Well," Mike says to Mr. Tate, "even in Durham, we down to the last factory."

"Can you believe it?"

"I was more surprised about out here," Mike says. "It wasn't that long ago there were three hundred thousand tobacco farms in this state. Now we got about sixty thousand."

"Three hundred thousand. When was that?"

"When you were a bit younger than me, I guess, sir."

"Back in the stone age," Mr. Hunt says. They all have a laugh about that.

"Even when I was a kid, tobacco was almost half the cash farm income, and it's down to a quarter."

"You still a kid."

"It wasn't too long ago," Mike says. "That's for sure."

"Well, Mike, you didn't have to go all the way to Duke to see how we've taken a beating out here. I could have told you that. They give me a degree for that?"

"They might, Mr. Hunt, I haven't quite figured them out yet, to tell you the truth."

Mr. Hunt and Mr. Tate laugh, hard, looking down the table at Mr. Olive. "I hope you getting your money's worth," Mr. Tate says.

"Me too," Clayton says.

"Me too," Mike says. Now seems like as good a time as any. "I get frustrated, sometimes, you know. I'm going to school with these." He shakes his head. "I mean, a lot of these people they take everything for granted. Been inside their whole lives, except to play tennis. Never worked a day. They got the blood, and money in the bank, and they're getting the right brand of education to match. But they don't know anything. And they gonna own companies. They'll run for office. They'll run the TV news and the papers and the magazines. And I'll tell you something. They don't care one bit about what's going on out here. Not one."

The table watches him. Beyond the table, too, he can almost hear the whole room listening, keeping up a low cover of banter for propriety's sake as they carefully overhear every word he says. A part of him wants to stop. A part of him doesn't want to hear himself anymore. But if he cannot say something here and now, then what the hell can he do?

"Tobacco's getting a bad deal right now," he hears himself say. "I think it's gonna get worse before it gets better. I want to be one who goes out there, to my classmates and the people like them, and say if you're going to make the future, *this* has to be a part of it." He hits the table with one pointed finger, twice.

"You not talking about the migrants, now," Mr. Tate says.

"Yes sir," Mike says. "I am. I'm talking about the whole thing and that includes them. They're in this with us, they're part of it. We got to take care of them on bottom the same way we want to get taken care of up top." He keeps his voice light as he can, as if he's describing an approaching cold front from the north. "When we want Congress or whoever to do us right, we just have to be sure we doing everything right, too."

He can't sit anymore and stands up, trying to look relaxed. There is something coming, something not yet spoken but building in the farmers at his table and maybe behind him as well. "Well, I'm going to get another little bit to eat," he says. "Anyone need anything?"

"Would you get me just a little pudding, Mike?" his mother says. He nods, and when he looks at her he sees, to his surprise, that she's proud of him, not because of what he's said but how he's said it. She thinks he's handling himself well, here, in the town's soft center.

"Sure, Momma." He moves off towards the buffet, leaving them quiet in his wake.

He fills his plate slowly, lingering over the coleslaw and potatoes. Am I a liar? he wonders. Am I going to be here when down the road arrives? I could be. I might. He closes his eyes for a moment, trying to pick a familiar voice out of the low murmur of the dining room. What will I say when I go back and someone wants to know what exactly I'm talking about? What kind of specifics can they live with? There are farmers who listen and farmers who don't, and when they don't, nothing seems to work, not even offering up a scapegoat for communal slander.

He's tried. "I mean, sir," he said to Blue Dickerson, back in July, "these crewleaders are not exactly your Better Business Bureau kind of guys, they—"

"You mean they're sons of bitches? Hell, Mike, you gotta be a mean son of a bitch to handle these boys they got, can't do it with ice cream and bunny rabbits."

"I suppose you can't, Mr. Dickerson. But think of it like this: take any kind of man, you, me, them, and look at if he isn't going to work better with someone bullying him, holding back his pay, or with a fair wage at the end of the day."

"They'll drink that money right away, won't give you a good piece of work for three days."

"If he's got a good dry bed with a shower, versus an old damp mattress on the ground? You don't take care of your plants, the roots might rot, you don't treat your tractor right, it breaks down on the busiest day of the year. It makes sense, you got to treat—"

"You really don't know what you're talking about, boy. What your father does out on his land is his business, and if he can afford to throw money round like that, fine. But it's nothing to do with mine, git?"

"They're family men, lots of them. They've women and children to think about, not just a bunch of men, the whole families. Family is important to them. They're like us—"

"They ain't like me."

"Well, *sir*." The word spit out of his mouth like a piece of paper ripping. "I guess they're farmers too, aren't they? They just don't have any land."

He wanted to stay and hold Blue's stare, then, but he didn't trust himself or Blue and turned away, feeling the other man's eyes in the small of his back.

We got to do better than that, Mike thinks, as he makes his way through Eddie's dining room towards the table, putting a half-smile on his face and readying himself for the worst, but when he sits down in his seat he finds the mood has changed, completely, is lighter and better than when he left. He does not know who is responsible but someone, maybe everyone, has decided to move on.

"Carolina's gonna whup us," George is saying, loud. "I'm not denying that. We just can't play any damn defense. I can't watch 'em. Y'all gotta understand what, what pain it is for a Tennessee boy to go to a school where they don't understand anything about football. They don't know how to watch it, don't know how to tailgate, don't know how to win." The table laughs. "But now," George says. "Basketball's a different story."

"Basketball," Mike joins in, "basketball, the Heels are in trouble."

"Get on."

"Got 'em last year," Mike said, counting off the wins, unfurling his fingers slowly.

"Won't happen again."

"Probably not."

"Make me a religious man, it does," George says. "Team they got."

The room thins out as they talk, with Elma moving behind the departing diners like a shadow, clearing tables. Then the farmers and their families at Mike's table rise, one by one, saying their goodbyes. George and Mike and the Olives are the last to leave. When they do, they drive one behind the other back to the Olives' house, and Mike and George sit on the front porch with Clayton and Dolores, looking out at the night and digesting.

5TH

DOLORES OLIVE STANDS in the kitchen, making biscuits. Some people swear by cutting butter into flour, but she melts hers, mixes it in quick, and never sees the difference. She's glad to be in the kitchen. Outside on the front porch, facing the road, her husband and son are sitting with the Mexican girl, the none of them saying a word.

What should I do? she wonders.

She stirs. The spoon clicks against the tin bowl, denting the silence of the house. She has never worried about him. A halo-headed boy waving to her from a tractor, holding on to his father as they growled down the rows. She has never worried about him with tractors, on playing fields, hunting, out late on a weekend night, at the quarry. Leaving home. He's been blessed. She knows that God chose him in some small way, and she's long known that Michael would do things, and think things, and understand things, that she would never do or think or understand. She knows, better than Clayton does, that these things will finally take him away from them. She watched him at Eddie's on Tuesday, sitting straight and handsome, grown and well-spoken and respectful. There was something in him that seemed to her still small and soft. Almost female. She worries whether God has been watching out for him as carefully outside of Jackson County. There's something in him that seems confused, and it confuses her too. Is it this girl? How did she happen?

Dolores remembers another girlfriend, brought home one weekend at the end of Michael's freshman year. Claire. She does not remember her last name. The girl visited them once, and then Mike didn't talk about her anymore. She was very pleasant and it was a very comfortable visit. She was tall and thin and pretty. From Richmond. Some family in Charlotte. Claire what?

The Mexican girl seems nice, from what Dolores has seen. Pretty too, and clean, considering where she lives, out in those trailers, the stains, the trash, the tilting roofs. Dolores does not know what the insides of the trailers look like. She's seen the outsides, though. And where the girl grew up? Those places were worse, weren't they? Maybe that's something to be appreciated, that the girl can look as nice as she does living in a place like that, and coming from her background. She checks her biscuit batter. She hopes their guest likes ham and green beans and sweet potatoes and biscuits. Mike has assured her anything she cooks will be fine, but she worries.

On the front porch, Clayton Olive sits and rubs his teeth with one finger, trying to think of something to say. He stares across the way at his neighbor's tobacco fields, where most of the leaves are already turning to yellow. Tobacco's on the downslope, really. Sweet potatoes. Five workers he might need but not more, maybe six. Eight most. What will Mike say when he tells him that it's time to cut back on the workers? He can hear the argument already. Well, he's not running a welfare farm out here. There are people in his camp this year whom Clayton knows, although not this family, not this girl's, and some of them are fine people but that's not a reason to choose them over your own. He's doing what he can. He's done a lot. Clayton begins to catalog the expenses, again, the expenses of the work on the camp, the pay, the food. He forgets that tonight is different from any other night on the porch, alone or with his wife, drinking sun tea, thinking. Her voice surprises him. It's part surprise and part her accent that he doesn't understand her the first time.

"Pardon?"

"You have a very beautiful house, Mr. Olive," she says again, smiling with white teeth that shine out from her dark face. She's a good-looking girl. Clayton understands a little bit what she's done to Mike, who's just a kid, after all, although he makes you forget it sometimes. Smart. Probably talk his way out of death and taxes both if you gave him a chance. It makes Clayton wonder about the value of smart all by itself.

"Well, thank you," Clayton says, looking at her, although not full on. He turns half sideways to examine his house and appreciate it with her, and he feels better for it. It is a beautiful house. The wood floors are tight and clean. The wide windows look out over the fields to the south. "We do like it." As he answers her, a thought he cannot prevent passes through him, like a spasm in the lower back—does she have an eye on his very beautiful house? On Mike? On Cottesville? A mute series of scenes plays out lightning-quick before his eyes. The swelled belly, the tears, the angry family, the honorable thing to do. Mike trapped in by a dark beauty at the ripe old age of twenty-one. He feels pieces of anger rising inside him, like a cough. He cannot even imagine the possibilities Mike seems to have spread before him. Dean's List, with honors. Duke University. He doesn't even know anyone who knows what that means. Except it seems like it means that Mike is doing something very very wrong with this girl. He and Dolores were young, but that was different. Their backgrounds agreed. They had a similar understanding about the way the world worked, although their future pleasantly surprised them. What kind of understanding can his son and this girl share? He knows the kind, and knows it doesn't last. Clayton thinks he knows what Mike wants (although why bring her home, why, just to piss them off?), but what does she want?

Clayton does not want to be thinking like that, but he can't prevent himself either. New territory. A part of him feels that he has to accept her, that if you raised a child the way he raised Mike, all encouragement, all pointing to progress and potential outside the only world you knew, then those lessons or lack thereof played a part in what happened next. There is a county full of people around him who, if they could see him there on the porch with his son and his Spanish girlfriend, would grin and point and say see-there-Clayton-I-told-you-so.

Well, let them say it, he thinks. I promised myself I wouldn't raise another poor country ignoramus, and I didn't. That if I had the chance to give him the best, I'd give it. He's a good kid,

good head, good heart, and the rest, Clayton thinks, has to
come.

He looks at Mike and for a moment wants to smile at his
good-looking boy, his college boy, to tell his son and himself:
Not to worry, it's all gonna be okay.

"Twenty minutes," Mike's mom calls from the kitchen, too
loud considering the quiet.

Twelve hundred seconds, Mike thinks, considering each one
in the silence, counting them down. He wonders if there's a
part of him that has wanted this evening from the start, even if
he knew how terrible it would be, maybe *because* he knew how
terrible it would be. Have it out. He sees in his father's face the
amazing difference between theory and practice, how everything changes when it's in his house, his family, his boy. All the
things that excite him about Hermelinda confuse his parents.
Her dark skin. Her accent. Her scent, her language, her childhood, her places, her family, her what she knows. But beyond
all the differences he thought that they'd like her, that she'd
make his mother laugh, and his father too, despite himself.
That she'd charm the socks off him if she had the chance. How
to give her the chance. He wonders if his father has it in him.
He finds himself wishing, not for the first time, that he was
older, that he could hold something like age out like a badge to
show them that he knows what he's doing, that he's not just letting his dick lead him around like a divining rod. He knows
that's what his dad is thinking. Well, we've all done that but
this is not that. I love her. What would happen if he could bring
himself to say that in a clear voice, to everyone, at once. I love
her. But what proof can you offer for that? Millions of men and
women have said it before, and millions of them were wrong.
Who do you get to testify on your behalf? Romeo? Grace
Kelly? Sandra Dee? He sneaks a glance at Hermelinda. She's sitting very straight in her chair with a calm look on her face.

"Mike tell you about the house, how we ended up here and

all? Now that's a story." His father returns from his reverie of
troubling sons and sweet potatoes and starts to speak. Mike
watches his father giving it the garrulous country try. Well,
that's a start. Maybe the old Southern hospitality will bend him
to feel genuinely hospitable towards the not so welcome guest.
This is their chance, now, before the weeks to come, before the
lawyer from Washington appears. Byron Coe. It's a name that
could be a Cottesville name, really, but instead is only a thin
and invisible voice on the other end of a phone line, a name on
the top of letterhead and faxes. What will a Byron Coe be like
in the flesh? Will he look like a future Mike? Will he arrive in
Jackson County and see what Mike sees? In his mind, Mike
picks through the documents, pictures, and interviews piled on
the desk at the Retreat Center, wondering which ones of them
will best convince the lawyer, make him stand up on his pol-
ished city tiptoes, look around Cottesville, and say: Okay, listen
up, folks, this is what happens next.

Hermelinda is listening to the story of the Olive house, how
once they had an old house and tiny piece of land crowded
with corn, beans, onions, tomatoes, peppers, and then suddenly
they were rich. That an old man gave them the land that made
them Olives and not Salmerons, when Mike was just a little
boy, because the old man liked Mike.

"He was a strange one," Clayton is saying. "You could just
say he was about crazy, I guess. But he didn't have any kids,
and he wanted. I don't know what he wanted. To make a kind
of legacy, anyway. He might have given it to his dog if they'd let
him. But he gave to Mike."

Is that a joke? Could that possibly be true? She looks to Mike
for confirmation. His face is closed. Elsewhere. She wonders
where. He has never told her anything about this, and she realizes she's never asked him, that she's always considered his position of privilege as the given starting point, an unquestioned
precondition of his life just as hers was no money, no land, no

guarantee of anything. She glances around the house behind her and reconsiders the living quarters of her family, the trailer in the field not far from here, the room in Nuevo Laredo, the small house in Ojinaga, the hut in Batopilas, and she wonders: Where is our deliverance? Where is the Salmerons' crazy rich old man? Not quite wanting to hear the answer, or the answer her father might give, her father, who shifted from foot to foot outside the tiny bathroom of the trailer while she primped inside for her dinner with the Olives, talking to her nonstop, briefing her for the evening like a field marshal.

"Don't speak until you are spoken to, Hermelinda. Be careful not to scare them with too much talk."

"Will you stop it, Papá?"

"Don't eat too much. Try not to use the bathroom. Be helpful. Ay, don't you have any other shoes than that?"

"Why don't *you* go to dinner, Papá? Okay?" And she meant that too. She wishes it now as she rises from her chair and excuses herself from the men.

Inside she finds the bathroom. She runs the cold water and washes her hands. She looks at her reflection in the large, clear mirror on the wall. It's the best view she's had of herself for a long time. Her hair looks more wild than it ever does in the tiny square of mirror perched on the windowsill in the trailer, and she remembers a far-off night when she and Lupita stood next to each other in a bathroom at the Nuevo Laredo club, borrowing hairspray from another classmate of theirs. That night is no more than four months into her past, but already it seems gone, improbable, as if it did not happen and could not happen and will surely not happen again. As if that life never existed. A life of rules and limits that she could understand. Even if they were poor, even if she was hungry, angry, she felt that there she had some control. In Nuevo Laredo she would never had got herself in such a mess.

She curses Mike. She curses Lupita, her father, anyone she

can think of, and then opens the cabinet to look for something to tame her hair. The products are all unfamiliar. It feels improper even lifting the bottles to examine them, and she worries that when she returns to the table Mrs. Olive will smell her and know. She finally replaces them all and pats back the wildest strands of hair with her damp hands. She smiles at herself, for practice, a tight close-lipped smile, and then wide, showing her teeth, and finally makes a gruesome face to try and jolt herself into a good mood. *"Ya, basta,"* she tells herself.

On her way back to the porch she passes the dining room, where Mike's mother is starting to set the table, and she stands in the doorway watching for a moment.

"Let me help you with that."

"Oh, yes, thank you."

There is an awkward moment when Mike's mother looks unsure about what to do, whether to hand the stack of silverware and plates to Hermelinda or leave them on the table, and the decision seems to paralyze her for a moment, until she sets everything down and stands back. "Thank you," she says again, and retreats into the kitchen. Hermelinda wishes she had waited until the mother set one place, just to know how Mrs. Olive likes it; she does not want to get it wrong. She looks around the room for clues, like there might be a picture of a model place setting on the wall, or a placemat with telltale indentations. After thinking about it for a little while, she decides to set the table the way she used to for Mr. Thompson and his family, back in Ojinaga, with a fork on top of the rectangle-folded cloth napkin on the left and the knife pointing blade in on the right, with the spoon on the outside. Plates stacked at one end of the table for the father.

When she finishes she is left with four large silver rings, the size of her forefinger touching her thumb. She tries them in different places on the table. She clusters them together in a group in the center, then puts each above a spoon like the dot on a little i. She gets angry at these circles of silver, as if they are some stupid test, and she is failing. Finally she carries them into the kitchen, where she surprises Mrs. Olive poking a large, pink, steaming ham.

"I'm sorry, but I didn't know what to do with these."

Mrs. Olive turns as pink as the ham and glances around them, as if there might be someone else listening. "Oh, I'm sorry, dear. Those are for, um, the napkins. You fold them and put them through. . . . I'm sorry, dear, how terrible of me, you must not, you . . . " Hermelinda watches Mrs. Olive's mouth moving as if her tongue has knotted up tight into a twisted rubber band.

"No, we don't have these rings. I've never seen this before, but they are very pretty." She feels tempted to joke with her, tell her some of the things she thought the rings were for—candles, butter, sharpening knives, decoration, magic tricks—but she thinks of her father and tries to stay quiet.

"Well, that's very nice of you to say. Just leave them there, honey. I'll take care of them." Hermelinda puts the napkin rings on the counter and stands there in the rich air of the kitchen for a moment, not wanting to leave.

"Is there anything more . . . ?"

"No, no, I'm fine, you can tell the boys we'll be ready in just a minute. Thank you, darling."

Hermelinda moves back to the front porch, feeling uneasy despite the darling, honey, dear.

Father and son still sit quietly beside each other on the porch. She stands in the doorway and sees Mike nod to himself, unaware that anyone is watching. Something crackles under his skin, she knows that beyond the flesh there is bad weather ranging from ear to toe and back again, and when he looks at her he looks sheepish for a moment, as if she's caught him at something nasty, but then he smiles, winks. She smiles back because she thinks, Well, that's why I like this boy, because he is all those things at once: an angry man, a little boy, a lover who smiles and winks.

THEY SIT AND eat ham. It is sweet and moist and melts in the mouth like meat candy. Clayton eats steadily, gaining momentum at the head of the table as piece after piece disappears into the fierce workings of his jaw. Dolores watches each place setting carefully, ready to replenish tea, beans, and meat at the first sign of space. Mike and Hermelinda face each other at the table, trying not to look at each other the whole time, trying not to make faces at each other, trying not to blow grotesque and lascivious kisses across the table. No one says anything, and Hermelinda likes that, it's like their own dinners: when you eat you eat and when you talk you talk. Mike knows it's too quiet, though, and so he begins to tell his mother about a conversation he had earlier in the day with Martha Joyner at the Migrant Head Start.

"She says hi, by the way."

"That's nice of her."

"She said what a boon it's been for them having the volunteers this year. How we've been a big help."

"Well, you know you have," Dolores says admiringly.

"Yes, it seems like it. And since it seems unlikely that Duke students will be out here next summer," not looking at his father, "although who knows," hearing the clank of a fork from his end of the table, "she was talking about recruiting people in Cottesville. You think that would go, Momma? Would you be interested in something like that?"

"I'm not sure."

"They're the most beautiful little kids, Mom." He stops, aware of Hermelinda, watching him. "You'd like it."

"Oh, I think you were enough for me, Mike, I have really no desire to start changing diapers again."

"They're older ones. No diapers. Just pure and unadulterated cuteness and terror, combined."

"Well, I hope that works out for Martha. I know she works hard." Dolores Olive ends the conversation there, because what she does not want to say is that she doesn't approve of the mothers who would leave their babies with a stranger at such an early age, even a woman like Martha Joyner. But she doesn't want to get into that again.

"Do you have brothers and sisters, dear?"

"Yes, Mrs. Olive. Two sisters and three brothers."

"And where are you?"

"I'm the oldest."

"Oh is that right?"

Suddenly, as if his last bite of food contained unsaid thoughts which Clayton half digested and now regurgitates, Mike's father turns to Hermelinda. He squints at her as if she were standing in front of a bright light.

"How old are you, Hermelinda?" The name sounds very ugly on his lips: Irma Linda.

"Nineteen. Next month."

"Nineteen," he repeats, as if diagnosing her with a disease.

"People think I'm older than that." Some explanation of her age seems expected of her, but she does not know what that explanation is. "Sometimes they think my mother and me are sisters."

Mike smiles, wondering if she made that up; he can't imagine anyone mistaking Mrs. Salmeron and Hermelinda for sisters. Dolores nods politely. "Nineteen," Clayton says again. "So you've finished high school?" There's a weight to his voice that suggests he already knows the answer, and that it's the wrong answer. Mike hears it, knows it well. He starts to say something, thinks better of it.

"No, Mr. Olive. I didn't get to finish high school."

"She went to an American high school, down in Texas."

"Oh."

"I would have finished this year but we left Laredo with only two months left in the school."

"That must be so *hard,* dear, moving around like that all the time."

"I didn't want to go." She shrugs. "We didn't have any relatives I could stay with to finish. I don't think my father would let that anyway. He likes our family together, all the time." Mrs. Olive nods appreciatively. "My father decided the best thing was for us to come here. You know jobs are very difficult right now in Mexico."

"I thought you were in Texas."

"We lived on the border. My house was in Mexico and my school was in Texas."

"That must be interesting," Mike's mother says.

"I've heard those border towns are rough places."

"It was okay."

"And where was that called again?"

"Laredo."

"There a lot of drugs down there?"

"Dad." Despite himself.

"I've seen something about that, I'm just asking."

"I don't know. I didn't see them."

"It can be dangerous down there, though."

"I don't know. More dangerous because there's a city, lot of people, but not so dangerous."

"You ever read about that place, Mike? You learn anything about down there up at Duke?"

"A little bit. Some. Learned more from Hermelinda, really, hearing her talk about it."

"Why exactly y'all leave?"

"It's better to come up here to work. My father and my brothers can make more money here than in Mexico. The dollar, you know, it's bigger than the peso."

"Well, it seems like your family's good workers and we're glad to have them," Clayton says, trying to remember which ones they all are, and also thinking about how much he pays out every day, and if they're making so much more here than down there, maybe he's paying too much, more than his neighbors now because of Mike, and he doesn't know, maybe that's too much.

"Thank you," Hermelinda says again, because Mike's father does not seem to hear her the first time.

"Clayton?"

"Oh, yes, fine," he says. "So, how did you get up here?"

"Señor Blanco?"

"Iggy drove you?"

She laughs.

"What?"

"Mike calls him Iggy too. It sounds a little funny to me."

"They call him Nacho."

"Nacho, uh-huh."

"Well, there you have it. But you met up with him."

"He was taking people north for work, and my father didn't have any jobs, so we came."

"They knew each other down there."

"Yes."

"What'd your father do before?"

"He was a farmer, you know, when we lived in Mexico."

"In Laredo?"

"No, in Batopilas."

"That's a funny-sounding name for a place."

Hermelinda laughs. "It is a very nice town. Very small. With a river and mountains."

"That does sound nice."

"A farmer, huh? What'd he farm?"

"Oh, the farm wasn't so big, not like yours."

"Well, we have been fortunate. Although I did start out, like anyone else, you know. They grow the same things down there?"

"It was very steep mountains, where we lived, so there were only some little spaces. It was my grandfather's land. You had to build, how do you call them, some steps for the plants."

"Terraces," Mike says.

"Steps, yeah, I know what you're talking about. That's hard farming, isn't it? What'd you all farm?"

"It was corn, beans, peppers, I think. I was pretty young when we were there."

"Why did y'all leave, uh, Bato. You know."

"My father lost the land."

"Oh dear. I'm so sorry."

"Thank you Mrs. Olive. It was very hard for him."

"I should think so. For all of you."

"I was still pretty young."

"Lost it? What, like in a poker game?"

"Forced out by some bank or something, Dad, you know how it is."

"I thought it was her grandfather's." He turns to Mike. "Listen, I'm just finding out a little about her and her family."

"There were enemies of my father in the town, they wanted the land, so they forced us to leave."

"That's terrible."

"Well, I mean, how do they exactly force a man to leave? I wouldn't leave my daddy's land, they'd have to kill me."

"Then they would kill you," Hermelinda says. Her voice is smooth and cool but Mike can hear the edge beneath it. "In Mexico."

Clayton shakes his head. "It sounds like it's pretty messed up down there."

"So it's no wonder people should want to come here," Mike says. "Right? For a better life."

"A different life," Hermelinda says.

"More jobs, I guess I'm saying."

"Yes."

"Well. People are from somewhere." Clayton picks up his fork for something to do, but his plate is empty. "I guess it won't be too long before you're going back down there, huh? Always good to get home."

"Can I get everyone some more ham?" Dolores says.

Clayton puts down his fork, shakes his head. No one says anything.

"How about you, Hermelinda? Ham?"

"No thank you, Mrs. Olive."

"We'll wrap that up," Clayton says, "you can take it back with you to your family." He pushes back his chair. "I'm going to set out on the porch a bit. Maybe some coffee, Dee." He walks stiffly out to the porch, rolling his shoulders as he goes.

"There's pie."

"Just coffee," Clayton says, disappearing.

They sit at the table for another minute, not sure of what to do.

"This is very nice," Hermelinda says, and Mike stares at her, wondering how she is able to get that off with a straight face.

Mike's mother thanks her and rises to clear the table, and Hermelinda follows. He hears them talking about Texas as they move into the kitchen, his mother telling about her sister who went to Texas, Austin if she remembers right, said it was beautiful, rolling hills of blue spring wildflowers, and clear-water creeks, much greener than she ever thought it would be.

"You must miss it."

"Yes, Mrs. Olive." Mike has never asked her this question. "I do miss it. It was very active, you know, and I had a very good friend there."

Mike listens to them from the dining room, feeling a little jealousy for Texas but mostly mad at his father. What did he expect? That was even pretty civil, all things considered. He wonders which direction to go, then walks out on the porch. He sits down next to his dad in a low-slung chair, feeling his meal press him down.

"Well, they're gonna be on their way, soon," Clayton says, and for a minute Mike forgets what he's talking about. "Couple more weeks, maybe."

"How many, you think?" Mike feels his own pulse, clear and fast, between his chin and his throat.

"Two, three. You'll be back in school, things will come back to normal."

"I hope not." He needs to tell him. "We haven't made much progress with the other," he almost says farmers, decides against it, "crewleaders."

"Well, that's the way it is, you know. People get set in their ways."

"We're going to push a little harder now. There's a lawyer coming down here soon. There may be a case."

Clayton looks at his son. "Goddammit," he says.

"There've been some bad things going on at some of the other camps. Things you wouldn't stand by and let happen."

"Michael," his father says, somewhere between a whisper and a hiss. "Sit there for just one moment, and think. Think, will you?"

"It's the only way I see."

"Whose land?"

"We're not sure yet."

"Whose?"

"Blue Dickerson's."

"Son of a bitch," Clayton says. "Mike, tell me something. Just who the hell you think you are?" Mike looks at his father, knowing there isn't any answer. "Are you even thinking?"

"I've been thinking awhile," Mike says.

"About what? Not about what it is out here. Not about what you're doing to your mother or that girl you're leading in all the wrong directions."

"She's not." Mike feels blood. "Just." He raises his hand in a gesture of seizure.

Clayton stands up and looks down at Mike. This is how Mike remembers him from childhood, tall and towering over him, and the son feels a wave of sadness rock through him before the other feeling returns.

"Go ahead," his father says, louder than he intends to. "What does this lawyer have to say about the half of these people who come to this country illegally, hey? How many of them have broken laws? What about the men that steal from me, cheat me? We gonna put them up on charges? They the ones you want? Those your people now, your heroes? Go head, then. Take your little poor girl and get out of here. I don't want to see you or her right now. I don't want to give you any more chances to try to embarrass your mother or me." He points a finger into the night. "Go." Mike doesn't move. "Get out of this house right now," Clayton says.

Mike rises without saying a word, walks into the kitchen, and takes Hermelinda by the arm, pulling her gently towards the door.

She departs as gracefully as she can, thanking Mrs. Olive, calling out to Clayton on the porch, "Good night, Mr. Olive. Thank you for everything." She follows Mike to the truck. She sits quietly beside him for a while before she suddenly turns and punches him in the arm, once, very hard, causing them to swerve from the dirt road and cut a crescent tire mark through the edge of the spent pepper field.

"I'm sorry, Hermelinda. It wasn't about you."

"No, it's always about you, I know. Always."

"I'm sorry." He tries to touch her but she gets out of the truck and begins to walk the last quarter mile back to the trailer. He jumps out and follows her, their shadows thrown long by the headlights of his truck, but she turns and says, "No, leave me alone." He stops. He gets back in the truck and watches her walking past the reach of his lights. He tries to remember the last time he cried, and why, and he wonders why he won't cry now. Wonders, if he did, what exactly would it be about? But he won't. He turns off the headlights, inching forward, watching her, making sure she gets back all right. Then he turns the truck around and heads back to the Catholic Retreat Center.

6TH

IT'S FRIDAY NIGHT. They've already taken a couple of laps around town in the Pinto, with Harvey yelling, "Get out of the house, you fucking zombies, ain't gonna kill you," and no one paying him any mind. He'd be surprised if they even heard him anymore.

They end up at the Stop N' Go, like they always do. The place is bustling, even for a Friday night, familiar cars and faces coming in and out, buying cold drinks, getting gas. This heat will make you thirsty, and Harvey is solving that problem with Bud number six. Or is it eight?

"How many we had?" he asks Ox, who's sitting on the other side of the Pinto's hood so that the entire car tilts his way.

Ox thinks it's one of Harvey jokes, riddles. "I don't know, Harvey, how many we had?" he repeats, grinning.

Harvey sees he isn't going to get an answer and doesn't really care. "Few less than enough," he tells Ox. "Ts'all I know." He bounces the car lightly on its shocks, leans back comfortably into his next sentence. "Clydesdales better be ready to ride tonight, 'cause this," he tips the red-and-white can towards his lips, "this is like pissing in the sand." His head tilts back and his Adam's apple bobs as he drinks, quickly, deeply. He pulls the can away and half-crushes it with his hand, turns it upside down to let the last drops fall to the pavement. "Gone."

They drink. It's just the two of them. Harvey doesn't know where the others are, his cousin Carl or Jimmy or Truett, any of them, but they'll be along. They're always along eventually. Got to get out into the world. If all you gonna do is be tired and work like slaves all day, why bother? Got to get out. If it wasn't so damn hot he might motivate over to Acton. Not much more there but at least some women to look at. Almost always one stray hottie over in Acton, with any kind of luck.

A big white truck pulls into the lot fast, and Harvey leans forward off the hood. Now what have we here? The driver door comes open at the pumps and one of the Duke girls steps out, the fine one, she's got the bod, this one. And pretty cool too, no stick up her ass like the rest of them, she'll talk to you, she's all right. Harvey met her back in the beginning of the summer, when she was standing over the hood of a metallic-green Saab, checking her oil. The hood of the car was hinged on the front and opened the wrong way out.

"Miss," he said, "pardon me for asking, but what the hell kind of car is that?" She laughed as he moved up beside her to check the innards. "Really. Is there any sense in it?"

"I don't know. It's not helping me out on the dirt roads out here, that's for sure."

"You got no clearance on that thing. What you need," Harvey said, "what you really need is a big ol' truck."

"I was thinking of that, actually. You want to buy my car?"

"Hell, no. I don't know who would buy that thing. Someone in Durham, I guess. Where you from?"

"Virginia."

"You not a Duke girl, are you?" He knew. She nodded, smiled half shyly. "Oh, man! I'm telling you, those lucky Duke boys. Mhmn. Well this is Tar Heel country, you know that now, but we're still pretty nice about it, nice people like you. What's your name?"

"Cynthia."

"Well I really am happy to meet you, Cynthia. I'm Harvey Dickerson, and I'm hoping I'm going to see you again."

"Maybe you will. We'll be here all summer. I'm with Mike Olive?"

"You're *with* him?"

"Well, we're out here, doing this thing, all of us, you know, I'm working at a health clinic for migrant workers. You know Mike, right?"

"I surely do know Mike. Yes I do."

"Everyone seems to." She put down the hood, made slowly towards the driver's door of the car.

"Well, I hope you'll come visit us again. Cynthia. It was really nice to meet you."

"It was nice to meet you too."

Goddamn right, Harvey thought, watching her bend and curve to slip into the low-slung car, waving her on her way.

It's her, again, and it's her truck. She bought it a while ago; he saw her in it a few times back in July. Waved. Shouted. Thumbs up. But she never stopped or got close enough for words until now. Harvey lifts his chin, waiting for her to look over, then he hears the other door open and shut, and sure enough, there's Mike Olive, who does not look over where he knows they are. Just like old times, hey Mikey boy? Harvey stands up off the hood and starts walking their way.

"Hey Mike," Harvey says with a grin for the Duke girl, leaning against the side of the truck. "You still curing the sick and enlightening children out there?" He winks at the girl. "Didn't think that would take all summer for a capable young man like you."

"Well, Harvey, you know, we been waiting for you to come help us out."

"Oh, I've been kind of busy. You got this truck looking good," Harvey says to the girl in a new key that's meant just for her. He's done with Olive, for now. "Looking real good. Miss, uh, Cynthia, isn't it."

"That's right," she says. "You've got a good memory."

"You all know each other." Mike smiles. "I guess that kind of figures."

"You know I ain't shy, Mike. Be down to my last tooth if I waited for you to introduce me to your friends. My old buddy here can be a little lax on the etiquette, at times. Here, let me get that." He steps forward and flips open the gas cap, puts the nozzle in place.

"Oh, really, that's okay." Cynthia laughs, she smiles. "I can do that."

"Oh, just let me give you the Harvey Dickerson full service treatment. Let me spoil you a little." She steps back, nods, glances at Mike, who's leaning against the truck on the other side, watching. "I bet Mike never spoils you at all."

"Don't want her to get a swelled head."

"She not that kind, you can tell. But she's got to get her due." Harvey smiles at her, props the throttle open on the pump. Mike turns and goes inside. Good boy.

"Go ahead and pop the hood, I'll check the fluids."

"Really," she says, "don't worry about it."

"You're not gonna make me do a half-assed job, are you?" he says, walking towards the front of the truck. "Just got this baby, know you gotta take care of it. When'd you check the oil last? I'll bet even money you down a quart."

"Probably," she says. She hesitates, then opens her door and pops the hood.

Harvey pulls out the dipstick, wiping it on the way with his receipt for the Bud. He puts it back and takes it out again. "A quart. What do you know." He leans over the engine. "That hose there is pretty good and cracked too." She moves up beside him. "You see it? You see the one?"

"Yeah." The gas pump numbers continue to whir and click.

"Now that's just one of those emission deals. You don't even need to replace it, you don't want to. Just stick a spark plug in there, stop the hole, and you're in business."

"Wouldn't that effect the emissions?"

"Not to speak of. 'Sides, you wear that nice perfume, I figure you got the right to some emissions."

"All right, Harvey. I'll know where to go when I deal with that hose." She puts down the hood, gently. "Are you always this friendly?" she says.

He picks up the hood again and drops it hard so it shuts. "Only since I learned to talk. Only if I like you. You seem pretty easy to like."

"Thank you. So do you."

The fuel pump clicks off, finished.

"Now that's a nice thing to say. Especially seeing how that sure as silk ain't what Mike told you."

"Well. He said you two never really got along too well."

"I wouldn't say never. It's that classic story of the poodle and the pauper." She looks at her hands. "We grew apart, I guess you'd say. A good bit apart." Harvey grins at her, spreads his arms wide. "Cain and Abel."

"That can happen."

"You know we were born an hour apart? Mike and I."

"Really?"

"That's right. Cottesville hospital, right down the road. October five, start your shopping now. Had our first fight right in the delivery room. Mike tried to strangle me with his umbilical cord."

"You're making that up."

"So what you all got going, tonight?"

"Working. Getting some sleep, I guess."

"Have a beer with us." He sees Mike swing out of the Stop N' Go door with a paper bag, heading for the truck. "Why not. It's hot. A little unwind."

Mike gets to the truck, looks expectantly at Cynthia. "Well," he says. "Harvey fix you up?"

"Come on, Mike, y'all are gonna come have a beer with us. We'll chalk it up for world peace."

"Thanks, Harvey." Mike swings the bag into the truck and rolls his thick bottom lip under his top in a little pout of denial. She's taking her cue, getting up into the truck. Something's got to be done. Harvey gets up alongside the truck and props his elbows on the driver's-side window.

"We can be a pretty fun bunch of rednecks, really," giving her his best smile. "Tell her, Mike."

"Can't argue with you there, Harvey."

"Sure you can. Come on, have a beer, we'll argue. Maybe I'll let you win. One beer, you can't go a hot summer without one cold beer with Harvey and Co. It ain't right. It's in the county constitution."

"I'm pretty beat," Mike says. He does have some circles under his eyes, but that's not really Harvey's concern.

"Friday night," Harvey says very slow. "Cold beer." He puts a little shiver in his voice. "Come on, that's gotta sound good. I'm buying."

Mike's looking down at the dashboard like he's ready to go to sleep right there, but then he looks up at Harvey, and Harvey thinks: Maybe. He hopes. Be nice to get her out of the car again, have another look at her.

"All right," Mike says. He and the girl both look surprised.

"Alllll right," Harvey congratulates them, his voice rising. He slaps the side of the truck lightly, a little pat on the ass, and steps back.

Cynthia pulls the truck around and they park next to the Pinto. By the time Harvey gets over there, they're out on the pavement and Mike is introducing Cynthia to Ox.

"Nice to meet you, Jeremy," she's saying, and Ox nods,

slowly, not knowing whether it's nice to meet her or not.

Harvey blinks to let him know it is and Ox smiles. "Hi," he says.

Harvey takes out a fiver and puts it in Ox's hand.

"What you drinking, Cynthia?" He says her name slowly, enjoying all the sounds and syllables.

"Budweiser's fine."

"We can do better than fine. What you want?"

"No, I mean I like Budweiser." She laughs and shows her white straight teeth. "A lot."

"You got a nice laugh," Harvey says. "Get us a six," he tells Ox. "Longnecks. Good laugh, smart, pretty, Virginia Bud girl. Man. You are a dangerous person, Cynthia. You gonna raise our standards out here for womankind and then where we gonna be? Wanting caviar and eating beans."

"You should write country songs," Cynthia says, laughing. He's doing good, she can't stop laughing.

"I should, shouldn't I. What rhymes with Cynthia?" They all think about that for a moment, and then the beers come back. Harvey opens two and hands them to Cynthia and Mike. They wait until he and Ox are ready, too, and then they all drink together. "Bottles," Harvey says. "Mike's always been a bottle man."

Mike smiles a small smile. "You remember that?"

"I remember everything. The first thing I forget hasn't happened to me yet. I remembered your name, didn't I?"

"You did," Cynthia says.

"I'm serious, I got a memory like you wouldn't believe. You were wearing white-and-blue Nikes the first time I saw you," he tells her, and she looks at him, and then at Mike. She laughs. "Triangle silver earrings," Harvey adds.

"A good memory for some things," Mike says.

"Come on, try me, Mike, anything you want."

"What books did we read freshman-year English? With Miss Manning?"

"Oh, now, Mike, what kind of question is that? Never much of a reader," Harvey explains to Cynthia. "Really, I didn't read book one. Ask me something important. All right. Hold on. Maybe I remember one book that year was called *The Jungle*."

"Yeah," Mike says. He's surprised. "That's right, we did read *The Jungle*."

"I know it. And I remember another book about those German boys in World War One."

"*All Quiet on the Western Front*. We read that freshman year?"

"Well, you did. I remember, it sounded pretty good, actually. You wrote a little paper on that. He got up and read us this little paper front of the class," Harvey says to the girl, who seems to be enjoying all this.

"That's pretty cute," she says.

"I didn't want to go up there."

"Oh, he was all proud. But we gonna bore our guest here," Harvey says, turning his sights back on Cynthia.

"No, I like hearing about it," she says. "You do have a good memory. I forget everything like that, all those little details."

"Ah," Harvey says, "I got all the details." He's about to say something else when cousin Carl pulls in beside them in the old orange Bronco, the engine rumbling loud and low. Mike nods at Carl, but Harvey can see something in his face change, and can see what's gonna happen in the way Mike tilts back his bottle of Bud. Like he realizes where he is, what he's doing.

"Thanks for the beer, Harvey."

"Where you running off to?"

"We got to get back. We got people waiting for us."

"Let 'em wait."

"See you, Jeremy," Mike says. "Carl."

"Bye," the girl says.

They get in the cab and nothing comes to Harvey for a second or two as he watches the truck drive out of the lot.

"Fucking Olive, man," Carl says, getting out of the Bronco. "What the fuck he doing?"

"He ain't doing nothing," Harvey says, pissed that she's gone, but what did he really expect? "You see that?" He taps Ox on the shoulder. "She was checking out the I."

"You snaking for a college girl, Harvey?"

"Losing your touch, Harvey?" Truett yells over from the passenger side, coming around.

"College, country, they all constructed pretty much the same, what I seen. But that one better than most."

"She wasn't that much."

"You probably right. I've just been out here in the wilderness too long. Girls round here dull as plastic picnic knives." Harvey opens another beer and sits back against the car.

"Some things never change," he tells his silent partner Ox, who has not moved since he got back from the beer run. "Olive running with another one he don't deserve."

"That ain't his, from what I heard," Carl says. He steps towards the beer. "Who the fuck got bottles?"

"So that ain't his, huh." Harvey's face stretches out wide in a smile. "Damn, I should of." He's thinking. "Well all right."

"Mike's on to darker meat these days."

Harvey stops drinking to hear that again. "Shit, you got all kinds of news, don't you, Carl. What is it you know about Mike and chocolate that the rest of us don't?"

"Naw, it's some Mexican girl. A buddy of mine in Acton saw them out there couple weeks ago."

"Who?"

"Billy Foote."

"Weeks ago?"

"I just run into him yesterday."

"No shit. Any good-looking?"

"Said pretty good-looking. For a poor ol' Mexican girl."

"Nice titties?"

Carl shrugs. "He said they were pretty good."

"Damn. Where'd he find her?"

"That's the thing. She's some daughter of one of the guys working for Olive."

"Out there? A migrant? Sheeet. That must be a pretty good deal. Thought he could keep that secret over in Acton. Well, that ain't gonna keep too long, is it?"

"I don't know what the deal is. The Olives seem to know about it already. She's been over to the house, I heard."

"The Mexican girl?"

"Yeah," Carl says. He sucks on his Bud too hard and sends the beer foaming over the top of the bottle and over his hand, but he doesn't seem to notice. "The full deal. Can you believe that shit? Mike gets hooked up with some poor Mexican. Off at Duke, with everything to choose. You imagine they get married? Give that land over some little brown kids, little brown Olives. On your daddy's land, Harvey, can you imagine?"

"It ain't my daddy's land."

"My daddy says, when they were living out there, old man Worten—"

"Blue don't know what he's talking about. It ain't Dickerson land. You believe everything you hear, Carl, your head's gonna just blow someday like a piece of popcorn."

"Well it ain't their land either. Rightly. And now you imagine they get married, all those Mexicans—"

"You probably would marry the first piece of ass that came your way. Out of plain gratitude. You don't know what you're talking about."

"Maybe he knocked her up."

"You just think of that? Right now?"

"No. What I heard. My brother thinks so too."

"I thought we finally shipped him off to Uncle Sam."

"Come on, Harvey. He still in Florida, but I called him up. He said exact same thing when I told him. We gonna have a bunch of Mexican Olives here before you know it. Mike's been planning it right from the start."

"Mike has." Carl nods. "Carl, that's got to be the stupidest thing I've ever heard. No contest."

"Why you think he's been poking around all these migrants? He's gonna stir something up, find something illegal—"

"What do you mean, illegal?"

"Some old law on some old book or something, he's gonna get us one way or another, and then, bam, the land, the Mexicans. He likes those Mexicans. He wants them in."

"Beer me."

"Mike puts us down, gets the Mexicans in here, hands everything over to them, and then just goes. He don't care about out here. All this used to be Mexico, he says, he wants to turn it back."

"You heard him say that?"

"My brother did. Something like that, he said, when he was back in May. Said he heard Olive talking all kinds of shit."

"No offense, Carl, but your brother's a dumbass, all right? A badass but a dumbass."

"He said he'd take Olive out if he was here."

"I don't doubt it. But I don't think the army's gonna give him leave for that."

"He's that close to going AWOL just to punch Mike out."

"I'll punch Mike out," says Ox.

"Shut up, both of you. Y'all go punch each other out. Am I living with the stupidest people in the world? Carl, you're dumb as a hubcap you believe your own logic or your brother. Make me ashamed to be a Dickerson sometimes. All of you sound like my drunken dad." He slurs in imitation. "Frucking Olives running the wurld." He spits.

"But what about Mike's—"

"Mike Olive is a pain in the ass. He'd like to think he's more than that, but he ain't, he's a little goldfish in a toilet bowl. You the one want to make him more."

Harvey sits down heavily on the hood of the Pinto, glares at his friends. They don't say anything. They're done with this for a little while. But Harvey can't help it; he's thinking about his dad, who will believe this shit, believe it all the way just as he believes that land is his by some shameful bastard right. A myth to explain why the Olives got rich while his daddy got nothing except mad as a half-smacked wasp. But fuck it. What he needs to think about is himself, and the truck driving Cynthia, and that deal with Mike and the Mexican girl. Why didn't he ever think of finding something like that?

9 TH

MIKE FEELS HIS throat tightening as they pass the house in one great Doppler rush. He barely dares to look at the modest blue-and-white building. It's a mean house, Blue's house, and Mike's never been in it. No reason to. No love, not ever, between Mike and Blue and Carl or the older brother, gone now, but in his day meaner and more muscular than the rest. Mike knows that the men are in the fields, even knows which fields (north plot, early August, bad drainage, fair soil), but he feels the house watching him as he drives by. Mrs. Dickerson must be inside somewhere, listening to the difference between the cars that crescendo, pass, and fade, and this car that doesn't drop off the map. She is listening and cataloging, putting mem-

ory knots in her knitting, checking the clock on the stovetop
and the position of the sun.

They slow and turn off onto the dirt road a half mile past the
house, and Mike is very aware of the engine of the car as it
posts notices in every direction. The sound carries east over the
fields. To the trees, to the house. It travels ahead of them into
the still-obscured migrant camp, where heads must be turning,
lifting, peeking from doorways.

"Every time I'm on this road, it feels like the wrong one,"
Raúl says. "There's something about it which makes it impossible to remember." They're closer to the camp, and a few people
have focused into view against the tree-green and concrete-gray
backdrop behind them.

"These old roads and fields all look alike." Mike squints and
tries to count the figures from a distance. He doesn't pay attention to what he's saying, and doesn't care that it isn't true.

They step out of the car onto the dry, cracked ground, hooking the stethoscopes loosely around their necks, carrying the
white medical kits with the red cross facing out. A woman
stands in the doorway of the nearest concrete barrack, watching them. She is round, but not fat. Her face is smooth and
wide, and from the car she looks like she's smiling. Everyone
else has disapeared. She leans against the doorway and
watches. She waits. She is not smiling.

"*Buenas,*" Raúl says. He asks her something and she shrugs,
shakes her head, steps back into the shadows. They hear children's voices, laughing or crying, and then a hushing whisper.
She does not appear again.

"Her husband has a fucked-up arm," Raúl says. "He was
supposed to come to the clinic today." He shakes his head.
"No show."

"He's at work."

Raúl nods.

"Can't afford it or won't let him?"

"Same thing." Raúl starts heading for the other barracks. He looks over at the crewleader's trailer, the generator off, closed up tight. "This guy's a real live son of a bitch."

The walls of the next barrack are crumbling around the door, as if a low-slung animal has been gnawing on it, every night. The concrete seems permanently stained or waterlogged. Beside the barracks there is, inexplicably, a sagging and rotted volleyball net, and beyond the net, starting at the server's spot, a huge pile of trash slopes to a triple peak. Clouds of flies orbit one another in exhausting ellipses. At the doorway of the barrack Raúl knocks, lightly, his fist making no sound as he taps it against the concrete. He clicks a hollow sound with his tongue. "Señora Antuñes?" He sticks his head inside, then quickly withdraws it, steps back. A small woman emerges from the damp darkness of the barrack. She is short and pregnant. Her skin is dark brown, deeply toasted. She looks nervously at Mike, who smiles his best stranger's smile.

"*Tu hijo?*" Raúl says. "*Está mejor?*"

As if on cue, a little boy, about four or five, appears at her side, holds his mother by the leg. The middles of his eyes seem enormous, full-grown, as he looks up at the two students, his mouth dangling open. There is a black fault line of dirt running across his lip.

"*Sí,*" she says. "*Un poco.*"

"What was wrong with him?" Mike asks Raúl.

"He was throwing up for two days."

"Food poisoning?"

"Something poisoning. Hard to be sure. This guy, Ruiz, won't let them go to the clinic."

"That's the crewleader?"

Raúl nods. "Dr. Waxman was going to come out, but it looks like he's better. *Bastante mejor, no?*" Raúl says.

"What do you think?" Mike asks.

"Oh, it could be anything." Raúl gestures towards a pool of water not far from the camp. The water is thickened by algae and scum. Foamy browns and foreign greens. "I don't even know where their water is coming from."

"I'm sure the south fields leach down to that pond," Mike says. "Fertilizers, pesticides, who knows."

"And you know the kids play in it."

Mike kneels down and looks at the boy, says hello, holds out his hand. The boy shrinks away from him, stays anchored to his mother's leg. "Hello," Mike says again. *"Cuantos años tienes?"* The boy presses his face hard against the leg, as if looking for a way in.

"We shouldn't stay too long," Raúl says. *"Señora, dígale lo que me dijo."*

"Sí? Ahora?" she says. Her eyes are too wide in the afternoon light, and they move too much, governed by a small internal earthquake. "But when can you help us," she asks, her Spanish slow but monotone, without the high rise and fall Mike is used to hearing.

"Soon, very soon," Raúl says. "Tell him how it started."

She shakes her head, and when she speaks, finally, her eyes are down and her lips barely move. "My husband said that Señor Ruiz was not paying us what he promised."

Mike listens for the whir of the tape recorder. He cannot hear it but he knows it's there.

"And what happened?" Raúl says.

"He hit my husband with a stick for tomatoes."

"A tomato stake?" Mike asks Raúl, who nods.

"He hit him," she says. "Then my husband said we were leaving. He asked Señor Ruiz to take us to the nearest town but Ruiz said no. So we asked another man who has a car." She points at a brown sedan parked under a tree and shakes her head. "They stopped us."

"Who?"

"Señor Ruiz. And other men."

"What kind of men?" Raúl says, looking at her hard. She's silent. "What kind?" he says again softly.

"White," she says.

"Was it the farmer?

"I don't know."

"Were they young, old?"

"One was older. Two were young, a big one and a small one." She looks at Raúl now, meeting his eyes, talking faster. "They wouldn't let us leave. I don't know where we would go, but . . . " She stops, and Mike can hear her breathing through her nose.

"How did they stop you?" Raúl asks.

"They had a truck," she says. "Orange. With white on the top. They put the truck in front of us. We had to go back. They told us not to leave again." She looks over Mike's shoulder again, but he keeps his eyes on her. "They had guns," she says. "They said they would shoot us if we tried to leave again."

"Who said that?" Mike says.

She shrugs. "Señor Ruiz said they would shoot us," she says.

They are quiet, looking at the brown sedan under the tree.

"They took something out of the car," she says. "It doesn't go."

"Señor Ruiz told you you owed him money," Raúl says, prompting her. "Right?"

"Eight hundred dollars," she says. "But he never pays us. He says there's four hundred dollars for bringing us from Mexico. One hundred for gas. One hundred fifty every week for food and our house." She waves her hand at the room behind her. "We work and we only owe him more and more money."

There is the sound of another engine and the two students stiffen, step instinctively away from the door of the barrack. They stare at the dirt road approach to the camp.

"It's a car passing on the big road," she says.

185 E R I C   M A R T I N

"She's right," Mike says, in English. They stand there, quiet, listening to the sound move away. "But we should go. Tell her," Mike says, trying to think what you could tell someone, what you could say, "tell her we're going to help her." Raúl tells her and she looks at Mike expectantly.

"When?" she asks. "You come here," she says, turning to Raúl, "you come and I tell you but nothing happens yet."

"I want to clear out the whole camp," Mike says to Raúl. "I want to be ready for that, I don't want to take just one family and leave the rest to suffer the consequences, you know?" He turns to the señora. "We have a place for you to stay." Mike finds each Spanish word with effort. "It is ready soon."

She looks at Raúl. "We do not have papers," she says.

"In this papers do not matter. The laws protect you. They punish people like Señor Ruiz and protect you, do you understand?"

"Is there someone else we can talk to?" Mike says. He watches the camp while Raúl asks the woman the question. Mike has been here once before and there is something different about the place this time. The signs of people have diminished. The color too. As if the place has been drained of blood.

"Another family tried to leave again yesterday," the woman is saying.

"In the car?"

"No. In the woods. They brought them back." They all look towards the woods together, into the dark tunnels beneath the trees. "They had dogs," she says.

"Jesus," Mike says.

"What's the other family's name?" Raúl asks.

She hesitates. "Orozco." She turns sideways, ready to disappear inside. "When are you coming?"

"Monday. Monday or Tuesday, we will take you then."

"Next week?" she says. Raúl nods and she says, "*Sí,*" like a long slow sigh. "*Sí,*" she says again, and disappears into the room behind her with her child.

"You got most of that?" Raúl asks.

"Yeah. Most."

"Should we go?"

"We're here," Mike says. "Let's see who else we can find." He heads for the third barrack.

"Do you know who it was?" Raúl says. He's following close behind.

"Sounds like Blue Dickerson's truck. I'd say Blue, Carl, maybe the older brother, but he's in Florida, last I heard. Ox, maybe, he'd be around. You'd think Harvey, but who knows." He's talking to himself.

There is a young woman in the next barrack, but she is not Señora Orozco.

"Remember us?" Raúl says. "We're from the health clinic?"

She steps towards his voice and squints. "Ah," she says. "Yes. From the clinic."

"Do you know where we can find Señora Orozco?"

The woman shakes her head, squints, leans in. "Are you doctors?"

"Yes, well, we're students. We need to talk to her."

"I have problems with my eye," the woman says. She peels back the lid and the students can clearly see a milky cloud over the pupil and iris.

"You need to come to the clinic," Mike says.

"I can't see anything with my eye."

"We can take you now."

"Mike," Raúl says.

"Fuck it," Mike says. "Fuck all this. We're taking her."

The woman backs away. "No, no, I can't go anywhere now."

"Tell her it's fine, we'll take care of it."

"No, no," she says. "Maybe next week. Yes," she says, "thank you."

"Is everything all right for you here, besides your eye?"

"Ah sí, todo bién," she says, and waves them away.

"No hay otras problemas?"

"No." She looks at them warily.

They circle around the camp once more, but they don't see anyone else, or hear anything either, as if everyone has gone below the ground or melted into the spaces between the walls and trees.

"Okay," Mike says. Raúl is already halfway to the car.

They drive slowly back to the paved road. As they drive past the Dickersons' farmhouse, Mike points his finger like a pistol and squeezes his thumb down like an imaginary hammer. His lips move but he makes no sound.

11TH

SHE IS LYING on her back, her arms outstretched in a cross. Her head rests on his lap, her eyes fixed on the ceiling as he runs his hands through her thick hair, working his way through the curls, the occasional snarls. Sometimes, as he follows a tangled line, he loses the path in the thickened intersections, and she moves his hand away before he can begin to work on the knot. She pulls the offending piece of hair in front of her face and separates each filament carefully, like charged wires. She smoothes them straight and then replaces his hand on her head so that he will continue to pet her.

"Were you sad?"

"When? I haven't been very happy last few days."

"But when I was walking away from you."

"I was happy when you finally came out of that damn trailer, that's for sure."

"I was only tired. Nothing to think about. But were you sad?"

"Yes, of course. Yes I was."

She has been avoiding him since their dinner, staying away from the clinic, refusing to emerge from the trailer when he's come to take her to work. He even sent Raúl, yesterday, to try to lure her out, but she just sat in bed and listened to him talk at her through the window the way you might listen to Hungarian or Chinese. Distant sounds, the strangeness, the rise and fall. Sick, she said, I'm sick. She didn't know if it was true but it did seem like her metabolism was falling, sharply, into a kind of summer hibernation, as if she'd stored enough life to withdraw until they were back in Mexico. Her heart beat slowly, she was sure of that. Sometimes she didn't feel it beating at all.

"Yes, sick, Señor Michael," her father said to him this morning outside the trailer, as she lay in the hot bunk inside, poaching in her sheets. She smelled like sickness now. Stagnant. "But she is very strong, yes, she will be well soon, she's going to laugh with us very soon, return to the clinic."

"They'll give her the time for sickness at the clinic. I am going to tell them to pay."

"Thank you, you are very kind, thank you."

"Tell her we miss her a lot." His Spanish has gotten better, Hermelinda thought. "We need her to come back. I miss her a lot too."

"Yes, I'll tell her." She could hear her father smiling.

Monday he'd left her two books, paperbacks, slick and brightly colored. Tuesday, yellow flowers. This morning a tiny radio that played music she didn't like.

"I don't want to work at the clinic anymore, Papá," she told her father. "I'm just getting sick there, with all the sick people who come."

Her father examined her.

"Why don't you want to work?"

"I'm afraid of getting more sick, that's all."

"Is that why?"

"You don't know, Papá, there's so much sickness at the clinic. We're going back soon, no?" She tried to remember what all the houses of their street in Laredo looked like, but she could barely remember theirs.

"You'll be fine, *mi'jita*. Everything is okay."

She looks up at Mike now. He is looking at the wall and she sees his chin and the bulge of his full lips and the tip of his nose. She sees the lightness of his hair, hanging down toward his eyes, his long lashes. She thinks about the nights she has been lying on the other side of the thin trailer wall while he waited outside for her to come out. Why did it take her so long to come out? She doesn't know. Time, she thinks. It seems like I spend all my time wasting time.

"You were sad, and I was sad. Well, that's good, at least," she says.

"I thought maybe you weren't going to see me again."

"I thought maybe too. But I changed my mind." She extends her arms above her head, hooking them loosely behind him. She says his name.

"Yes?"

"I think you are a nicer person upside down. Maybe next time we go to dinner with your parents it can be upside down."

He looks down at her and laughs but it doesn't sound like a laugh to her.

"I want to go for a drive," she says. "A very long, long drive."

"I can't tonight. I have to go back to Durham."

"I'll come with you."

"Okay."

"I will tell my parents that now I have to meet your grandparents."

"Ah yes, my grandparents."

"They believe that I had a nice dinner at your house, I'm sure they'll believe that. Why not?"

"Did you really tell them that?"

"Oh, yes, I talked about the ham and the furniture for a long time. Papá is very interested in these things."

"I'm sorry, Hermelinda," he says. "I'm really sorry."

"Me too. You didn't do a good job."

"I know it." He leans down and kisses her on the forehead.

"What are we going to do in Durham? Is there dancing?"

"Well. I don't know. There's one dance place I know of. But I have to meet with my professors early tomorrow morning, and a guy from the law school in the afternoon. Tomorrow's a full day."

"Is the lawyer coming tomorrow?"

"No, no, not the one you're thinking of."

"The one you talk and talk about."

"Not him. He'll be here on Monday. I'm getting ready for him."

"Will you bring him out to examine us? If you do I will complain to him about how you treat me. About bad dinners."

Beside them, the light has moved to the edge of the floor and is beginning to climb the walls. Dusty plankton drift through the bright corridors of sunlight as the sun stoops towards the western tops of trees.

"What kind of dancing?" she says.

He has to think for a moment. "Modern stuff, you know. I've only been there once."

"What do you do all the nights in Durham?"

"Drink beer, go to parties. Have dinner with friends, things like that. And study."

"No dancing."

"Not really."

"I don't know these kind of parties with no dancing. It's stupid."

He laughs. "I guess it is."

"I think I'm ready to go to university. Don't you think?"

"Yes. We'll pack you up in my bags and bring you back to school."

The mention of school and the insinuation of the month to come stops them both for a moment, and they try to veer around that black hole again, avoiding what is coming at them, day by day. Their eyes slide into one another and they know they are going to fail.

"You would like to do that, no?"

"Yes, I would."

"Well, maybe the university is not for me. I imagine you do not have so many poor Mexican girls there."

"No," Mike says.

"To clean the bathroom, maybe."

"You could go, Hermelinda. You're smart enough. If," Mike says, and knocks his knuckles against his upper lip several times.

"It doesn't matter."

"Texas has a good university."

"It doesn't matter."

"Don't say that."

"It doesn't." She twists and moves away from him, to get into the sun. "Tell me about the lawyer. Is he who you want to be?"

"I don't know him yet. Maybe he's a jerk."

"You talked to him."

"Yes."

"You think he is a jerk?"

"I guess it doesn't matter if he is or not if he can help us get this crewleader," Mike says.

"What is his name?"

"Juan Carlos Ruiz." He seems surprised by the question.

"Tell me," she says. She leans back against the wall, her face framed by a rising patch of light.

"He's got eleven men working for him, and twenty-four people altogether in the camp. He has a bad reputation. The farmer he's working for is a bad man. It's just all bad, the whole situation."

"Where are the people from?"

"Mexico."

"Where?"

"Veracruz, I think."

"And what do they say?"

"They say he doesn't pay them. He cheats them. He locks them up at night. He hits them."

"You know this?"

"They told us. We even put it on tape, recorded it."

"The crewleader knows?"

Mike shakes his head. "We've been going from the clinic, you know, during the day, when he's gone."

"He knows. He knows what's going on."

"Well." Mike is thinking. "I don't know. Maybe not."

"So you are going to change him."

"I can't change him. I can get his ass thrown in jail. Maybe the farmer." He shuts his eyes. "I don't know."

"The lawyer," she says. He nods. "It's bad?"

"It's all bad. That's not true," he scolds himself. "Some places, I mean, it's okay, but others I don't even know where to start."

"You think he goes to jail it makes things better?"

"Don't you think?"

"There will be someone else."

"I know it. That's why," he says, "that's why we have to put someone's head on a stake."

She doesn't understand him, but she doesn't like the sound of it either. She waits for him to explain, but he's on to something else.

"If you thought," he says, "that the only way to take care of your family and yourself was to harm other people, would you do it?"

"I don't know."

"But you would think about it. And if you decided you had to do it, it would be a difficult decision, wouldn't it?"

"I don't know. I think so."

"What about people who don't find it difficult? Who commit acts of . . . " He's looking for the word, or hesitating, she doesn't know which. "Evil," he says finally. "People who do damage for their own reasons, for their own good, for money or power."

"It's a big question," she says.

"Yeah," he says. He looks at her and then looks away. "I don't understand it. I know that makes me naive, but deep down, I don't really get it."

"It's just true," she says. "It doesn't matter if you understand or not."

"It does matter. If you're going to do something about it, it matters."

"You can't do anything about it."

"I don't know about that."

"Mike," she says, "can I ask you a very important question?" She is making fun of him but he hasn't figured it out yet. He turns to her and she gets the full front of his clear blue eyes, looking at her and only her. "Mike," she says again. "How did you get to be so serious?"

He turns a little red, and then recovers, starts to speak, then stops, shrugs. "I honestly don't know, but it must be your fault," he says, joking now, playing the game. "I'm sure of it. Lovers always seem serious, don't they? I mean, the famous ones?"

"No. They're always smiling and laughing. And climbing on top of the other."

"I must be thinking of the doomed ones," he says. "Pyramus, Tristam, Leander . . . " He trails off.

"Who?"

"Stories."

"I like stories."

"Not these stories."

"Why not?"

"They're good stories. But they come to a bad end."

"Those can be good stories too. Sometimes the best. But tell me a story, anything, I want something for me to think about when I go to sleep tonight all alone in my hot trailer and you're away dancing in Durham. Take me somewhere," she says. "The beach." She closes her eyes and leans back against him. "Sand," she says.

Behind her, she can sense his eyes wrinkling up at the edges. His hands feel good and cool against her sides. He kisses her near the ear, and she twists around until she is sitting on his lap, her legs wrapped around his waist.

"Tell me."

"I don't want to go."

"Tell me, quickly."

"Okay. I love you." He pulls her against him, wrapping his arms around her so that they seem to encircle her again and again, like a long length of silk rope. "Once upon a time," he says, and she hears him in the air and in the vibrations of his chest.

14TH

BY FOUR IN the afternoon the thermometers are bickering over the heat: ninety-nine, one-oh-one, one-oh-four. In the Olive fields Hermelinda's father squats in the shade of Clayton Olive's big truck, drinking warm water slowly. Above him Clayton stands, legs spread wider than his shoulders, waiting for the next bucket. A young man hoists a full bucket into the air and lets go, so that it is suspended against gravity for just an instant and then Clayton catches it, cups the rim of the bucket with a united brace of thick, strong fingers, and lets the bucket tilt to the pile below him. The sweet potatoes roll and rumble to a settlement, shaking their dirt off like swimmers as they bounce and fall. With one hand Clayton swings the empty bucket down again. With the same hand, like a magician, he holds a sudden fairground ticket between his fingers. The ticket is yellow, with black all-cap lettering of the word OLIVE. There is no interruption in flow or momentum as the man accepts the empty bucket and ticket and turns smoothly back to the fields.

The pantomime is old and familiar from peppers, from cucumbers, from the year after year that Clayton has worked the fields with hundreds of other faces unlinked to names, but at the same time that everything is repetition and sameness Clayton feels a difference. It's the first year he's kept one group of workers around for the whole summer. Not so long ago, sweet potatoes meant black men working the fields. Year after year, no matter how many more Mexicans kept arriving, the sweet potato harvest was always the domain of the blacks and the time of year when Clayton felt that nothing had changed, that he was twenty years old again working the fields beside black men under an awful August sun. That was the Jackson County he knew, when he was poor and landless, when the language was the same and color was a clear silver line between white and black, when it seemed like everyone knew for better or worse where they stood with one another. He was never one to spend his energies on hatred, not for anyone, certainly not for the hardworking men on either side of him advancing down the long rows of another man's field, nor for the bossman in the truck above them, fatter and cooler with advantage. Black and white were different and they always would be but they also had time on their side, a history and a shared time of year after year for a hundred years and more, and in that much time no matter what you say about your fellowman you are going to come to some kind of understanding. Black and white had a past, but Mexicans?

Clayton checks the sun, wipes his drenched brow with one drenched sleeve, calculates the potatoes in the truck bed, and his face tightens slightly in displeasure. He spots Francisco Salmeron squatting in the shadows and nods at the field.

"Hey, come on," Clayton says. "Let's go, we're slow today, let's go." From the front of the truck, the crewleader Ignacio hears the farmer speak, and peeks his head around the corner and sees Francisco. *"Vámanos, Francisco,"* Ignacio says, *"Ya despiértate."* When Francisco stands and moves low and reptilian towards his fellow workers, Clayton sees his face for a brief upturned moment and recognizes him as the father of the girl, the one his son has taken on like any other of his pet projects, like the damaged birds and stranded deer dogs over the years. He has taken on this girl in pure opposition to his past, with the further incentive of beauty, of lust, of being young and full of stupid, unreasonable want. And with her his son considers that he has adopted this whole population of small brown men who speak a different language, and although Clayton cannot speak the language and his Michael can, Clayton knows he understands these men better than his son does. Clayton understands that some of them are fathers and husbands first and some of them are felons and rapists and some of them are lazy and some proud and some angry and some lucky to be alive, lucky to have work. He understands that some of them have made sacrifices for their too large families, that they carry the burden of that responsibility to the fields each day, the mouths to feed and bodies to clothe. Some of them have left their families behind and, lonely as that might be, are grateful to escape their cramped screaming homes for these three to four months of the year, to be away and out in the world of drinking and talking and men, simple work and sweat without having to worry about their children and wives. Others are missing those self-same girls and boys and women, and still others have brought their families with them out of love and some out of lack of trust—of their woman, of their fellowmen at home. Most of all, Clayton understands that the men are country men, that they have grown up on land as he's grown up on land, and he knows how hard they can work, how hard you have to work when you work in the earth and do not own it.

A division has occurred sometime in history, and in this life, in this now, Clayton is the bossman and they are the workers, just as in other lives there are Mexican bossmen and workers in their countries, far away, and since that is the way it has fallen out here they must work hard for him and he must pay. If he is to pay them as much as Mike says he must pay them, then they had better work steady and hard. Until now the year has been a good one, despite his son, despite the Mexican girl, despite the rumblings and displeasure of his neighbors, and he knows that soon his son will be gone again and everything will settle back to normal and his house will be a little lonely, as it has been since Mike left home. Dolores will cook too much and make meals that are not for him but for their missing son, and Clayton will feel something for his wife and for his absent Mike but in all he looks forward to that quiet, to those dull evenings and afternoons. Even with the tumult that seems to follow Mike around like a strange and lingering scent, the year has been a good one—good crops, and this a good crew working for him until the sweet potatoes when suddenly all the pistons in the Mexicans' arms and legs have seemed to freeze and stop. Saturday, so they are tired, no doubt, he's tired too. He'd like to be on a cool porch, drinking sweet tea. They should be grateful for the work. More work, more money. But they need to work. Until now he has thought that all Mike's shifts and demands and shenanigans have moved things for the good on Olive land. The men know how he works and what he likes, and for his part, Clayton understands the ways in which to show them respect, and the ways that respect means as much to them as the pay handed over for each Olive ticket counted out. So when the men stop working hard and the human conveyor belt from dirt to truck bed seems to shudder to a halt, Clayton wonders what is wrong, what is brewing. It's only when he slips into the cab of the truck to switch shifts with the crewleader that he experiences a mild nausea and realizes the astonishing fact of the heat. Well, damn, it's August and it's hot and maybe that's it, maybe Mexicans can't take the thick wet Carolina heat like a Southern country boy, or like a black man. Or maybe they don't really have sweet potatoes in Mexico, don't know what they're doing. He takes a long slow draft of water from the thermos under the seat and smoothes his thinning hair back under his cap.

At the far edge of the field, Alejandro Salmeron ignores his elders, takes off his shirt, and slinks into the shade of the encroaching woods, where he sits in the shadows, brings his eyes down to slits, and rests. Today is his birthday. He is seventeen today, whatever that means. Back on the border he is pretty sure it would mean something, but here is only another stooped day with old men and white men and dirt and nothing like becoming seventeen where he is from. No clean white shirt belted under a stiff pair of jeans, his boots shined to respectability as evening sets in and he scrubs his mechanic's hands before walking slow and watchful down to the pool hall for a drink, a beer from Don Castillo's cold freezer, cold to shake your teeth and lengthen your face, brought out for this special occasion, for Alejandro! as bottles are raised to the dull yellow light and click against one another to punctuate the laughs and friendly jeers. With midnight, or far deeper into the night, the boys and men crowd around him, whisking him outside where a truck already rumbles deep and healthy, a truck he knows perhaps, has rebored the engine late last week and now it returns to take him out like an old grateful friend. He is loaded into the back by friendly arms and company, and they drive out towards the desert until that circle of lights appears, *ay, mira,* Boys' Town, the only English a Mexican man needs to know, this double helix of light, and there, lining every inch of the figure-eight ribbon, are girls, women, creatures extraordinary and fancy, blondes and gringas and dark Indians from the south, beauties from Guerrero, from *el D.F.,* from Michoacán, their hips thrust out, their hands reaching to tug at his shirt, as if testing the fabric, touching his face, rubbing his crotch, touching him. *Vamos, guapo. Ay, lo bueno que te voy a hacer.* While his friends laugh and hoot and council, no, not that one, wait, we will do better than that, we will find you something perfect, and they do just in time, rescuing him only barely from the wide jaw and thunderous thighs of a huge doorway matron pulling him in by the belt loop. The tornado of loose flesh scowls as he escapes her orbit. He is brought tip to tip with a young woman, a woman, yes, but young too. The other men stand apart and leave him with the woman discovered, paid for, offered up. He climbs narrow stairs to a narrow room and there she undresses, peeling off her one silky thin layer to reveal a body of curves, of full breasts and dark nipples, the flat stomach plain giving way to the trim triangle valley of her sex, shaved down and plucked, maintained like a championship soccer field, and she sits on the edge of the bed and spreads her legs wide to let him look while she rubs her coffee thighs in long strokes and slow circles and watches him watch her, and when she says *vente* he moves for her and when it is over and he is out on the streets again it is as if the whole street has been waiting for him and a cry goes up, an enormous sound, a laugh, *ya eres hombre!* and with the woman moving away, squeezing his arm one last time, smiling, kissing his cheek, he looks back at the world and thinks, *Sí, así soy.*

Seventeen.

Alejandro sees that the men are working their way to the next row and he knows his father is looking around for him, suspecting. He does not return. He stays low and moves back into the woods and walks in the cool corridors beneath the trees, pressing a straight line through the underbrush in his long dark pants which he occasionally reaches down to adjust or crimp or move his stiffness to one side or the other. Fronds brush against his bare chest like feather dusters and he keeps on, wanting to escape the light, the hum of the truck, the voices of the men behind him, looking for a place where he can close his eyes and touch himself and return to his Boys' Town girl.

Just when he thinks he has arrived, when he has already started to lower his pants and lean his head against a tree, at that guilty moment he hears voices. A man and a woman. At first he thinks it is his fantasy until the woman speaks again and he recognizes the lilt even if he cannot understand the words, because his English has never been good apart from the basics—carburetor, alternator, piston, one two three four—and never as good as hers, this sister whom he hears speaking to him from the jungle somewhere in front of him.

He eases his pants up, zips, crouches, and steps forward delicately over the twigs and roots, not knowing what to expect but listening. She speaks again and it is as if her voice behaves like a beam of light cast into the shadows because suddenly where there were only trees before he sees a shed and a truck parked in a narrow track beside it. The shed tilts wildly, like a man punched one too many times, leaning into and against the woods around it for support. Vines and branches brush against its sides, cover its roof, holding the place together. The plants and trees are so dense around it that only when Alejandro approaches very near does he realize that the building is not completely buried in the woods but actually stands at the edge of the trees; the far side of the shed faces more fields, more rows, more crops, more open land owned by the red-faced man always waiting for them at the truck, always waiting. Although he has never seen this building before in his life, Alejandro cannot know for sure if he has worked the adjacent fields and merely missed this concealed structure, nestled in on three sides into the camouflage of the pines.

His sister's voice is inside. He moves up to the hut, squatting under one vine-wrapped dust-filmed window. When she speaks again he rises slightly and peers within.

The two of them are leaning back against one wall with a small space between them. He's wearing a pale blue shirt unbuttoned almost to the waist. He looks like an American movie star; something about his posture, his messy blond hair, the blue eyes matching the blue shirt, the hairless chest carefully displayed. He sits still, his hand rocking back and forth, slowly, wrist propped against his knee. Beside him, Hermelinda sits with the straps of her dress sliding down her arms, exposing her neck, her collarbone, the foothills of her breasts. They have stopped speaking. Alejandro's eyes pan across the small room, and he sees the blanket spread carefully out on the floor near the other side of the room. And he knows. He knows but he does not know what to do. He crouches down beneath the window and looks down at his feet, as if expecting to find an answer: a stick, a gun, a length of pipe.

His sister speaks. He looks up over the ledge and sees her standing. They are leaving. She reaches down and pulls the farmer's son to his feet, and he stands up, lazily, and Alejandro wants to hit the lazy bastard as hard as he can, in the face. Get up you stupid piece of shit. He does not know why, but he begins to move around the shed, towards the doors, where they are walking too, where they will swing out into the sunlight, and he moves quickly, to meet them there. He listens. As he passes another window, he glances inside and they are gone. He freezes. He cannot hear them anymore. Have they managed to slip by him somehow? What will they do with him, what will the farmer's son do with all of them now that he knows?

Alejandro is near the doors now. Still closed. He doesn't know what to think but when he looks inside again, he sees them. They kneel on the blanket, facing each other, and the son is moving his hands up her back and stroking her hair. Her hands are in his shirt somewhere. They are drifting down, now, until they are lying on the blanket, and Hermelinda is working her way out of the dress. Alejandro speaks, hisses to himself, utters a word he would never tolerate in anyone else about his sister. Inside, the two bodies yawn and stretch and crash together. They touch sadly, sweetly, and move against each other while at the window Alejandro's dark unblinking eyes watch and watch.

15TH

SHE WAKES UP early, when the rest of the camp is still sleeping. She gets out of the room as best she can, climbing in measured shifts and holds from the top bunk, avoiding the limbs of her sleeping sisters below. She toes her way through the main room of the trailer, siding past her working brothers, who do not move. They will sleep as far as they can into their only day of rest.

Outside it is wet and cool, almost misty. She pulls on a jacket from Laredo, given her by a Laredo boy. Laredo. She struggles to remember his name. It has been only three months since she was there. She sits on the stairs, wraps the jacket tight around her, pulls up her legs. Clint. She thinks.

By the time the others wake up, she is washing clothes in the metal basin, scrubbing the stained pants of her brothers, her father's mangled shirts. The pathetic remains of socks have to soak gently, so that they do not disintegrate completely. She washes the work clothes first, and hangs them up just as the sun is working its way over the trees around the camp.

They're eating in the trailer: beans and tortillas. A little piece of meat from the day before. Hermelinda shakes her head at the plate her father waves her way. "I ate already," she lies. She does not know what to do. She has been spoiled by the mornings of fresh fruit at the clinic, the melons, peaches, oranges, the bananas that appear on her desk. Maybe she will go back this week. Mike wants her to. She wants to, right now, not for the money or for Mike but for the simple fact of fresh fruit.

"Come back," he said to her in the shed.

"I don't want to work anymore. Because it's going to end and that's what I think about, so make it just end now."

"No," Mike said.

"What do you mean?"

"You're still here."

"No," she said, but he didn't seem to hear her.

"I'm sure Waxman will write you a recommendation, maybe we can get you a . . . " He got lost in his own unsuccessful thoughts. "There must be a way."

"For what? What do you think there is a way for?"

"What if there was a job at the clinic, or up in D.C. with the migrant East Coast—"

"Mike, be quiet. I am not going to leave my family. I'm not what you think. There are so many differences, you have to think. Think all the differences and then you'll know what can happen and what can't happen."

"I don't want to think about that."

"You don't have a choice."

"We could—"

She put her hand on his mouth, shushed him. She could not listen to it, whatever it might be.

That is not what she wants to remember. What he might have said. Instead she remembers the kiss, the blanket, the afternoon. She breathes in once, and holds it, and then lets it out slowly.

She takes the dishes outside with Camilla and they wash them, quickly, shaking the drops off like sparks, laying the plates and pans out to dry. The center of the camp is full of children now, older and younger, kicked out into the day, washing and cleaning. The adults are inside. Sleeping. Not sleeping. Rebecca finishes the wash, and Hermelinda hangs the pieces up one by one. She has already washed her own clothes, her underwear. She doesn't let the others see her soiled clothes anymore. They are hers, they are private. She is sure that they would reveal secrets in their stains. The only things left are the sheets inside, but the trailer door is closed, and Hermelinda decides the sheets can wait.

Now there is nothing to do. Alejandro smokes. Pedro and a friend play underneath one of the trailers, until Hermelinda tells them to come out, brushing the cobwebs and dirt roughly from their hair. They sneak back under a little while later. She tries to read one of the books Mike has given her. There is a young girl and her brother with a broken arm and a small friend and a lawyer father and a ghost next door and words on every page she doesn't know. Reckon. Viscous. Taciturn. Auspicious. She tries to read it, though, she does not give up. Sometimes she looks up the words, and sometimes she lets them roll over her. The book girl is in trouble but you know she is going to grow up fine. Hermelinda feels that there are meanings in the book, not only in the words, but in the town and the history and the names, that she cannot understand, that no one could understand unless they lived in America their whole lives and absorbed it, day after day, through the ears and nose and skin.

"That book was so familiar to me, even the first time I read it," Mike told her. "Everything about the town, the people, I knew them all. And the father, I wished . . . Well, I'll let you read, maybe it will be something entirely different to you."

She reads slowly and with effort, although she knows the book cannot mean anything to her.

Sometimes she puts the book down, carefully, keeping the clean pages uncreased, and thinks about what it would be like to be an American girl. The pictures of Mike's university look like a castle in the forest, with high walls and huge stones. There are gardens and girls and boys like Mike in T-shirts and shorts. They look like children in the pictures, smooth-faced and inno-cent and pale. Can she imagine walking beside Michael to a class in one of these castles, among these children who smile and sit poised seriously with a pencil against their lips, their hair long and straight and shiny? Rich. What do they worry about? How many of these girls has Mike wrinkled up his eyes for? How many touched at the base of their backs? Why, then, Hermelinda?

Her father emerges from the trailer, blinking, and she puts down the book and goes to get the sheets. Her sisters bring the dishes back inside.

The day goes on, with reading and waiting and with work. Hermelinda travels the wide routes between the day and the past and her mind, watching herself from several feet above as she moves from task to task to inactivity. She thinks about Mike, she thinks about the absence of Mike. Sometimes she remembers Lupita, or Don Eduardo's store in Batopilas, or the old hacienda across the river. Sometimes she thinks about noth-ing. She allows herself only rarely to worry about when the blood will come again. Four days today but four is still only late. She cannot depend on anything, she thinks: not Mike, not her family, not even bad luck. Mike won't come tonight, but she wishes he would. She likes to listen to him, to watch him. He is in this book, she thinks, he said himself, and she reads, watching for him, forcing herself into the words that are not her words. She wishes, as she sits on the trailer stoop on Sunday, that she were, this moment, this instant, someone else.

16TH

Mr. Byron Coe arrives at 2:45 p.m. in a brand-new dark blue Volvo sedan. It looks like a tank as it rolls into the driveway of the Catholic Retreat Center and jolts to a stop next to the soft gray contours of Raúl's Accord. Mike is on the porch, waiting and sweating in the heat. The minute he sees the slowly moving Volvo on the road, he knows it's Coe, and something makes Mike stand and duck into the building quickly. He stands beside the doorway for a moment, listening to the car door shut and the footsteps on the gravel walk. He waits for the steps to grow closer and then swings easily through the screen door with a loose smile on his face, one hand in his pocket, one extended to the newcomer.

Byron Coe is short, about forty. He has enormous bushy eyebrows, almost extraterrestrial in volume, which flare off over his eyes like dragonflies. His complexion is ruddy, his eyes small and pitch-black. He walks with quick, purposeful steps; there is no mistaking him for anything but a man of the city. He wears a dark suit and carries an expensive-looking leather bag in his left hand. The other hand holds a mostly empty plastic bottle of spring water. There is no hand for Mike to shake.

"Michael?" the lawyer says, and Mike nods.

"Mr. Coe."

"Byron's fine," Coe says. "Can I get inside? I'm not very good with the heat." Mike sees it's true, spots the wet film that has already formed on the older man's brow and just above his thin upper lip.

"Been pretty hot in D.C., too, I guess," Mike says, stepping to one side. The lawyer grunts. "Please, come in."

They walk through the Retreat Center, and although Coe barely seems to notice the space around him, Mike, for the first time in weeks, observes the familiar surroundings in minutiae. He smells summer camp and Sunday school, damp walls and stairways. Summer camp, that's what it is. Summer camp for playful little leftist girls and boys. He sees the dirty floorboards, the aging terra-cotta curtains bunched at the sides of windows, the not very white walls, the too big doorways. The two of them pass the rec room, where George and another student are playing Ping-Pong. At the moment they pass, George wins what must be a big point. He throws his paddle up in the air, pumps both fists twice, and hollers "Yes!" at the top of his lungs as the paddle clatters to the table. Mike winces and glances at Coe, but the older man's gaze does not seem to veer even a single degree off straight ahead. Coe says nothing until the door is closed behind them in the air-conditioned office, where Mike offers him a chair and turns the wall unit up to high.

"Ah," Coe says, barely audible over the roar of the air-conditioning. He takes off his suit coat and drapes it over the chair. "That's better."

Mike hovers near the desk for a moment, wondering where to sit, and while he wonders he simply stands, hands on his hips, watching Byron Coe out of the sides of his eyes and looking over his papers in the file room of his head. How does he feel? He feels fine. His mentors at Duke, the professor at the law school, they all think there's a good chance he'll be able to get what he wants. He wonders what to start with: the state health codes? federal labor code? the interviews? an overview? For two months he has been writing and rewriting summaries and reports with this moment in mind. He has done his home-work. He knows as much about migrants in North Carolina as anyone he's talked to. Read books and articles in the library at Duke, gathered statistical records from state and federal agen-cies. He has pleaded with farmers and neighbors in hopes that it would not come to this, all the while knowing that another part of him, a deeper, angrier part, was hoping for exactly this.

Coe coughs. The noise seems innocent enough, but it wipes every thought out of Mike's head, like the beginning of a spelling bee. He wants to say something. He leans on the corner of the desk, holds the edge of the desktop with both hands, smiles at Coe. "If you missed lunch we've got a pretty good barbecue place in town," he says.

The lawyer has zipped open his leather bag and removed a yellow legal pad covered with notes scribbled in blue hiero-glyphic cursive. He pulls a pair of reading glasses from his breast pocket, puts them on, and faces Mike.

"Excuse me?" Coe says. His voice is very Northern, very flat.

"Carolina barbecue," Mike says. Coe is just looking at him, his head tilted like a dog hearing a strange and mystifying sound. "Shredded or chopped," Mike explains. "East Carolina pork barbecue, best thing there is, little vinegar, a little heat, pepper and salt, you'll never look at a pig the same way again. It's just in town, and I'd be happy to drive us in for a bite. It's not the worst place to talk." The words come fast and choppy, the way they do when he gets nervous, making him sound like several people at once, but at least his mind has started again. Take his guest down to Eddie's, get him fed. Have him look around and get a sense of place, of who and what they're dealing with, here.

"Michael," Coe says, twisting a silver pen in his hands and clicking it ready, "I'd like to try to get back to Washington tonight if I can, so if we could, let's just start right in."

"Tonight?" The word is incomprehensible to Mike. "Oh, I . . ." He stares first at Coe and then at the careful pile of documents sitting next to him on the desk, as if he might find an answer to his disbelief there. He recovers quickly, though, and tells Coe, in an even voice, "I think you might have to stay through tomorrow at least, if we're going to get out to the camps."

Coe looks at him, glares might even be the word, and Mike feels the weight of the fact that they have not gotten off to a good start. He tries again. "Why don't I tell you what we've got."

"Fine," Coe says. He leans back in his chair.

Mike talks and watches Coe carefully. The camps. Health conditions. Pay. Drugs. Coe doesn't indicate a thing, and Mike can almost swear he doesn't move, doesn't blink. A wonder pigeons don't shit on the guy, he thinks. He moves now from the general to the specific, says the name Blue Dickerson. He slows down.

"We have a difficult and potentially dangerous situation in this camp. Between the farmer and the crewleader, I'm afraid for the people." Coe is listening, he can feel it, he can see it in the lawyer's small eyes, which move from his eyes to his mouth to the pad on the lawyer's knee and then back again. Only the eyes. The head still hasn't moved.

"I think that's the place," Mike says. "I think you, we, would have a very good case there. There's lots of documentation here, we have some interviews, tapes. We'll probably need depositions, I don't know. I'm curious to see what you think."

Mike finishes and then waits for a response, but Coe seems to be waiting for something else, so Mike picks up the folder nearest him, glances at its contents, and hands it to the lawyer. "We've compiled this survey on the health conditions in the camps, part our fieldwork and part Dr. Waxman's evaluations. Since we felt there was only so much that came across with statistics, we've included some of the testimony from migrant workers too." He stands at Coe's shoulder, watching him examine the documents, leaning over and looking at the too familiar pages, like a returned traveler showing prized vacation pictures to a stranger. Coe looks carefully at the first few pages, and then flips through the rest of the eighteen-page report as if it were an animated flip book.

"We have some tapes," Mike says. "We transcribed the most interesting ones—the pages are tucked in the back there. You kinda got to just skim, though, we haven't had time to edit."

"And those?" Coe points to the leaning tower of documents on the desk.

"It's sort of a, what, an evaluation of the educational experience of migrant children to help round out the picture of the population. That's more for us. There's some stuff in there on prenatal care for mothers, and a survey on STDs, that's probably more—"

"Do you mind if I just look at them?"

"No, I hope you will."

Coe takes the entire stack of papers in his lap and begins to read. Mike sits and watches for half an hour or so, but when he checks the clock only eleven minutes have passed. It is quiet except for the sound of the air conditioner bellowing away as it turns the back of Mike's neck cool and clammy in the continuous blast.

Mike stands up. "I'll let you look over everything on your own. We can talk after, I can answer your questions, whatever you want."

"Fine."

"I'll be in the kitchen if you get finished before I get back."

"Okay."

"It's downstairs."

"Uh-huh."

Mike shuts the door to the office and steps out into the humid hallway, which is open to the interior courtyard of the Retreat Center. Cynthia and one of the other students are sitting in the grass in the shade, sipping something with ice out of tall glasses and talking. Mike watches them for a minute, and can imagine that all of them are back on campus, carefree, sitting on the lawns, talking about a test or a party or a plan for spring break. He doesn't know whether to feel nostalgia or disgust. Both. He walks down to the kitchen, where he sits down at one of the tables to wait. When Sarah says his name he is elsewhere, not asleep but not quite awake either, and as soon as she breaks the spell he looks at his watch. Almost four. Coe has been in there for nearly an hour now. Mike doesn't know where he himself has been.

"Mike," Sarah says again. "He here?"

Mike nods, points upstairs.

"You get sent out to the hall for bad behavior?"

"Yeah, something like that."

"What's he like?"

"I'm not really sure. He hasn't said much yet. I gave him a quick overview and now he's just reading."

"You think we'll get him out to the camps today?"

"He says he's going back tonight."

"He's not going back tonight."

"No he's not, is he? I'll let you break the news to him." That reminds him. "We need to call over to Acton to get him a room. I don't think staying with my parents is going to work out."

"No?"

"No. Still no Camp David since I brought Hermelinda to the house." He seldom says her name around Sarah, and tries to gauge the level of disapproval in her response.

"I'm sorry."

"We'll get through it." The platitude sounds nice to him, he even believes it, and he leaves it at that.

"Well, I'll call over there right now. What's the place called?"

"King's Inn."

"Ah, yes. How could I forget that."

"I'll check on the good counselor."

From the end of the hallway, he can see that the door is cracked open, and as he approaches he hears talking inside. He starts to knock on the door, then opens it. Raúl is sitting across from Mr. Coe, gesticulating wildly and talking very fast. Mike is not very happy about that. Raúl is excitable, and from what he's seen of Coe, this is not a man made comfortable by multiple tellings of the same story. Lawyers, Sarah has told him, can be particularly sensitive to that sort of thing.

He interrupts Raúl immediately. "Did you have enough time to look at everything you wanted to look at?" he says, stepping almost in front of his classmate.

"I was explaining to Byron the urgency of the situation at the Dickerson camp. I think we should go after criminal charges there first, and then have the class-action—"

"Raúl," Mike says, trying to figure out something subtle to say to stop him, and deciding very quickly and simply. "Shut up."

Raúl looks at Mike with some murder in his eyes.

"That's why we've asked Mr. Coe to come down," Mike says, trying not to sound like a kindergarten teacher, "to tell us what *he* thinks is the best thing to do. He has been good enough to make this trip to share his expertise in these matters with us, and I think we can benefit most from that by listening, not proposing." Not yet, Mike thinks, as an addendum. He hopes this ridiculous speech has made Coe more comfortable, more inclined to give their ideas a chance. He hopes Raúl won't try to strangle him in his sleep tonight.

Coe clears his throat. "Where," he says, and then he stops, and for the first time Mike has seen, the lawyer smiles, looking past him to the doorway where Sarah is standing.

"I'm Sarah Levin," she says. "We're very glad you could make it down, Mr. Coe."

Coe smiles. "Byron," he says.

"Byron."

He stands and shakes her hand, looks at her and smiles

again. "I can see it," he says. "Your father," he says, "you look a lot like your father."

"You know my father?" Sarah says.

"Oh, no, only from TV, pictures, you know. What a great lawyer. Really amazing lawyer."

Sarah looks annoyed, but only for the briefest moment before a more politic look takes over her features again. "Don't I know it. You think I won any dinner-table arguments growing up?"

"Oh you probably won a few."

"A very few."

"Well, Sarah," he says, setting his sights on her as if she were the only other person in the room, "maybe you can boil this thing down for me. I'm looking at your documentation, and while some of it is quite good, there don't seem to be any specific cases that we could go after and stand a good chance on. See," he continues, rising from his chair and pacing the room professorially, "there are only a few cases we take on each year, because they involve so much time and personnel and we have little of either. When I spoke with your father, very briefly, I had the sense there was a particularly specific and severe case that we would be investigating. Perhaps I misunderstood him. When we spoke, Michael, I was also under the impression that the situation was worse than what I've seen so far. I didn't really expect . . . all this." He pats Mike's pile of papers with one hand.

"I can see how that might dilute things, but if you look at the camp I was talking about."

"Even that one."

"With all due respect, sir, we haven't taken you out there yet."

"Yes, well, maybe we should go, then, if you think it's worth our while." They all stare at him. "You've done some good work here, I'm not saying you haven't, but in terms of the kind of test case we look for . . . I'm afraid I have my doubts."

"The debt schemes?" Mike says. "It's not just the one, there are three or four camps we mention there that—"

"Almost impossible to go on the debt thing alone. Because so much of it is unofficial labor, there's very little documentation to go on. If there's the drug use you say, there's less chance of getting good testimony and witnesses that can stand up to discreditation."

"I think the sanitary conditions by themselves. I know those are usually only fines for the farmer but—"

"That's a state issue—"

"We know, but it could be made federal if the state is failing to enforce—"

"Well, that's like filing for an appeal before the case is tried. No, you'd have to go to a state inspector for the Bureau of Health for that, there's nothing legal that can be done before a formal complaint or a request for inspection, and even then." Coe places his legal pad down on the desk, puts his pen on top of it.

"But we know those health codes can be flexible to the extent than an inspector wants to interpret. It seems like the failure to inspect would allow us to—"

"The request has to have been made. And the records of same."

"Okay." Mike starts over. "Forget about all that. Then focus on the civil rights stuff, at the Dickerson camp. The one I was telling you about."

"It doesn't seem completely clear."

"What are you saying, then?" Raúl asks.

"He's saying there's nothing he can do for us," Sarah says. "That we have some interesting facts and figures that do not necessarily translate into the law."

Coe nods, looks at Sarah. "That is in fact a good part of what I am saying."

"That's typical. I guess I should have expected this."

Coe shrugs. "Your father, I think, would agree with me on this."

"Oh, I'm sure he would."

"I would go ahead on the state complaint, if I were you. See what happens. And at the very least, you have the kind of documentation to help you get more money to pressure them if they stall. Or to do more research. Or to apply pressure on the local level, keep plugging away, create a pattern of involvement. If you can find a sympathetic ear at the state level, that's going to be the best thing for you. Washington should only be after that. And that's probably a good way down the road."

"Local politics isn't going to change a thing," Raúl says. "Not here anyway."

"Mr. Coe," Mike says, calming himself, working up a slight but serious smile, "I wouldn't have dragged you down here if I thought there was another way. I understand that the legal route is not easy or pleasant. But as Raúl says, I think only an outside sword is going to make anything happen here."

"Well, I'm sorry to be the one to tell you this, but this kind of situation unfortunately does not give itself well . . . " He clears his throat, starts again. "These problems are not ones easily addressed by the law."

"I don't understand. What exactly do you people do then?"

Raúl's voice is a little wild now, but Coe doesn't flinch. "There are cases," he says, "we've brought four cases before the courts this year. This is an area, unfortunately, where you have to pick your battles."

"We've picked ours," Mike says.

They're all staring at Coe now. He nods and purses his lips briefly. "It's hard, without experience, to have an accurate idea how long these things take. I have to say one of my chief concerns here is time. We need cases that are sustainable. How long are you all going to be out here? A few more weeks? Tops?"

"I grew up here," Michael says. "This is my home."

"All right. But what about the rest of the team? What about

when school starts for you again? Not to mention the migrant workers, we're late in the season, I know that. It's such a fluid population—"

"That's why—"

"That's why you wanted to turn it over to us, I understand. And that's why I'm saying no. From what I've seen, no. Because our chances of coming in here cold and getting something after you all leave, and on the eve of the migrant workers' departure, with a Mexican population especially, the chance is not very good."

Mike doesn't know what he's about to say then, only it's not going to be calm or nice, when Raúl stands up and takes a step towards Coe.

"Okay," Raúl says, "this camp. People are getting beaten out there."

"That was not clear."

"Not clear."

"Listen, I'm not saying it sounds good out there. But the fact of someone getting poked with a stick is not going to be the thing to bring the house down."

"How about women? What has to happen to them?" Raúl hesitates and looks at Mike. "Maybe you all need to know what's really going on."

They're all watching him now.

"How about if they beat a woman badly? They beat her? Touched her? While the husband watched?"

"Raúl," Mike says.

"They threatened to kill her child, if she told anyone? Their little baby, for Christ's sake." The spit comes off Raúl's lip as he talks, his head juts forward at the three of them. The muscle of his jaw bulges out of his cheek, tight. "Punched her. Bent her arm back."

"Raúl," Mike says again. "What are you talking about?"

"Blue Dickerson."

"Raúl."

"It starts like that," Raúl says, pointing at the papers, leaning into his stare at Coe, "with no money being paid to workers, the kids kept from school, people prevented from getting medical care. Like a slave camp. You have your good slaves and your bad slaves. Your good ones behave themselves and there's no trouble. But your bad ones, they get into trouble. Then they get threatened. Try to leave. Get smacked around. Do we wait until someone gets killed?" Raúl looks at Mike.

"Raúl," Mike says, "it's not going to help to—" He doesn't know how to finish the sentence.

"You don't know. Something happened over the weekend."

"The crewleader?" Mike asks.

"Him. And three white men."

"Listen," Coe says, looking from Raúl to Mike and settling back to Raúl again. "I want to make something very clear. I want you to make sure you're not exaggerating. That's not going to help anyone at this point."

"I'm not exaggerating. I'm just forcing you and everyone else to deal with the reality of what's going on."

"Calm down for a minute. So we're talking about another incident? A man and woman assaulted in one of the migrant camps? Injured?"

"Yes."

"And this is at this camp of a man named Blue Dickerson, is that correct?"

"There. And probably other places too. But there that I know of. There that we have people ready to testify in a court of law."

Everyone examines Raúl for a long minute before Coe breaks the silence. "I'm listening," he says, and sits down, clicks his pen ready again, and balances the legal pad against his knees.

THEY CARAVAN TO the Dickerson camp, five of them in two cars. Coe insists on driving, as if he doesn't trust them, as if this might just be a trap. They watch him warily in their mirrors, half expecting him to fork away from them down another road, out of sight. Raúl is with Coe, as hostage, and they can see him sitting still in the passenger seat, although it's hard to tell whether he's talking or not. Sarah's car is silent except for a slight rattle from under the chassis—some part of the exhaust system shaken loose by bumpy roads and gravel. After a particularly loud rattle, Sarah looks at Mike and that is what he tells her.

"The exhaust. Not something to worry about. Easy fix." She nods.

Mike's mind is not on the road ahead of them. On their way out the door at the Catholic Retreat Center, he took Raúl by the elbow, pulled him lightly back into the doorway while the others went towards the cars.

"Is it true?" Mike said.

"What?"

"I'm asking."

"It's true. As true as anything else has been around here," Raúl said, his face hardening at the edges, the brow furrowed, the eyebrows tilting down like divining rods.

"Oh shit," Mike said.

"That's what happened. You'll see."

It took a moment for Mike to bury his panic, but then he was back. "Okay. What are we going to do? We've got to get them out of there. As soon as we can."

Raúl nods.

"How did you leave things with them?"

"I didn't know. I told them, I told him not to go to work tomorrow, and we'll get them then, after Ruiz has taken everyone else out to the fields. I didn't know if we wanted a direct, you know, confrontation."

Mike glances at his watch. "It's five-thirty. Was the husband home today?"

Raúl shakes his head slowly. "He went to work."

"I thought he was hurt."

"He went to work."

"Okay. This is it then. We'll go out there, and we'll check it out. If we can get them out tonight, then we will. If not we'll come back tomorrow morning, get them then. Will that work?"

"I told them tomorrow."

"Sooner the better."

They are close now, coming up to the slight rise before Blue Dickerson's house will swing into view, and Mike decides something.

"Slow down," he tells Sarah. "Turn here." They drive carefully down a dirt track through uncultivated fields, a grazing land between the Dickersons' and the Bowmans', until they hit a stand of trees where the cars won't be seen. Mike gets out. Raúl and Coe are already out of the car, too, standing and waiting.

"We'll walk in through here. It's about half a mile. We'll do it fast, and then if everything's clear, we'll come back and go get them together. I'll run over and check it out and come back."

"I'll come with you," Raúl says. "They know me better. Someone's got to talk to them."

"Okay."

The two of them run through the trees, Raúl following, and Mike has to slow down a little, can't let out his stride the way he'd like to with his classmate trailing behind. He hasn't run in the woods for a long time; it reminds him of the late nights in high school when he was somewhere he wasn't supposed to be, up to some kind of not-supposed-to-do. He focuses on the step in front of him, the trees whipping by, the branches reaching for his face. He runs.

"Jesus, wait up," Raúl is saying behind him, hissing, barely audible over the beat of Mike's blood, huffing, gasping for air. Mike lets him get close, and then keeps going.

They come up to the camp from the trash pile side, and slow down. Mike walks carefully now, for silence, avoiding branches, although there's music coming from the camp, and the sound of an engine running too. He moves around and squats beside a tree. From there he can see the clearing and the barracks pretty well without being seen himself. Raúl breathes heavily beside him.

Mike nudges him and shakes his head. "They're back," he mouths.

The men have come home. Two of them are sitting on the hood of the brown sedan, not too far from the students, drinking beer. Several others are sitting down against the wall of one of the barracks, their knees tucked up, their heads down. No women in sight. The crewleader, Ruiz, is in the center of the clearing talking to Blue Dickerson and his boy Carl, the farmer and son leaning against their orange truck, none of them looking happy. Beyond them are two vans, one white, the other a metallic red and silver, the windows tinted and bubbled, with some sort of fantasy horses and unicorn detail on the back. The white van is white only in theory; a film of red dust clings to the wheels and windows and sides and hood.

Raúl turns to go, but Mike grabs his arm, holds up a finger. Carl has left the conversation and moves to the driver's-side door of the truck. He gets in and turns off the engine. It's quieter now and Mike feels exposed, and now he nods and the two students move away from the camp. When they've got far enough away Mike begins to run again, faster than before, and he reaches the others before Raúl.

"We can't get in there now," Mike tells Coe and the others. "Dickerson and his kid are there. I think if we try now, I don't know. I don't think it's a good idea. I don't think a face-to-face out here, or now, is good for anyone."

"We'll wait," Sarah says.

"No," Mike says. "You can hear everything out here at night. That would be even worse, to have . . . anything happen at night." He can say the words but he doesn't even know what they mean. What do they mean? What would happen? But they don't know the woods and they don't know the fields and how anything seems possible at night. They don't know what history has done before, in places like Jackson County, at night, or if they know it is only with their heads and not with their whole selves. Mike can feel what has happened before in these fields.

Raúl has emerged from the trees now and stands with hands on his knees, trying for air.

"No, we'll have to wait until tomorrow." Mike glances at Coe, but the lawyer is nodding, maybe because he agrees, or maybe because he just wants to get the hell out of here, right now.

"All right," Coe says. He is deferring now, he is giving them the benefit of the doubt, and now, out in the middle of he knows not where, has come to realize that there seems to be danger in their situation. If he weren't scared himself, Mike would feel pleasure in keeping the lawyer out here for a little while, scared.

"How about the police?" Coe says.

"We could. But the sheriff will protect Blue, I think. Warn them and then no evidence. I guarantee it. We'll go tomorrow, early." The truck, he thinks, if they have to carry stuff. And maybe something for the brown car, get it going, maybe Raúl knows what it needs. They must have taken something simple. Distributor cap. What else? George had better come out here too. What else. A gun?

"Did you see that van, Mike?" Raúl says. "The one with the horses on it. Texas plates. I'd never seen it before."

"What do you think?"

"I don't know. Some more workers, maybe? Was that Blue Dickerson there at the camp?"

"It was."

"He looks like a mean motherfucker," Raúl says. "He actually looks like someone who could do it." Raúl almost sounds surprised.

"Yeah." Mike knows what he's talking about, but he's not so sure himself. Complicity, yes. But despite everything, he wonders, as they drive down the dirt track and back to the main road, what can the worst really and finally be?

17TH

THEY MEET IN the parking lot of the Catholic Retreat Center at five in the morning. Coe is there, drinking coffee out of a very large cup, and George, and Sarah and Raúl. They talk for a moment and decide on the cars: Mike's truck, Cynthia's truck, Sarah's car, Raúl's. Coe rides with Mike in the truck, George and Sarah and Raúl each alone.

They drive. Mike has spent the night at his parents' house, slipping in late after dark, padding up to his room knowing that his parents, sleeping or no, heard him come in, that they know he is there. He wanted them to know. That this was still his home, despite the cracks opening up in the county, in the house, in the dining-room table downstairs, in the front porch where fathers and sons sometimes sat and talked. He went to his parents' house to find a moment of calm, but there in his childhood room could find no more reason to sleep than anywhere else. The old trappings of his youth did not comfort him but instead reminded him of how much this new feeling of helplessness, this understanding that destiny was being calculated to a sum that existed entirely out of his control, reminded

him of being a child again. It was this child in him that took
him downstairs to the phone, to stare at it, wanting to dial the
numbers, to get Carl Dickerson on the other line, not a friend
but still Carl, still the boy who flipped him the ball to start a
double play, still someone he knew, has always known. Hey
Carl, he wanted to say, shit, I know it's late, but what's happening, I mean what's going on? This is crazy, Carl, it's crazy. And
Carl: Aw, Mike, that's not right, that's not true, it's a misunder-
standing, what it is. But that conversation could not exist.

He'd gone back to his room and stared out of his window
east towards the migrant camp on his father's land where
Hermelinda was sleeping, and for a long moment he found he
could not summon up her image, and wondered: Maybe she
can't exist either. He could not remember what she looked like,
or how her voice sounded; he could not remember the texture
of her skin. When he finally managed to conjure her up, he did
not know whether to believe himself, and did not know
whether he had ever spoken to her, let alone lain with her in the
machinery shed in his father's fields. It was as if he had
invented her. He had invented the entire world going on behind
the fields, just as he had invented his past. Now all those
worlds had been reinvented in a new brutal and doomed image
that seemed immediately permanent and irreversible.

He is still thinking about all of these inventions when Coe
speaks, bringing Mike back to the road and the dotted yellow
line being devoured by the hood of the truck.

"This is not what you expected," Coe says.

Mike glances at the lawyer, who, despite his initial claims
yesterday that he had no intention of spending the night, is
wearing a different suit. It's dark, wool, defies the climate and
the place. It's a good choice. He looks more like authority in
this one.

"No," Mike said, although it's not as simple as that.
Complicity, he thinks again. I'm not sure if I ever thought more.

If you'd told me that my neighbors were locking their workers up, chasing them down in the woods with dogs, firing guns outside the camp at night, striking them, slapping a woman to the ground in front of a husband, all to protect some sense of right, some sense of their own authority, I might have said: Hell, yeah, they might be mean enough, they might be capable of that. But I also would have told you to pull your prejudices in check. I would have told you that didn't happen. That they were selfish and narrow but they weren't bad people. Not incapable of compassion or change. Not evil.

"I don't want to waste any time," Coe says. "First thing is to verify the account, just be sure there isn't any confusion, that they want to go. Then we take everyone out, go back to the Center. I'll do interviews in the afternoon. After that, if we need to alert the authorities, we'll do it." The lawyer looks over at Mike, sees something in his face that softens his hard, even voice. "I know it's nerve-racking, but I don't anticipate a problem right now. There's usually no problem at this stage in the game. Later, perhaps. I'll do the hard talking if there's talking to be done. I'm the one no one will know what to make of. I'm the lawyer, and people, for better or worse, are scared of lawyers."

Ahead of them now, Mike can see Blue Dickerson's house sitting squat and watchful over the fields scrolled out south beneath it. He squints for a flash of color in front of the house, Blue's Bronco or Ox's Pinto or anything, but it's far, it's dark, and if he maybe sees orange and white he also sees every other known color too. Is Harvey over there? Will someone drive down to meet them? If they did, what really would they do? Mike's a Cottesville boy, and no matter what else happens that is going to have to count for something. He feels the thick weight of doubt in his chest, his stomach, his neck.

The truck's tires spit rocks into the fields to either side of the dirt track as they turn onto Blue Dickerson's land. Sarah is behind them, and behind her Raúl bullying along in the Honda, following close, like an impatient driver who would pass them all if he could. The Dickerson house finally jerks out of sight as they enter the trees and then, in another small moment, the dirt clearing of the camp.

Something has changed. Mike's first thought is that a kind of war has been waged there, a bloody and violent encounter leaving no survivors, no witnesses. He gets out of the truck.

For a moment he is standing alone in the clearing amid the barracks, with the red dust stirred up around him drizzling upwards through the static air before falling and drifting like a fine mist to ground. Mike squints through the screen of dust and looks deep into the woods beyond, where he sees Carl and Blue Dickerson and Ox and Harvey too, a couple other of the boys, their guns resting easily in their arms, grinning, and then they raise and fire together into the air a funereal salute, "Get back on in, we ain't done with you yet," and the crewleader Ruiz smiling gray and brown and gold teeth and yelling in his own language, *"Quédanse, me deben dinero, quédanse,"* and then Ox's dogs fly whining and gnashing into the thick where a Mexican couple stand hiding with their baby, and there's Mike's own father Clayton Olive with the heft of an ax coming down hard on the husband's head, dropping him while the mob nudges Ox towards the tiny woman, goading him on, get her, Ox, get her, Ox unfurling his enormous member and the men howling like it's a back-alley donkey show, and when the woman's face turns towards Mike he sees Hermelinda, her stomach swollen, her mouth moving for sounds of help, but unheard in the din, while Carl yells get Mike get him he's turned into a goddamn Mexican.

Mike shakes the vision away and looks back to Mr. Byron Coe, who is stepping out of the truck, coughing, straightening his tie, sweeping the barracks and the clearing with a percipient eye, and he hears Coe's voice from the night before, *If there's proof we will get involved and they are going to jail,* and Raúl,

It's true and they will. They will tell you how the men beat him, how they slapped her to the ground, how they took the child and tossed it through the air, and if he gave them any more trouble they'd get clumsy and drop the baby next time. And locked them in the barracks all weekend. Starved them, like dogs.

Well, that's a case, all right.

And Mike's own attendant thoughts: Is this what I want? Is this what I have always wanted?

Raúl walks ahead of them and the rest of them follow like ducklings until Coe puts up one hand and Mike and Sarah and George stop. "Wait here," he says, indicating a spot in the clearing as if he knows it well, and stepping after Raúl to the far barracks. It is very quiet. Mike has the feeling of walking into an ambush—the emptiness of the camp speaks to him of people elsewhere, waiting. They watch Coe and Raúl go.

"There's a crowbar in the truck," Mike says, and George looks at him unhappily. They check behind them. Only Sarah seems really calm. Maybe she's naive; maybe she knows something they don't. She walks over to the nearest barrack and looks inside. Her arms cross as she stands in the open doorway. "Shit," she says.

At the other barrack, Raúl and Coe are disappearing inside, and they emerge again after a few seconds. They look back at Mike and George and Sarah, and then turn and talk to each other. Raúl points at the crewleader's trailer. Coe heads for the trailer without hesitation, and Mike moves back to the truck. He picks up the crowbar and holds it there, concealed under the lip of the truck. He examines the tendons in his hand, in his wrist, bulging out when he holds it. When he lifts his head up, he notices. The brown car is gone. The red-and-silver van of the other day is gone. There are no cars in the camp, no clothes hanging on lines.

Coe peers into the trailer, shades the window with his hands, and then begins to walk slowly back towards the rest. As he returns, Mike realizes that he is not only disappointed but simultaneously relieved. He walks to the back of the truck, away from the others, hiding his face from them because he's afraid what they might see there. He feels something true and dark rising inside him, a terrible brew of anger or joy or shame. He puts one hand on the rail of the truck, the blood pounding in his neck.

"They're gone," Raúl says, because someone has to say it. Mike turns, and they all look around the camp at the stained concrete, the paths of cigarette butts, plastic wrappers, and aluminum cans, the crooked bunks leaning against the dirty walls in the shadows.

"That van, I knew it, that van," Raúl says. His face is red.

"All of them? Everyone?"

"Cleared out."

"Well," Coe says. He looks around the camp one more time, as if checking for something he might have missed. "I'm sorry." He takes a few steps towards the truck, glances back at the students. "Let's go. There's nothing here. There's nothing."

"But—"

"Listen," Coe says. He points at the barracks. "They left. I am sorry."

"Maybe we can find them."

"Maybe." Coe is coddling them now, sweeping them back to the cars with his voice, his eyes, his outstretched arms.

"We've got pictures," Raúl says. "We'll have license plate numbers in there."

"You want to call the police?"

"Hell, yes."

"And tell them what?"

"They've been kidnapped."

"Raúl, they haven't been kidnapped. They were here, and then they left. If you know more than that, it's your choice. You can call the police, and should, if you think it's necessary."

"You don't think it's necessary. You don't give a shit," Raúl says, sending the word at Coe like a knife tearing flesh.

"Look, I'm sorry," Coe says, his voice steady and flat. "I was willing, but, well, where are the locks, for one?" He points around at the barracks. "I looked at all these doors and there aren't any locks on them, no sign of them, either. And the conditions. That's an ugly pile of trash back there, but there's much worse. People should live better than this, but there's much worse. We went out to ones in South Carolina . . . you wouldn't believe it." He addresses Sarah now. "There was one where some old boy had four men locked in a bunker half the size of that one. They tried to escape, understandably, but they were in the middle of the swamp, there was no place to go. After that he chained them to iron rings on the wall at night. The floor was covered with their shit. He fed them once a day. He kept them chained together in the fields. Slavery?" He looks at Raúl, as if referring to a conversation the two of them have had. "That was slavery. They finally made it out. They ran through the swamp for two days before they found a road. The trucker who reported them in didn't stop, thought they were jailbirds on the run. When the cops found them they were starving, half eaten up by bugs. They still had red marks on their wrists and ankles." He's giving his closing argument now, leans back against the door of the truck. "We went into that trial with pictures, the testimony of all four workers, the cops, the trucker, a couple of utility workers who'd seen the farmer threatening his guys with a shotgun, and we still had trouble getting him. Although you'll be happy to know we got him, and we put him away." He takes off his jacket, folds it neatly, drapes it over one arm. "I'm telling you this to make you understand that when I say we've got nothing here, I unfortunately know what I'm talking about. There aren't physical, incontrovertible signs of that sort of thing. Maybe the families left in that van and the crewleader went the other way. Maybe the farmer was the one at fault and they all got away. I don't know what happened here." Coe pauses, giving them another chance to speak, but no one speaks. "You don't know what happened here," he says finally. He looks at Mike. "You grew up here. The best thing you can do is make sure that your own backyard is clean. You want to go and find the farmer and see what happened, that's what you should do. But if you want change, there are other ways. I'm a lawyer and I believe in the law, and I'm still one to say that there are many, many other ways. Sometimes, better ways. You negotiate. Provide services. You let time do some of the dirty work, make your case to friends, neighbors, enemies. Because the only lasting kind of change I've ever seen happens when a community is convinced, or becomes convinced, that it wants things to change."

"I want it. What do you think I've been doing this—"

"Yes, yes," Coe says. "I can see you have. But how long have you been trying? How long do you think these things take? Do you think you can tuck it into a summer term in the country?"

"I'm not running away from anything, Mr. Coe. But they won't listen to me," he says, "and they have to listen to the law."

"Maybe. But the law is complicated, and the law is demanding, and in this case, I'm afraid it doesn't help us. We've got nothing. You kids are smart, and you've got some considerable resources, but before you go cashing in your cards you have to know what the stakes are. They were here yesterday, and they're gone today. Maybe that's a coincidence, and maybe you did something out here to stir things up. I don't know if it had the effect you hoped for. I don't know what the result of it will be. I hope it's a good one. It can be. Means that for better or for worse, someone's paying attention to you. Listen," Coe says, although they are doing nothing if not listening, "it's encouraging to know that young people like you even give a damn, I'll say that much. You'll get there, I believe you will, if you keep it up."

Mike wanders away from them as Coe speaks and moves over to one of the bunkers. Inside he sees a few mattresses, a single sock, and pieces of plastic. The smell is dusty, but not human. He looks back at Coe. He is standing in front of the others, lined in a row. The lawyer looks like a troop leader addressing his young Scouts. He turns and gets in the passenger side of Mike's truck.

"Come on," George calls out to Mike. "Let's go."

They drive out of the camp in silence. At the road, the others turn left, heading back to the Center, and Mike keeps the truck idling but stopped, hesitating until they are out of sight. Coe taps his knee nervously.

"Don't give up," he says.

"Oh, I won't," Mike says.

"The documentation you have is good, and I know that we want to have a copy of everything when you're done. Anyone who has anything to do with migrants would want it. It's a damn good start, something you can really build on. You should put it together in one package, and when you do, remember: stick to facts. Stick to testimony. Transcripts are good. Don't feel, at least try not to feel anything until you are done. This is the tough moral of the lawyer, the investigator, the documentarian. Things are bad, and you know it, so don't try to make things worse than they are."

"It's hard to imagine." He puts the truck in gear and pulls out quickly, turning right and driving up the hill towards the Dickersons' house. "If you don't mind there's a quick errand I would like to run while we're out here."

Coe is about to say something, but he decides against it.

They crest the hill. Blue Dickerson's Bronco is in the drive-way, next to his wife's little Chevy. Mike parks the truck with a jerk and hops out.

"This will just take a minute," he says. He leaves the engine running.

It's four quick steps over to the doorway. They know he's there but he knocks anyway. The door opens and it's Blue. It's dark inside and Mike sees Blue through a gray haze. He smells the too intimate smell of Blue Dickerson's house, of the food they will eat, of the furniture they sit on, the beds they sleep in. Blue's thin Dickerson face sharpens. There is something metallic about him.

"Where'd they go?" Mike says.

"Get off my property," Blue says.

"Where'd they go, Mr. Dickerson?"

Blue looks past Mike at Coe in the car. "You tell me," he says. He shuts the door. Mike hears the catch.

He walks over to his truck and takes the crowbar out of the back and swings it once, hard, against the side of the Dickersons' Bronco. The side panel dents in, and Mike feels something like a shock pass through his fingertips, his arms, his shoulder, his chest. He steps forward and looks at the windshield, holding the bar tight, and then walks quickly back to his own truck and gets in. Coe doesn't say a word on the way back to the Center, and Mike is not sure he would hear him if he did.

18TH

THE MAN IS IN the kitchen again, making nitric acid. This is the worst part. There is nothing complicated about this step; in many ways the process is far less dangerous than the combinations that will follow, but the man is nervous nonetheless. He is uncomfortable with gases. The threat of a liquid, a solid, is something he can more clearly understand, but a gas? Where is a gas? He remembers a night this winter, coughing on his knees outside in the damp coastal air, trying to free his lungs of something he could not see or smell, trying to shake the panic.

He breathes shallow through his mouth now as he measures out the sodium nitrate and adds it to the sulfuric acid he leached out of an old battery earlier in the week. He adjusts a low flame on the Bunsen burner, which heats a glass retort shaped like a bulbous inverted pipe. The soup begins to bubble, and he steps away from the cluttered table, moves to the small windows over the kitchen sink, stands on his toes and leans and breathes the outside air. It's a hot night, the air heated and held by the buildings all around him, and he can feel the outside pouring in and swirling with the cool conditioned air of the kitchen like oil in vinegar.

When he turns back to the room he can see the bulb of the retort reddening like a ruptured blood vessel, about to pop, he knows it won't but that's how it always looks to him, no matter how ridiculous he knows it to be. The gas is very poisonous, though, there's nothing ridiculous about that. The worst way to go, he thinks, imagining, on poison gas, choking to conclusion, eaten up from within. Better to go out big and fast, shot in battle, wrapped in flames. Kaboom. Kablooie.

The gas is starting to condense now, and red droplets form in the long tapered glass neck and crawl down the slow slant towards the beaker, which sits surrounded by ice water in a large "Gators!" thermos cup. He checks the beaker frequently, and as soon as there's enough nitric acid he kills the flame and then goes outside and sits on his front stoop for a while, breathing deeply. He is far from done, but the worst, for him, is over.

When he returns to the makeshift laboratory, he cleans the kitchen table and the retort and feels better. There's a late night sports guy on the radio tonight, and although he doesn't give a shit about sports there is something likable about the host's voice—calm, focused, funny, connected. From a dry closet he removes a tray where the ammonia and formaldehyde have evaporated and crystallized, and he listens to the host as he measures out the crystals and slowly stirs them into the nitric acid. He checks the thermometer frequently, but it's fine, it's good, and when all the crystals are in he keeps stirring. In radio-land some black guy is on the line criticizing the American League pitching. He laughs out loud listening as the host dis-patches this guy quickly, revealing the nigger's all-show-no-fact verbal swagger for what it is, dressing him down, scolding him. Of course, he himself doesn't know everything about baseball, but then he isn't calling in, now, is he? No. He's not.

After twenty minutes of stirring he pours the solution into cold water and crushed ice, and then filters out the new crystals which have formed. He washes the crystals in water again and then checks the acidity on litmus paper. Almost seven, almost perfect. He doesn't have to boil them again. He spreads the crystals out carefully in a shallow pan, like shards of precious shells, and puts them on the little breakfast table to dry.

Now he begins to work more quickly, not in any hurry, but hitting a rhythm, feeling comfortable and relaxed, and even admiring himself as he works. He pours gasoline and oil into the top part of a large, deep double boiler, then adds clear plas-tic sandwich bags to melt into the mixture. He blends in the treated and dried guncotton, watching the acid bubble on the surface, and when the cotton has disappeared he puts in another plastic bag, and then another. The brown roux begins to thicken against his spoon as he stirs, and he sets it aside to cool. In a white ceramic bowl he mixes a sticky mass of mineral oil and lecithin, then collects his crystals from the far side of the room. He talks over the sports guy now, reciting his actions as he performs them, as if doing a cooking show for an invisible audience. When he sets aside the plastic dough and steps back, the table does in fact look like the setting of an enormous buffet, with leftover ingredients in beakers and tubes and the finished dishes waiting for their final presentation. A nice platter. A garnish. He returns to his plastic-bag roux, pours and scrapes it into a plastic mold—the kind his mother once used to freeze fruit juice or Kool-Aid into homemade popsicles for him and Carl. He gets two popsicles' worth out of the double boiler and puts the mold in the small refrigerator to cool.

Now he must wait. He goes upstairs and washes his hands, takes a shower, opens a cold beer, and sits on his front stoop, looking out at the moonlight hitting the water of the Gulf, looking west towards the rest of America, which he has not seen. He thought the army might take him there, but so far it has got him only as far as Florida, a hotter, wetter version of North Carolina. Living in a dingy army apartment like some nigger in the projects. He knows that there is a lot more of America to see, but sometimes he's not sure whether he wants to see it or not. There are landscapes he knows from pictures and television which seem vast, empty, impressive, but he knows you cannot go and believe the romanticism of pictures. There are pictures in books of fall forests half an hour from his childhood house, and those pictures are at least as pretty as this moonlit evening orchestrating itself before his eyes, with the water shifting like mercury, bobbing the boats in their moorings. He's seen those fall forest pictures and knows the tendency of pictures to exaggerate, and so he wonders about all of the pictures he has seen of America, this country which is real and which is his and is as fucked up as any country could want to be. When the South itself is such a mess, he doesn't see any reason elsewhere America should be any better. Although a part of him wonders, and hopes.

He finishes his beer and rubs at a grease spot on his elbow that he missed in the shower. It's hard to erase every trace of his days spent in the shop working on jeeps and transports and even tanks, fixing on command for his country. He works with idiots, blind men, fools, works with them and for them, fixes while they complain about the weather, the army, the girls, the economy, the laws of physics, their pay, their rank, their duty, anything they can think of. Complain and do nothing is their preferred way to live a life. Uneducated, uninterested, uninvolved. The college boys are the stupidest of all, arriving as officers and not knowing jack about jack but thinking they do, which is what he tells his brother on the phone: watch out for these college boys. They think they know but they don't. They have the world down as they see it but they haven't seen much. There are other things out there, ladies and gents, so at least know what you're talking about or shut your fucking trap. That's what he tends to think.

He goes back inside, but he isn't tired. He sits back on the couch, the one new thing in this ratty apartment, the only thing he's added to his stuff that the place came with, standard stuff. A nice couch, too, cost him and worth it. He turns on the television with the sound down low and looks through the newest issue of the *Southern Call*, which arrived today, and which he has been expecting for a week. He turns straight to the letters. They occupy a good half of every issue, which annoyed him until he started writing letters himself. They've yet to publish one, although he got a nice note from the editor a while back, thanking him for his interest. He doesn't have to look very far before he's found what he's looking for:

SPIC-ING THE SOUTHERN SOUP?

Thanks to R. E. Burden for his analytical and statistical insight on the Hispanic situation in "The Southern Invasion of the South." I would like to point out one statistical error, however: according to a recent regional survey by *Storm of the South*, Miami is actually 67% Spanish-dominated, rather than the optimistic but still shocking 51% reported by

Burden. Furthermore it turns out this "lost city" is domi-
nated not only by Cubans but significant numbers of
cocaine-pushing trigger-happy Colombians.

Roger Miller, Milton, GA

Thanks Roger for your update! I am told that anyone who
has had to spend time in Miami knows instinctively that
your numbers are regrettably right.

R.E.B.

While I agree with Mr. Burden's statement that the
Confederate States must contain the sudden influx of
Mexicans, that pretty much seems a pipedream to me. If the
national border can't keep them out, how can regional or
state boundaries hope to do so?

David Vines, Edenton, NC

What about a prohibition on those who use Hispanic labor
and thus encourage migration and settlement into our region?
Also state enforcement of national immigration laws would go
a long way since many of the unwelcome guests are illegals.

R.E.B.

It made me sick to read the excerpts from the communist
Spanish press in R. E. Burden's article. The sheer number of
these leftist rags and the voracity of their so-called writers
proves that the Brown Skin colonization of the South is not a
migration but an orchestrated plan by the leaders of Mexico
and their operatives. This is not osmosis but a lethal injection, and it must be stopped!

Foster Perkins, Orton, TX
(formerly of Tyler, NC)

Mexican leaders and their operatives? I doubt it, although I
do agree with you that there are plenty of 'voracious' pro-
Hispanic groups and sympathizers working disruptively
throughout the South. They are the ones who need to be

focused on, not the Mexican government. Unfortunately, the problem is much closer to home.

R.E.B

The editors would like to thank everyone for their thoughtful and well-written letters on the Burden article. Your responses were insightful and overwhelming, and we regret that we are unable to print them all.

He puts the journal aside. His, in fact, was one of the insightful, well-written letters which the overwhelmed editors of the *Southern Call* regret they were unable to print. Which sucks. Because his was relevant about what's going on here and now, not in any theoretical way, but what's really going on, to him, to his own family and neighbors. Looking at the published letters on the creased newsprint before him, he realizes his letter was probably too long, although he worked to pare it down to a bare minimum, two and a half pages typed. In any case, it was and is certainly a better letter than the short David Vines letter about containment. His own letter ended on that note, explaining how if there were a way to isolate the problem in the southwestern United States, in the way that most of the Indians are concentrated there, then the South and other regions would be able to tolerate that kind of compartmentalized cultural pluralism. He doesn't know, and did not claim to know in his letter, whether there is such a way. What he does know is that there's no use trying to explain this stuff to his family—what they know about the outside world, about politics, about the forces which threaten them from the outside, what they know about all that you could write on the back of a candy wrapper. If I was still there, he thinks, if I was still there, as he's told his brother on the phone six, seven times, this wouldn't have got this far, tell you that.

—And what would you do?

—That's the thing about the grandpas and you little punks, don't know how to act. Just ignorant. Olive come in there like he done and the all of you don't do anything.

—We're taking care of it. We're gonna do something.

—You ain't gonna do shit. I'm gonna have to come home to keep y'all getting beaten up by some little smart-ass college boy. Make sure you don't let our farm get taken away.

He turns on the TV and flips around, and as luck would have it there's a rerun of a documentary on the Alamo, with costumes and actors and music and reenactments. Although he's seen it before, he has forgotten the exact details, and finds himself watching intently. Goddamn, he thinks, those boys put up a good fight, considering. If the reinforcements hadn't been unlucky, if the wagon wheel hadn't broken, if the oxen hadn't wandered off into the scrub, if they'd got more powder, a few more men, they would have kicked Santa Ana's ass all up and down the Rio Grande. They did everything they could, but all the circumstances were against them. He watches. A slight trickle of sweat creeps down his neck and disappears beneath the rim of his T-shirt. In the kitchen, liquids are forming into solids.

When the show is over he decides to call his brother again, the penultimate act, fuck the time of night, it's time to talk about it is what it is, to ask him something, but his mother answers and he hangs up. He dials again, and puts the receiver to his ear.

"This is Clarisse," says a black girl. "What city?"

"Cottesville."

There's a pause. "Yes?"

"Number and address for Olive."

There's another pause, and then the girl says, "I have a Clayton Olive in Cottesville at Box 257, R.R. #1?"

"That's just fine," he says.

19TH

SHE HEARS THE bass cough of the truck break above the quiet hum of late afternoon as she stands out between the trailers pulling laundry off the line. She folds a dry green blanket carefully, raising her hands high to keep the soft fringe out of the dirt. Behind her, the truck is bouncing over the last bump before the camp, and she listens to the hollow pop of the tires on the dry ground, listens to the engine cut and die. The bass cough, the afternoon hum, the hollow pop: she wonders when she will listen to these commonplace sounds and not hear the sound of Mike. When will we leave? she thinks. When will this Mike end?

"Hermelinda."

She turns and sees him, walking towards her, and he's looking at her but she feels the gaze miss her, as if he were searching for her in a crowd. Maybe I've already left, she thinks, maybe I've been gone for days.

She hands the blanket to him as he steps in close, and they walk over to the stumps outside her trailer and sit. Her mother opens the trailer door, examining them, making her watchful presence known before letting the door bang shut again.

Mike sits with the blanket on his lap, trying to say something. "I'm sorry I haven't been here," he says. "I don't think a good thing's happened since I saw you last."

"Nothing's happened," she says.

"Nothing's better, sometimes." He looks down at the blanket, wondering what to do with it. "Right now nothing's as good as it gets."

"I'm sorry," she says. She doesn't ask him what's wrong, what's happened, because she knows he is going to tell her anyway. She watches him and waits.

Then, unexpectedly, he smiles and leans towards her, folding the blanket one square smaller and putting it out of his way on the stump beside him. "There are things I want to tell you," he says. "Let's go. Let's get out of here."

"It's not possible," she says.

"Tonight?"

"No, it's not possible," she says again. He nods and his face goes soft. She can't help it, she wonders what he's thinking. What he feels when he leans back and looks at her and then away. She wonders if he notices the part of her that has begun to hate him for all the possibilities he has dragged in front of her, for the slice of the American dream her parents see in him and his attention. Her father, her crazy father does not doubt Mike's intentions, but she doubts them. She knows he is a child and has no idea what to do. She knows what America is more than her father can, and she knows it's something very different from Mexico. The rules are different. The rules are that the young make up their own rules.

Do I tell him my secret? she thinks. Do I tell and then see what that will make him, what he will say or do? Eight days. He is not so stupid, he knows something is wrong. Ask me, she thinks, I won't answer but please ask me.

From the road behind them, the lopsided rumble of the Olives' big truck grows, and the men are back earlier than usual, dropping from the truck bed like winter flies. Mike's father is there and Hermelinda's too. The two children look at their respective fathers, Clayton standing beside the truck, Francisco making a beeline for the trailer.

"Michael," Clayton calls out to him, waving him over with one big hand. From behind him, Hermelinda's brother appears, with a piece of machinery in his hand. He follows Clayton's wave and finds Mike, and Mike sees Alejandro put down the part and watch him, kneading his oily hands against one another.

"You should go," Hermelinda says. Her brother is stepping towards them now, slowly, with hesitation but with purpose, too.

"I'm supposed to be in Durham again tomorrow," Mike says. "I'll come find you on Saturday." She shakes her head. "Saturday," he says again, and she doesn't have the strength to shake her head that one more time.

"Go," she says, standing and straightening her skirt.

"Okay." Mike leans forward and she freezes, he's going to kiss her right there in the teaming middle of the camp, but instead he whispers in her ear. "I love you," he says. "I do I do." And despite the world around them she reaches out and holds him, squeezes him hard. Surprised, he holds her too until she releases him. Everyone's staring at them except for Clayton, looking away to examine the wheel of his truck, and Alejandro, digging a ditch in the dirt with his eyes. They separate, and the camp moves again as Mike turns and walks back to the truck. Hermelinda watches him go. Then she takes the blanket off the stump and into her arms and walks to the trailer, her eyes pinned to a spot on the door. She refuses to cry as she climbs the trailer stairs and goes inside to help her mother prepare the evening meal.

20TH

"FRIDAY," GEORGE WHIPKEY drawls across the room. They are sitting on the floor drinking beer, sweating it out, a perfect loop. Beer and salt and lime and they have been drinking for a few hours. "Freaky freaky Friday." George opens his mouth to reveal a jutting mishmash of false teeth jury-rigged out of a lime peel. He crosses and bugs his eyes, moans a wraith's moan through the splayed green teeth. He leans towards Mike, grins. "Aaaarg," he says. "Boo."

Mike hasn't been paying attention. He glances over at George and sees the teeth and tries to smile. The smile goes away and he takes a breath that tells George he's about to ask a serious question and George waves him off.

"Uhn-uh. No. Shut up."

Mike closes his mouth.

"Nothing personal. But it's Friday." He hands him another beer. "That's the last one," George says, "just in case you have any doubts about how I really feel about you."

Mike accepts the beer, pops it open, takes a long pull. "Now what the hell do we do?" he says, staring at the wall in front of him.

"We buy some more beer, for starts."

The Catholic Retreat Center is very quiet. No doors slam, no voices sound through the halls or the courtyard. No one is cooking anything downstairs.

"Okay. Let's go."

The parking lot of the Catholic Retreat Center is empty too. Everyone has gone back to Durham for the weekend. There's a meeting tomorrow morning, early, with the university sponsors, the professors who have nurtured Sarah and Mike along the years. The people who put up the money for the summer. They want to know what the gang's been doing. They are living out their activist years all over again through the kids, living out their dreams of creating a new kind of activist, different from their generation's. This one will have teeth and fangs and dress respectably and penetrate the state, the courts, the establishment. This breed that they hope Mike and Sarah will become will accomplish more than theirs ever could. They have helped Mike get money and connections and all the rest, and Mike has charmed them all silly along the way. They love him, and he's the one they want to see, he's their man. But Mike can't bring himself to go. He has claimed illness, something vile and intestinal. Something with the involuntary release of fluids. The rest

of the students travel under vows of silence which he is not at
all sure they will keep.

"We've got another week of work to do, I'll talk to them
then." He'll call the university press, let them know everything
is all right. The information side of things is moving right
along. It is the activist side that shames him.

Sarah knows him, knows how his mind works, disagrees.
"It's ridiculous," she tells Mike before she leaves. "You are not
pathetic. There are too many things outside our control, you
know that. There's still work to do at the health clinic, and the
Head Start, so if you can just stop moping about your revolu-
tion for a moment and look around, you'll see that it's not for
nothing. But maybe we were too ambitious. Involved in too
many things at once." She doesn't say anything about
Hermelinda, but he wonders if that's what she's talking about.

"Nothing lasts," Mike says. "Everything we're doing here,
it's over and done like that." He snaps his fingers. "They're
gone, and then we're gone, and the only thing that isn't gone is
Blue Dickerson. So, what, we get a nice document out of it?
Who gives a shit? We didn't change anything."

"Come on, Mike. It's not true, for one, and you sound like a
petulant little kid."

She's right and that pisses him off even more, but now she's
gone, all of them are gone and Mike's with the only guy he can
bear to see, who doesn't want to talk about it, doesn't want to
know. Tennessee George and his camera and his beer and his
lovely neutral eyes.

They drive to town. As they pull into the Stop N' Go, Mike
senses the barely perceptible shift of Harvey's crew sitting on
their hoods in the parking lot. It's a warning, a sign. Something
old and instinctive in Mike wakes up. In high school this was a
premonition that told him to beat it, to get out of the path of
Harvey and Ox. All through the years, the instinct's kept him
safe and out of trouble. A night like this when he would pull

into this parking lot and feel that same heat coming off his neighbors, he knew to keep driving, away from any sort of situation which could be made bad, fast. He turns to George to tell him, at least tell him about the crowbar, the Dickersons' truck, but decides against it. He knows that George may have the ability to make things worse. They step out of the car and the boys in the lot murmur and Harvey says, "Looky here, the circus must be in town. It's the geek and the fat man." When his buddies laugh the hoods of the cars bounce up and down as if the cars are laughing too.

The two Duke kids move through the store and debate beer while Harvey and company jaw outside. "Drove them off? How drove them off?" Harvey is asking Ox again.

"I don't know. One day they were there and then Olive went out with his friends and come Wednesday they weren't there." The words come out slow, as if every syllable takes its internal and physical toll on the taciturn giant.

"Well where'd they go?"

Ox shrugs.

"It don't surprise me. But hitting Carl's truck," Harvey laughs to himself, "that kind of surprises me, it must have been a picture to see ol' Mike doing something like that. We'll have to inquire about that tonight." He takes another long pull from his beer as Carl pulls into the lot. "Speak of the devil. From the horse's mouth. Get over here, Carl!" Harvey's cousin gets out of his Bronco to join the boys. He catches a can in midflight, opening it absently, not seeming to notice the foam that blossoms out over his knuckles and hand.

"Ox tell you, then?"

"Shit, I heard it twelve different ways from eight different people."

"You heard about that." He points to the dent in the Bronco, stabbing at it with his finger three times fast.

"That and the rest of it."

"The truck, though, Harvey." Then Carl sees Mike inside the Stop N' Go. He stops. "Shit. You assholes. He's right in there."

"Hold up. He ain't going nowhere. Tell us what did he do to your workers?"

"Told them to leave. Told them they shouldn't be working for my pa."

"Why the hell he do that?"

"Just to get at us."

"That ain't right," says Jimmy, to fill the silence that follows.

"Right?" Harvey says. "That ain't even in the same neighborhood as right. Don't really make any sense though, either." He looks at Carl. "What's he got wrong for Uncle Blue?"

"He doesn't have reasons. Just to put us down."

"He always has reasons. He thinks so anyway."

"My poppa said you all had some trouble with those workers anyway," Jimmy says. Carl nods. "Bad batch, huh. Least they got you through the tobacco. That'll happen. Remember that year when—"

"Jimmy, shut up. Swear, you and your poppa could open yourselves an AM station talk so much." Harvey doesn't look at anyone as he speaks, keeps his eyes fixed on Mike and the masquerading good ol' boy inside. He watches them pay for their beer.

"Let's take care of Olive," Harvey tells Carl, rising off the hood of the Pinto.

"Oh, we're taking care of it," Carl says.

"Well, I'll just take care of it again," Harvey says, and when he sees George and Mike heading towards the Stop N' Go doors Harvey starts walking and then Ox rises too, a step behind him but following step for step.

The other boys lean forward, but stay put.

Mike and George exit the store. Harvey and Ox walk. Slowly, inevitably, a triangle completes itself as the two couples converge on a single point a few yards away from George's dull red hatchback, while Harvey's boys watch, and the clerks and customers in the Stop N' Go watch. A few feet away from the tip of the triangle the two parties stop.

"Hey Mikey boy." Harvey shifts lazy and relaxed to a leaning stance, as if propped up against the frame of a phantom doorway. He hooks one thumb into the rim of his jeans, lets the other thin arm dangle free. "How's tricks?"

"Harvey." Mike glances at Harvey, at Ox, at the boys beyond, at George's car.

"What you all doing tonight?"

"Not much." Mike nods vaguely towards the twelve pack of beer in George's hands.

"Maybe a little auto body work? Heard you been dabbling in that, of late."

"Well. Only where I find occasion for it. Actually, you know what, Harvey? I regret that."

"Yeah? I figured you might. Well. What's done is done. I guess we're all involved now."

"Oh you are?"

"Sure, Mike. Family, you know. That's to do with me."

Mike straightens, digs his toes into his spot. The jaw tightens, the eyes slit slightly, the head tilts on an irritated axis. "Is that right? What else it gotta do with you, Harvey, tell me?"

"You tell me."

To the left and behind Harvey, Ox Bowman stands slightly stooped, his arms crossed down front of him, hands joined like an acolyte. His face is passive, blank. He does not seem to blink. The only thing in his face that moves is the lips, or jaw, it's hard to tell—it's as if he's chewing something very slightly, very slowly. At the other end of Ox's silent, dull stare, George Whipkey holds the twelve-pack in the crook of his arm, like an oversized football, and now he lets the cold, steaming cardboard box slide through his hands, catches the cutout handhold at one end, and rests the box lengthways up on the ground. He takes a very small step forward to bring himself even with Mike and statues himself there, standing straight, arms hanging loose at his side.

"Funny, Harvey, I can't imagine there's anything goes on for a hundred miles that you don't know about. So are you lying, or are you slipping, that's the question."

"Naw." Harvey smiles a thin smile, shakes his head. "The question, see—and I'm afraid, Mikey, it might be less a question than a problem—is that I think I do know what's going on. I'm ninety-nine point nine nine nine percent sure. But see, what I know, I don't want to know, and I'm hoping that you can tell me otherwise. Despite the odds. Despite everything. I've never liked you, Mike, but you still a Cottesville boy, ain't you? That's what I'm asking. That's what I'm wasting my time talking to you for. On a perfectly good Friday night."

"What exactly are you asking me? Just for the record."

"For the whole box set. What you and your boyfriends been doing on my uncle's land. What all you and your buddies been doing poking around our fields, our homes, our workers, who gave you what right and why and how. How about it, Mike? You trying to ruin Carl and his pa? You trying to bring everyone down, keep you and yours on high, that it? It seems kind of simple to me, but maybe you getting simple in your old age."

"Why don't you ask Carl?" Mike says, "Or Jeremy, maybe he was there too," nodding at Ox, who does not flinch at the sound of his given name but continues to stare. "Ask Jeremy what's going on. Or maybe you don't need to ask, Harvey. Maybe you were out there with them."

"Aw, now Mike, you shouldn't get your panties in an uproar over this. You're getting very upset over some simple questions, and when you get upset I get upset and that makes two of us and I know that ain't good for anyone's health."

"Upset? Well. This place is enough to make anyone upset got eyes and ears."

"Well, Mike, I'm not a doctor, but it sounds to me the only prescription for that is you can just get the fuck out of Dodge." The word *fuck* snaps like a cymbal clash amid Harvey's even talky tones, and Mike starts. "I ever tell you my theory about you, Mike?" Mike's hands, known to him or not, are curling into fists and then relaxing, close and release. "I have this theory, that some people are born in the right place and right time, and that some of the poor unlucky bastards among us are brought into this world out of sorts. And they just never get used to it. They never find the where they belong, and it makes it unhappy going for them. And some of these folk, like yourself, when they get unhappy, they decide to make everyone else, all those right people in the right place in the right time, they decide to try to make them unhappy too. Now, Michael, I don't know where your place is, or when your time is, the future, the past, the once upon a time, New Jersey, I dunno, but we both know where it isn't."

Mike rubs his lips with one hand. "That's not the worst theory I ever heard," he says after a pause, "but I have this theory too. My theory says that this is my place as much as it is yours, whether we like it or not."

"No," Harvey says. "That's the thing, see, it's not."

"I'd let you have it, Harvey, as far as I'm concerned. If it was just a matter of y'all out here stewing in your own ugly juices. But no. Now we got your boy there and his pappy and whoever all else beating the shit out of these Mexicans, robbing them, treating them like the slaves they wish they still all had. And the weird thing is, Harvey, I don't know if you were in on it or not." Mike steps closer to Harvey. "There's no reason, but I always thought you were better than that. And them." He looks past Harvey now at Carl and Jimmy and Truett sitting on the hood of the car, watching. "You have a good time, Jeremy? Did you enjoy that, Jimmy? Which one of you pushed around the woman? You slap her around a little, Truett? You like squeezing her up, Carl? Now Carl, was it your idea, or were you going along with your pa?" He steps back. "Did you all have a nice time playing keep-away with the baby?" Mike hears and barely recognizes his own voice, these spitting words that seem to be rushing from him on their own power. He wonders what this voice is going to say next.

Harvey hears it too. "He finally lost it," Harvey says. "Lost it, and gone suicidal, too, talking about our family. You hearing this, Carl? This is you and yours he's slinging." He turns back to his cousin, who takes a few steps forward, looking wary. "That's right, better get up here, Carl, your brother ain't here to lay down the law anymore." Some of the guys laugh and Carl keeps coming until he's standing beside and behind Ox.

"And you. Harvey," Mike says, not seeming to notice anything but Harvey, now. "Hard to believe it could happen without you." Mike's voice has slowed down again, acquired a kind of cemetery calm. "Did you tell everyone what to do? Did you bring your dogs? Track them through the woods? Did you tell your uncle he'd better send them off away when you realized what you'd done?"

"Mike. These fantasies of yours are pretty complicated. You sure you can keep them all straight?"

"Be nice if they were. Bad dreams."

"Come on, Mike, where'd you send them off to?"

"I wish I knew where they were. I wish they were still here to stand in front of y'all and point out which ones. Because we were ready to take you out, put you in court, and let them point. We were going to lock somebody up."

Harvey looks at him.

"Court," Harvey says. He laughs a brittle laugh. "Oh, Mike, you in even deeper shit than I thought."

"I wish I was, Harvey. I wish I was in deep shit because I'd found a way to make sure it didn't happen again. But I haven't, not yet." He shakes his head and then looks at them one by one: Harvey, Ox, Carl, the rest of them, his old classmates, teammates, maybe even a once pal. "You know, I've been talking to your daddies all summer. And I guess I figured that they couldn't see it on account of their age. So that I almost reconciled myself to the fact that they couldn't understand. But y'all, Carl, Jimmy, Harvey, you see it even less than they do. I never thought y'all would be the ones wouldn't change."

All of them are up off the cars and coming now, but Harvey puts a hand out and they stop.

"It doesn't matter," Mike says. "Change is gonna get here like anywhere else. And it's gonna eat y'all up."

Harvey starts laughing then, hard. He claps his hands together twice, and at the cracking sound Ox blinks a few times and stops his mysterious chewing. George takes a deep breath. Even Mike seems confused by the sudden noise of Harvey's hands, and for a small moment his face contracts in shame or guilt or fear. And Harvey laughs. "Amen, preacher boy. Play ball." He checks over his shoulder but no one else will laugh so he turns back to Mike and says, "S'okay, Mr. High and Mighty, I understand why you out there on Blue's land, working over those Mexicans. Looking for some more of that shit-colored pussy, big bossman giving it to the Mexican girls what choice she got anyway I hear they suck some good cock don't they Mikey boy pretty low to go but I can see how you reduced to that, I remember your old Cordelia Potts, love of your life, she always said it was just the cutest little smallest cutest little thing, but I guess it don't matter with some poor-ass Mexican, a little Chiquita banana I'm here to help y'all if you help me, yeah, that right, down on your knees," and then Mike takes a step back and says, "No, Harvey, uhn-uh," and turns away, his face blank and frozen, as he starts to walk back to George's car.

Harvey watches him go, and then takes a slight running start and spits, and everyone watches the beeline gob strike Mike on the back of his head, Mike who doesn't turn around but keeps walking until he hears something and spins to see Harvey lying on the ground where George has thrown him.

There is a moment of suspended breath, like a line of swimmers readying for the dive, and then Ox comes, grabs at George's shirt with one enormous hand but meets his elbow instead, an elbow and then an electric-quick hand to the neck, George quicker than anyone could have imagined, quicker than Mike knew but George has always known, just as he has known that he would one day be in this parking lot or somewhere nearby, bloody and bloodying.

Mike tries to get back to them but it is too late. The crowd comes and moves in a quick amoebic sway around the two fighters, and hands hold Mike in place while in the center George fires and punches, furiously, fast, the blows missing and hitting and landing but unable to reach the head, taking the wind out of the giant, pressing the advantage of the dervish, the low swinging power of every fight George has ever been in, plenty, both lost and won, and knowing that he needs to take this huge farmboy out now, NOW, or face the consequences of his size and strength which he can feel already as one hand wraps around the shoulder of his shirt. George snaps the shoulder away, gets off an enormous pop from the right hand as he almost jumps off the ground and hits Ox. George feels the crack of his hand and the farmboy's face and knows something is broken, a hand or a nose or a tooth, something that was not meant to give has given way. He sees that moment like a photograph, at once a live animal in midstrike and an observer above the fight, looking at himself, recording the angle of their arms, the connection of fist and face.

The crowd sings and sways, a shifting ring, as Ox staggers back slightly, bringing George with him, giving involuntarily to the punch. A falling space opens behind Ox, a coffin of space in the crowd, as Harvey, and Donny in the Stop N' Go shirt and Zebulon Hough in for chips and Coke and Lilli Hollister filling

up her daddy's Chevy and Jimmy and Truett and Carl
Dickerson and paralyzed Mike all watch the impact, wait for
the consequence, the counterstrike. No one steps into the circle.

Ox bleeds. His nose, cocked and crooked by the punch,
sprays blood in a wild goatee around his mouth, leaking across
his lips and down his chin. But he holds on. He has reached out
even as the Duke boy withdraws the scoring hand and grabbed
the arm, finally, at the elbow, and he holds on, and when his
opponent is unable to withdraw Ox puts another hand around
the other arm, at the forearm, and suddenly they are immobi-
lized, the both of them, straining with full force against the
other, except that now Ox feels his size and strength eating
away at the smaller man. He leans, he pulls, he presses.

George does not hesitate. Caught, he wrestles in this losing
battle for only the briefest moment before he lowers his head
and charges, head down, into the stomach of the giant, and
when he does Ox lowers the Duke boy's shoulders and raises
his own knee into the wide face, twice, very hard, and then
pulls back. George drops to the ground like a marionette
clipped from strings. When he starts to move again, Ox takes a
step forward and starts to kick him.

Tough motherfucker, Harvey thinks, looking down at
George on the ground, getting halfway up, getting kicked, getting up, muttering the while, indecipherable. Carl is standing
over the kid, too, yelling "Take that you fucker" and worse.

George falls and Mike kicks and punches in every direction,
breaking free of Jimmy and Truett and Dale, and he vaults
through the crowd, as Ox continues to kick and Harvey says,
"All right," and Ox kicks the Duke kid one more time and
Harvey says, "ALL RIGHT," as Mike arrives and puts himself
between Ox and the barely mobile George. Ox turns to Harvey,
bloody, nods, steps back and looks at Carl, and when he does
Harvey sees dumb murder in both those sets of eyes, fading
only slowly, and he wonders.

"Move back," Mike says, and when no one moves he takes a step towards bloody Ox, and says it again. "Move back."

Ox doesn't move. "Mike," Harvey says, shaking his head like a sage. "Listen to me. You don't want none. Time to cut your losses. Run."

"I'm not going anywhere, Harvey. You want to beat me? You want your giant to take me out? You all want something? You want a sacrifice. Go ahead, come on. Fuck all y'all. Move back." Ox doesn't move. "I don't care, I don't even care, I'll fight every one of you if you don't move back right now. I'll fight you until you'll have to kill me to make me stop. Get that, Ox, you gonna have to kill me." He's screaming now, the spit spraying from his mouth and falling in a mist through the bright lot light.

Harvey examines Mike for a minute. "It's okay," he tells Ox.

Ox steps back. Mike moves to George then, bends down, and when he does Harvey nods and Ox steps forward and kicks Mike in the ass, sends him tripping and then flying over his buddy, and then they all fall on him, Carl and Ox and Jimmy as Harvey watches and the crowd yells contradictions. Mike fights back at first but there's no use and he curls up tight into a ball while they punch and kick a few times and then run back to their cars, leaving the two students lying in the grease and gas and oil of the Stop N' Go parking lot, with the crowd retreated and the heat from the day still seeping up out of the pavement. Mike uncurls himself slowly as they leave, checking himself for damage. Some cuts, scrapes, bruises, but he feels mostly intact. He rises quickly, the blacktop's radiation warming his skinned hands as he pushes off the ground, and moves towards his spitting, muttering friend. "George," he says, quietly, then louder. "George, you okay?"

21ST

He RETURNS FROM Durham late in the afternoon to find Father Joe waiting for him on the steps of the north entrance. He has not seen Father Joe for a time, but now here he is, putting himself in the doorway and looking at Mike expectantly as if they had an appointment for which he is late.

"You all right?"

"I am. Little nicked up, but I'm okay. Thanks."

"And your friend?" Father Joe said.

"He's been better. But he's a tough one, he's gonna be fine. Considering."

"Where is, uh . . ." Father Joe says, and Mike doesn't know if there's a name he's forgotten or if he is referring to everyone else at once. He decides the latter.

"Durham, too. They'll be back tomorrow night."

"That," Father Joe says, "is what I would like to talk to you about."

And afterwards Mike feels as if he's been slapped, as if someone else has taken aim and kicked him in the ass. The father wants them out; he wants to shut the doors on them, to send them back to their student lives immediately, to get them out of Cottesville and out of the Center for sure.

"We have another week," Mike says. "One week."

"I'll refund a part, if that's what you want."

"That's not what I want. We're not gonna just go, like that. We're going to finish this out."

"Not here you're not."

"Yes here we are, sir." Mike speaks softly. "I'm sorry, Father Joe, I know you must be . . . feeling pressure from folks."

"It's not about anyone else. I just want you out."

"Well," Mike says. "It's a week." The father stares at Mike but Mike holds his ground, looking back at Joe down into the heat of one eye then the other. "Please," Mike says. "If we go off now, what's the moral of that story?"

"What you're looking for," Father Joe starts, then stops himself. "Listen, I'm not going to argue it. It just takes time, Mike, sometimes."

"Not just time."

"No. Other things too. But dammit! I mean, look at me. How long it take *me* to carve a place out here? The Mexicans, you know what, they gonna take a long time, it's the way it is." He shakes his head again, fast, as if throwing off a chill.

"How much time? How long will it be with no one taking their side? You think it's just going to happen?" Mike steps past Father Joe, making the other man turn. "They're your people too, they need your help, so don't try to sweep us under the rug."

"I'm not having this conversation," Father Joe says. "You're in my house, in my good grace, and I'm asking you to leave."

"I'm sorry," Mike says. He starts off down the hall, but Joe blocks his way.

"Listen, you can go down to your daddy's house, I don't care, but you're out of here. Now give me the keys."

"No."

Father Joe stares at Mike for a long moment, and Mike feels as if he's watching two Father Joes fight for control of the body: a forgiving religious man and a man of property; a compassionate man and a country man who will not be told no on his own land. Mike does not know who wins exactly, except that he stands his ground and Father Joe turns around and bangs through the front door like a southern wind, away.

Mike heads through the Center to the office, sits among his papers and thinks about George lying in Mike's bed in Durham, watching cable or something, stitched and sutured and dulled by pharmaceuticals. Sarah and Raúl and the others coming by Mike's apartment to see the damage done and talk about themselves in the living room.

And Mike didn't stay. They're talking and fretting in Durham but he's come back to Cottesville, because to be anywhere else is the defeat everyone is looking for. To leave is to confirm the prevailing ideas about the way life works. He looks at the phone, thinks about calling the others, to check in, to make sure of their return. They've all said they're coming back, they won't run away, they'll finish the summer together. Stand out here hated and be a living voice opposed.

"What's another week going to do?" Raúl said. "What are we going to be able to do for the migrants, anymore? They're not going to let us on their land. The workers won't want to talk to us for being scared. The law's not going to help us. What's the point?"

"The point is that we have to be there," Mike said, thinking: If there's more to this, we need to be sure it comes down on us and not on anyone else.

But tonight there is no one left to argue with, with the others still in Durham and Mike in Cottesville alone. There may be lots of reasons he thinks he's here, but mostly he just wants to see Hermelinda.

Hermelinda is there, not far from him, not in miles at least or in states or continents, but far. Far enough to wonder where he's been, and if he's coming tonight. She worries, not about him or herself, or her stomach, which maybe is swelling she isn't sure in the thick wet heat that makes her feel like she is swelling and bloating always, but she worries about her family. Her father, her mother, her sisters, her brothers. She worries about the weight of their expectations that she, with her Mike, with her dinners at the house, with her job at the clinic, with her English and her breasts and hair and big black eyes, somehow she is going to deliver them all from ignominy, from poverty. She watches her family's expectations grow even as she realizes the preposterous state of affairs—could anyone really believe her screwing a farmer's son in a toolshed is some kind of guarantee of a future? She has never thought of it that way. She has tried not to think of it in any way except the way their bodies feel together, and the sweat that comes slicking off his body onto her, he does sweat, this pretty Anglo boy, and the way his yellow hair looks against her brown thigh when he goes gliding down her body. Has there been more to it than that? I love myself, Hermelinda thinks, I love who I am but why am I Hermelinda and not a Sarah or Elizabeth or Carolyn, a comfortable white girl with education and apartments and money and wealthy parents far away? She lives another quick moment as a student at Mike's university, walking among the castles of stone and short bright green clipped grass, thumbing open thick books packed with tiny, serious print. Winking at Mike down the aisle of an enormous, towering library. She cannot sustain that for long before she sees herself as Mike's parents must see her: a poor, Mexican girl, a dark girl with dark designs, a beggar, an Indian. Beggar, *india, La Tacuache del Cobre* all over again.

What does she want? Not a house, not a child. Not a man for hers forever, not a big American car with bright chrome wheels and lions roaring under the hood, not a closet full of short bright summer dresses. They interest her, she can see herself having them, and can even imagine and see the person she might be with those things, but what she wants has more to do with a sensation. Is it freedom? Pleasure? Love? Independence? She can't name it, but feels that it lingers out of her reach, and out of her family's understanding, even out of Mike's understanding.

So while Mike drives towards Hermelinda through the night, Hermelinda sits in her hot trailer thinking of the absence of Mike, and Alejandro, her brother, sits across from her and stares and thinks his own brand of brutal thoughts, while the rest of the family sleeps. He watches his sister. His eyes slide over the curve of his sister's hips to her lap as he replays the

carnal scene of the machine shed and tells himself for the hun-
dredth time that there is shame, that his family's honor has
been besmirched.

Alejandro rises and moves outside, and when, a few minutes
later, Hermelinda leaves the trailer in silence, he is out of sight,
off smoking somewhere. She moves away from the trailers,
starts through the woods until she hits the faint trail, and then
follows it, checking behind her as she goes. She walks and
walks. She is five minutes from the trailer when he grabs her.

He has a hand over her mouth, very tight, and with the other
pulls her body back against his, pinning her arms on both sides.
She raises one foot, ready to kick back into his shin, but instead
she relaxes, sinks back heavily against him, and he holds her
there, limp. He takes his hand off her mouth, wraps it around
her neck, holds her firmly but gently. He is breathing hard
through his nose.

"Let me go, Alejandro," she says softly.

"I can't," he says. "I can't let you."

"Let me go, brother."

"For what?"

"For me."

"So you can . . . so he can . . . " He has not relaxed. His
hand shifts against her neck.

"Alejandro," she says. "We'll leave here soon," Hermelinda
hears herself say, "we'll leave and we'll never come back. We'll
never see any of this again. It'll all be gone, he'll be gone, and
that's what should be. But right now, I have to see him now."

"No," Alejandro says. "No. It's better not to see him. You
can't." He lets her go, and she turns and looks at him. "I'm
your family," he says. "Don't go."

"Do you remember?" she says. "Do you remember when we
were little and Papá came home from prison? How I yelled to
him from the mountain and you tried to stop me, and we fought
because you were scared for him? Scared he would go away

again. Do you remember that?" Her brother nods, slowly. "I remember," she says, "you were so scared because you thought we would lose our family. And it seemed possible then."

"I remember."

"But here we are," Hermelinda says. "It's not possible, anymore. You are not going to lose me." He's shaking his head without even knowing, biting his lip in on one side.

"No."

She hesitates, and then says it. "I love him, you know? But this is the last time. You don't have to understand but you have to let me go."

She starts to turn and he grabs her arm. "If you go," he says, and she sees for the first time the machete hanging on his belt loop at the back. "I'll cut him."

"You don't want to do that."

"I want to," he hisses. "I want to very much. I would do it." He holds her arm firm. "Come back with me." He's pleading now. "I won't cut him. I won't say anything. We'll go soon, we'll be back in Laredo." She pushes his arm away but he grabs her again. "Please, Herme. Don't let me kill him." He pulls and this time she comes. They walk sideways and slowly through the trees, and he does not let go until they are back inside the trailer again.

22ND

"THE LORD'S DAY," says Father Joe, looking out from his modified pulpit set no bigger or grander than a lemonade stand at the front of a room, but despite the modest surroundings he is pleased as he restates himself, looking out over the crowd.

"The day of the Lord, and this is where we belong. I am glad to see so many of you here today. Welcome."

So many is thirty-eight people, the most Father Joe has ever seen in this shotgun church of his, and he doesn't know why, but the half-full room softens him. He feels compassion welling up in him and regrets the words he cast towards the young Olive yesterday. He understands that was wrong, that he spoke out of fear, and that is what he talks about today in his sermon: fear. Who stood by and watched Christ crucified on the cross, who bit their tongue or held back their protesting hand out of fear? Which of us has not shied away from the church, from the service and the confession, for fear of facing our sins, for fear of facing the Lord? Father Joe rails against fear, the original power of darkness, the enemy of love, and although he does not know how much of it the mostly Mexicans sitting in the fold-out chairs understand, he seems to see some of them nodding along with the beat of his sermon.

Today there are baptisms to perform. Two families have brought their infants, and the entire congregation stays, gathers around, delighted by the moment. His three families of white regulars smile and coo at the Mexican babies, and afterwards the men shake hands in the back of the church as they sip coffee and eat Tastykakes. For the first time he can remember, no one leaves immediately. They sit in the back of the room, talking and sipping and eating, and Father Joe feels them all joined by faith, this anomalous Catholic faith in the Carolina hinterland. In his heart he thanks God and the Mexicans for this feeling, for the opportunity to experience purpose and love.

And right then, in the middle of his satisfaction, Father Joe thinks about leaving Cottesville. He does not decide for sure, but for the first time in a long time he can picture himself far from here, with family perhaps, holding this last service in his memory as the culmination of his years in Jackson County. Later tonight, he will eat dinner at the Groves' house, a Sunday dinner with them and their extended family, a crowd of people in the dining room of that big white house almost in the middle of town, not Catholics but good people, friendly, and while he compliments the food and eats and banters the regular light banter of small-town Cottesville, he will think of his family's beach house. The ocean. The porch. The wind leaning against the old building, creaking the joints, shaking the screens. He won't figure out why this day, this almost perfect day in his many years here in Cottesville, infuses him with a feeling of completion, but he will accept another slice of pecan pie, and wonder whether he will feel the same way tomorrow.

Hermelinda watches the father baptize the baby José Peredes Hidalgo. She stands with her family and the Hidalgos, who live in the trailer next to hers, and she can forget for a moment where she is. In the here and now she's happy, not for herself and not for the baby or the family but for all of them, and this familial and familiar feeling dates from childhood, when she was young and the order of everything seemed uncomplicated and natural. She catches her brother's eye and he smiles at her, as if in this moment of nostalgia he has traveled with her, year for year and step for step, and stands in the town square in Batopilas, or lingers in the shade of a squat tree on the Ojinaga side of the muddy Rio Grande. In that moment she does not resent him for his love, she even thinks, briefly, that perhaps he is right. She has not seen Alejandro smile in a long time, and without even thinking about it she reaches out and takes his hand. He stiffens a little but they remain there, hands linked, watching the priest.

Even as the baptism is ending and Father Joe's small flock heads for the coffee and cake, the Baptist church back in Cottesville proper still holds its full crowd in off the hot noon street. The Olives are there, and Mike too; it's the first time he has been to church since he left for college. Over those years he has refused Christmas and Easter but this morning he dressed without being invited or asked, joined his amazed parents in their kitchen without a word. He sits through the service, which is not nearly so awful as he remembers, and although much of the preaching seems like bombast to him, there are whole sentences and phrases and biblical riffs that make sense. When it stops making sense, he drifts off into his own reveries, revisiting the scene of the shed where he sat and waited and thought about Hermelinda in her absence, knowing that she was less than a mile away but feeling it might as well be a hundred, a thousand. Feeling sorry and angry and sad, and then he is back in church, listening again. He hears the preacher, and hearing him realizes that the meaning of church is looking for meaning itself, looking for it alone but also side by side with neighbors, friends, enemies, and the total effect of the experience on him is strange, unfamiliar. He feels something vague which is spiritual, or religious, he thinks, even if it doesn't match up to a specific doctrine or denomination. Whether it's faith or hope or neither it's something enough so that when he emerges from the pew at service's end and finds himself shoulder to shoulder with Harvey Dickerson in the center aisle, he observes himself extending a hand, an offering.

Harvey takes it. He does not know why he takes it. He wonders what his father will say to him later, standing behind him, or his uncle, watching, what Ox will say, and at the same time he doesn't fancy explaining himself. "Church," he'll say. "Day of rest." When he takes Mike's hand and shakes it, they say nothing, but Harvey feels his stomach dip a little, a dip of doubt. It's not that he doubts the right of the situation, the impropriety of Mike, the infidelity of the young Olive. The doubt is bigger than that. Despite himself, Harvey finds himself wondering a little bit about the future of Jackson County. What if Olive's right, what if it's right that there are changes coming from the beyond and the people that don't change get left behind, again, and although Harvey's line of thinking doesn't get much more specific than that, he shakes the hand.

Clayton stares, and is proud of his son. The sight of Mike shaking hands with Harvey after the weekend bout is a sight of dignity.

Brackford and Blue Dickerson are disgusted.

Ox Bowman confused.

Cousin Carl scared.

Martha Joyner, thinking of her migrant kids at the Head Start, exasperated and relieved. "Time these boys stopped acting like boys," knowing it's the little things that keep a community together or rip it apart.

Sunday shifts into the afternoon, with people in their homes and piling plates high with summer spoils, centerpieces of yams and roasted pork. The handshake is discussed. Crops talked about. The end of the season anticipated. Mike and his Duke students debated.

They did mean well, I believe. They just didn't know what they were doing.

Dolores says she's as nice a girl as you could meet, even if she Mexican.

Beautiful girl. Saw her out at Acton.

Be over, anyway, 'fore long. Be leaving soon.

There's a point about the worker barracks. Bad. Live there what do you expect?

Good about getting the kids in school.

Can't argue with a health clinic.

Way it explained to me, sounded like common sense.

Went about everything all wrong.

Learn some English.

Learn some Spanish.

Wanted to sue somebody, can you believe it?

He put out that hand, he know they done wrong.

Has some good points.

Not going to get any easier. Any better for us, we all stick together.

Was something bad going on out there, what I hear.

In the meanwhile, Mike has driven out to Hermelinda's camp, but the Salmerons are not to be found, and for a moment he thinks they are gone until Iggy, the crewleader, tells him otherwise.

"Church," Iggy says.

"How 'bout that. I was there this morning."

"You go to church?" Iggy grins.

"I did this morning."

"I know about that," Iggy says, and they chat on a little bit before Mike goes back to his truck. He sits there for a little while and then writes a note on the back of a gas receipt, puts it on the steps of Hermelinda's trailer with a rock on it. He drives back to the Center.

For Mike, in this calm eye in the storm, there doesn't seem to be any reason that things can't get better, no reason that time and character will not win out. That the legacy of years and place and color and class and wealth might start to resolve themselves, to sand off their rough abrasive edges because of a fight and a handshake.

Mike pulls into the Center's parking lot, kills the engine, but doesn't get out of the car. He looks out into the tobacco fields past the Center and tells himself a story: A boy returns home, cranes his head around, and with his new inside-outside eyes says, Something is wrong here. Some believe him. Some suspect him. He ignores everyone and everything he knows. He turns on his friends, his family, his enemies. He falls in love despite them all. He arms himself with documents, with far-off allies, with strangers, with ideas from other places and other times. He prepares for battle.

Some of his neighbors ready themselves for battle, digging into the shadowed trenches on their own land.

And then the battle slips away. It slips away into disappearances, into quiet trysts, into pieces of paper, into an evening fight between boys, into churches, and when it is over there seems like some possibility that it all adds up to something decent after all.

Outside of Mike's truck, all over Jackson County, that is what Sunday night would like everyone to think. But that is not the way.

23RD

THE DOOR OPENS, swings down like a drawbridge, and when it closes again the package sits in the cramped heated darkness with two envelopes. One of the envelopes contains a bill from Duke University, a bill with numbers fantastic, and that bill, despite everything (the size of the numbers, the tumult of the summer, the regrets, the doubts, the combustion), will be paid promptly and on time. The other envelope is addressed to Dolores Olive in a curly, messy hand. It may be a card from a relative, or a handwritten note from an old friend. In any case, no one is ever going to read it.

The package is an elongated rectangle, an amazing and precise fit into the bay of the mailbox. Across the face of the box a computer-printed mailing label has been taped on tight and says: Clayton Olive, R.R. #1, Box 257, Cottesville, NC. There is a border, perhaps, a double line of trim around the return address. Black printing, blue border, red trim? Maybe the return address is Barron's Seed Company, Wattleboro, KY. Maybe it says: FRAGILE KEEP COOL. Surely it says: THIS END UP.

Inside the box, a battery is linked by two wires to the dual prongs of a metal pin. The current dances out in either direction, trying to complete a loop. The current reaches each fork

of the pin and hurries towards the clip where the heads of the
two sides join. The heads are fed by the wires and are ready to
conduct the current across except for a thin plastic chip which
separates the two contact points.

Under what circumstances would that chip depart and leave
the two contact points free to connect?

For instance: if the box were opened from the top, the move-
ment of the cardboard would pull one of six wires looped
through the thin plastic disc. Those six wires are taut and
tightly taped and glued to the underside of the cardboard top.
If that top opens, as it should, as packages are meant to be
opened, the wires pull and the chip withdraws, slips from the
tensioned grip of the metal pin. The heads click and connect
and the current goes and the circuit is complete.

The box sits in darkness and waits for the mailbox door to
open. But the door does not open. Instead there is the rough
approach of an engine, and a voice that shouts: "Goddamn there
goes Dickerson again with a moon shot over centerfield wall!"
Then the side of the mailbox collapses violently and it leaps from
its longtime post. The top of the box is jarred, twisted, and the
plastic chip between the current is wrenched and finally, after all
the precarious miles, removes itself. The current stretches and
kicks itself through the contacts, and the circuit is complete.

Crack. Explode.

24TH

IN THE SAME moment that Mike smells something, something foul that stirs him from sleep, Father Joe, clad only in
underwear and a long shirt, sweeps into the bunk room like a

sirocco, yelling, "Get out, everyone out!" and Mike's first thought is not of himself or Sarah or Cynthia or Raúl or the rest of them but the papers, the computer disks, the spoils of the summer sitting in the office. He reaches down and pulls on his pants as the others race from the room, and throws his shirt on as he steps into the hallway. Father Joe has already gone for the other bunkroom, for the women, and the hall is all smoke and classmates out there. They are ahead of him a little bit, in various stages of undress, and Mike follows them down the stairs. At the bottom of the stairs he can feel the heat pouring past, but instead of cutting through the kitchen with the rest he takes a hard turn and runs down the hallway towards the heat. It's the east side of the building that's on fire, he calculates, the side facing the road, the common rooms, the Ping-Pong room, who knows what else. He reaches the office door and pushes it open. For an instant he sees the room as it is, shrunken and smoking, with the papers curling on the desk and the months of interviews rolling themselves up and yellowing like ancient maps, but that is only an instant before he feels the room inhale the oxygen all around him in one quick gasp and then everything, his entire world, ignites. The flames leap out past his body and when he jumps back hard into what he thinks will be thin air a pair of strong arms are pulling him out and away. He shrugs himself out of the arms and runs, the arms running beside him, as they whip through the hallways. They hit the back doors together, half dragging each other into the open air, and stumble like old boxers across the dry dirt. Mike and Father Joe stop and breathe and cough and check themselves for damage. Over the crest of the roof, at the front of the building, they can see flames flicking towards the sky.

In the parking lot, Sarah is counting heads, and when she sees Mike and Father Joe coming towards the group she says, "That's it, that's everyone." All the students are examining one another like grooming monkeys, looking for signs of serious hurt and finding none. They stand and watch it burn. Cars and trucks begin to arrive behind them, but there's nothing anyone can do. It seems like a long time before the fire unit from Cottesville sirens its way to the front of the crowd. The students and Mike and the neighbors watch the Center burn. There is no wind, not a wisp of it, as if the whole earth were holding its breath, so despite the long flames the fire does not spread beyond the structure itself. All along the edge of the property the fields are visible, as the fire puts a smoke-filtered orange haze over the tobacco and watermelon rows. The plants closest to the building are wilting in the heat but do not burn. Mike watches.

"Everyone all right?" comes the familiar voice from behind him.

"Yes," Mike tells his father, not taking his eyes off the flames. They're beautiful, he thinks, staring into their black and shifting centers, blinding himself. He stares, and feels the slow, soft pressure of Hermelinda's arms around him, and for a moment he is in the center of the flame with her, standing in the dark migrant camp last night, entwined. He hears her whisper his name. He smells her skin and hair and breath.

One of the firemen brusques by Mike, hits him shoulder to shoulder, and spins him like a revolving door, and what Mike sees as he turns is not Hermelinda but the bewilderment and horror of his fellow students, one by one. There's a picture, he thinks, George is going to hate to have missed this one, back in Durham with his ribs, watching the late movie or whatever. A picture that would be a testament to the fact that they can't believe it, not really, that they don't believe in these kinds of consequences. Mike believes, though, and feels it down where his deepest breaths go, he knew it before Blue Dickerson, and the Stop N' Go, and the mailbox, something in him has always known about the violence of this land that roams unchecked in the August darkness of Jackson County. He has felt it in the

vibrations of his arm as he swung the crowbar to the side of the
Dickersons' truck and in the blows that rained down upon him
in the lot of the Stop N' Go. How many steps is it from a truck
to a knee to a head? He looks beyond the students and there he
sees the face of Brackford Dickerson standing next to his
brother Blue, and Mr. Bowman, and Carl, and Jimmy, and he
looks to the place where Ox would be standing, where Harvey
should be. There is Zebulon Hough, his postal pants pulled on
in haste, mumbling to himself, already telling himself this story
of the fire and trying to bring it into line with a larger moral,
and there is Eddie too, shaking his head. Jake and Martha
Joyner stand beside him, watching like the rest. Mr. Tate, Mr.
Hunt. They are all there, all of them except dead Harvey,
wounded Ox, the wives told to stay in bed or tucked in tight of
their own accord. Everyone is there, again, for the third time in
two days: the mailbox, the hospital, the Catholic Retreat
Center. He sees his father now standing alone, and beyond his
father he sees his father's land, that section of Worten's old
plantation called the Nile where a million silent roots are grop-
ing downwards into the rich soil, where plants will be stripped
and killed and rise again year after year after year, where he
and his father and Harvey and Brack and Iggy and Francisco
and Alejandro and Manuel have all worked at one time or
another, and he wonders: Who will be working there in a hundred or a hundred hundred years? What will they grow? Will
Cottesville have another Eddie, a Harvey, a Clayton, a Mike?
He keeps turning until he has come full circle and again is
watching the men dwarfed by the fire as they work the hoses.
They spray, but the building burns quickly, in a mad dance of
soot and orange.

"I'm sorry, Joe," Mike says. "I'm going to do everything in
my power—"

"What power? What are you going to do? You've already
done plenty, you ignorant fool."

Mike watches Joe for a moment but the father has nothing more to say. Then Mike nods, once, and walks away from the crowd, disappearing into the fields beyond the burning building. Sarah sees him go, swears softly to herself, and starts after him.

"Let him go," Mike's father says. "I'll look after him. You take care of these others."

The building burns. The poinciana cracks and pops and curls and disapears into ash, as the walls shrink and fade behind a film of flames. When it is finally over, only the charred skeleton of the Center remains. The lone tree still stands in the middle of the phantom courtyard, its leaves and limbs burned off, the green wood spitting and popping in the heat. The Cottesville collected retreat to their trucks, and their headlights angle and slice through the smoke as they back up and turn towards home.

When Mike returns from the blackness to the pavement of the parking lot, the students are gone as well. He stands next to his father, watching the men pull in their hoses.

"Sarah said to call her at her apartment," Mike's father says. "They all headed back to Durham."

"That's good, that's a good idea."

His father nods. "Everyone's all right."

"Joe did good," Mike says. His father has turned and is stepping back towards his truck. Mike follows him slowly. "I don't think they were trying to kill," Mike says, "whoever did it. Just put the fear in us."

"There's plenty of fear to go around, I guess," Clayton says. They reach the truck and stop, stand there for another while before his father speaks again. "Let's go home. Your momma's back there."

WHEN THEY WALK in the front door it's almost four in the morning. Clayton locks the door behind them. In the sudden clean of the immaculate hallway, they can smell themselves, the soot and smoke on their clothes and in their hair. They must smell like that last tree standing, Mike thinks, they smell like the smoke winding up through the lights of the fire truck into the sky. In the hallway for a moment, they hesitate, unsure of what to do, and then his father says, "Wait here," and climbs the stairs to the second floor.

Mike wanders into the living room. There, on the mantel, are pictures of him and his family. He knows the pictures as well as he knows every other inch of the house, but when he puts both hands on the mantel and examines them now, he feels he's walked into the wrong house. He hardly recognizes anyone. In the first picture on the left, his father is unbelievably young, young and tall and standing alone, looking serious, almost grim, a look he takes to the next picture, where Clayton is sitting in a chair beside Mike's mother. Another picture over, in the middle of the mantel, his father is the same and Mike's mother has gone plump, and now here's the beginning of Mike. Little Mike grins out at him, cocky as a little prince, and then grows before his eyes from picture to picture, like a jerky cartoon frame by frame. The last picture in the series was taken at the end of his freshman year in front of the gothic scape of the Duke Chapel, and despite the photograph's fact of his same eyes and nose and chin it's hard for Mike to place this young man on the same continuum with the Mike standing in this living room, standing and stinking, wondering what to do.

He moves away from the mantel and starts to sit on the couch, thinks better of it in his filthy state, and finally settles down on the bare floor, crossing his legs Indian-style, making sure his body does not smear or smudge anything carpeted or upholstered.

When his father comes back downstairs, he's wearing a fresh knit shirt, short-sleeved and green, and is carrying his shotgun. He sits on the couch and puts the gun across his knees.

"I told your momma you're all right," Clayton says.

Mike nods. "Good. Okay." They study each other, the boy sitting on the floor, cross-legged, the father sitting stiff and straight on the couch, looking down at his son.

"I have to live here, Mike."

"I know it."

"Okay." His father looks at his hands, and then raises his head, and his face is heavy, the skin sagging off his cheeks and jowls, and his eyes look like they hurt. All the youth of the picture-studded mantel is gone, and Mike wonders how long that's been so. His father accepts the gaze and then says quietly, "You have to go."

"When?"

"Tomorrow." The word sits between them, hangs like a feather on a current of air.

"What," Mike starts, looks down at his hands spread out against the dull red rug, "what did you think I was going to be? Turn out? Not like this, I guess."

"I don't know. But you know what, I'm not worried about you." Mike looks at his father with surprise and relief, but his father is more serious and stern and hard than any picture on any wall. "Listen, stop thinking about yourself, all right? For just one minute. And not the workers, either, because you got yourself mixed up with them. Put yourself aside for a second, can you do that?"

"All right," Mike says, just to say something, staring at his hands.

"I can make peace," Clayton says, "and I'm going to. You can do a lot of things, and you will, I think, but you can't make peace, right here, right now. You have to go."

"Okay," Mike says.

"But tonight you stay here." Clayton rises, reaches out with one hand beneath a lampshade, and turns off the light, and Mike finds himself squinting in the sudden dark.

"I think you understand," Mike says. He still can't see his

father, yet, and somehow it makes everything easier. "I mean, we have some arguments but I can't help feeling you're on my side."

Clayton stays quiet and still.

"And not just as a father," Mike says. "As a person. You're a different person from them, and I don't know why."

Clayton doesn't answer right away but when he does it sounds like he's been thinking about what to say.

"We're lucky to have what we have and maybe even to end up who we are. You know, there things that made it possible. We're all of us weak, I think, but maybe when good things come then finally you find the strength to thank God, and you find a little slice of what Christ felt for everyone, no matter who they are. And that's the Dickersons and Bowmans and that's the migrants too."

Mike can see a shadow now, and he watches the shadow that is his father move around the couch towards the front of the house. "I'm proud of you," Clayton says in the dark. "I think you'll do things people don't do. But it's not going to be here. Or not for a long time, anyway. If I can accept that, then you can too." His father has reached the window, and he leans and stoops, peering out through the curtains at the road.

Mike hears it now, as he has heard a thousand cars on a thousand nights roaring by their house on County Route 1012, bound for somewhere, except that this sound does not dissolve but hums to a low rumble in front of the house. Clayton moves into the hallway and turns off the outside light on the front porch, as Mike stands and goes to the window. He can see the orange Bronco stopped on Route 1012, and he hears his father unlock the front door and step out onto the porch. Clayton puts a hand back to let the screen door slap closed softly in his wake.

Mike goes to the door and watches his father walking down the pathway towards the black circle in the grass near the once exploded mailbox, where on the pocked and singed pavement Blue Dickerson's truck idles with its lights off. Clayton walks with his gun pointed down at the ground, his hand wrapped around the middle near the trigger. And Mike closes his eyes and expects to see blood, but instead he finds images of tan girls drinking beer on well-kept university lawns and multicolored backpacks and fancy bikes, and bespectacled professors with ridiculous vocabularies. No Mexicans, no rednecks, no dirt, no tobacco, no blood, no Cottesville. And then his mind empties of all thoughts and images and as he opens his eyes he is walking, in long quick steps, out the front door which smacks like a cymbal behind him and down the stairs towards his father and the idling truck, where the men are already talking under the murmur of the big Ford V-8.

"Why the hell you want to do that?" Mike can hear Brack Dickerson, and he calculates the other shape as Blue, driving. The cab is so dark inside that he cannot see faces, only shapes.

"Has to be something. Your boy's already dead over it. Because maybe if it was more even from the start, it never would have got so bad."

"What if I just told you to go to hell?" Brack sounds hard and spiteful as he repeats himself, but there is also confusion in his voice, in his voice if not his eyes, which Mike can see now, burning out of the truck at him as he comes even with his father, shoulder to shoulder. Clayton doesn't look at his son.

"You could do that," Clayton says. "That's a choice."

"It could have been him," Brackford says.

He leans out of the car, into the dim light, and Mike cannot remember ever seeing Brack the way he is seeing him now. He sees Harvey there, in the man's eyes, he sees the hardness of Harvey but not the lyric and he is surprised to be thinking it but he thinks, It's worse than losing one of theirs. They lost the best one and they know it.

"It wasn't," Clayton says. "It was your boy. Could have been mine. It could have been me, it could have been you, it could have been you, Blue." The driver shifts on the far side of

B.D. "It could have been Carl, or your other boy. It could still be all of us, we could all just kill each other and get our endings over with. It could have been your land to begin with, and I'm the one sitting in the car tonight with another can of gasoline, you out here. There a million could haves but what we got left is what we got to go on. I'm determined to do it. I will do it. I live here, Brackford, you know that. I live here."

"And him?"

"It's not about him right now. Maybe never was."

In the outskirts of his vision Mike sees the smallest motion and realizes it's his father's hand tightening on the shotgun, the fingers moving into place, the tendons of the hand bulging out over the knuckles from the strain.

"You have my word, Brack," Clayton says. "You know me and I ain't going anywhere. And I know you too. Do I have yours?"

Brack looks behind them at the house Clayton built, where Mike's mother is sleeping. Beyond the house, modern drying sheds sit like parked RVs, and beyond that the long fields grow. Maybe he sees all that before he speaks. Maybe he makes a sort of calculation.

"All right, Clayton," Brack says. "That's the way it's going to be."

"Your word?"

"My word."

"Blue? You vouch for yours?" There's a sound from the driver's side but it's not enough for Clayton. "Blue?"

"Got my word."

"Okay." Clayton's hand relaxes and the gun slides down, the barrel thumps lightly on the ground.

The truck pops into gear. Brack's eyes squint for a moment, and he leans out the window, and for a moment Mike thinks he is going to spit, but instead he looks down and around at the charred grass and earth where the bomb exploded, two days hence. He examines the blackened pavement where his son split and lay and bled to death. He coughs and swallows and coughs again and then the truck jerks forward, off the road onto the shoulder, and then swings in a wide circle and speeds off past the father and son standing in front of their house.

They turn and walk back towards the house. Clayton looks old, stooped and tired, and the gun looks like a cane in his hands. Mike waits, and when they reach the foot of the porch, his father tells him.

"I gave him the Nile," Clayton says. "I'm gonna give it to them."

Mike stares.

"You don't want it," his father says. "I don't want it anymore either. I've got enough without it."

"No."

"I know what I have. It's still a hundred acres for tobacco for us. Plus three twenty-five more of peppers and the rest. You think we deserve it more than them? Maybe. It could be. And it might not."

"You can't do that."

"You want it? You going to come get it? You going to make it into something more than dirt? No, you're not."

"They," Mike says. He can't get any further.

"Harvey's dead," Clayton said. "For no reason at all."

"Harvey is dead because," Mike says. "Because of evil."

"Evil? Well." Clayton looks out over the fields below the house while Mike waits for him to speak again. "It still seems kind of arbitrary, doesn't it. Come on, Mike, it's not so goddamn simple."

Clayton's voice is shaking, a little bit, and Mike's hands are shaking too. He puts them under his arms to keep them steady, like a man standing in the cold. "Do you remember when you brought me out to the migrant camp to fix a roof when I was a kid?" he says.

"Brought you out lots of times."

"No, this was the first, I think. We were out there and you were talking to these guys and you put me up on the roof to nail it down. They were all back from work, tired, hanging out, laughing at me. I couldn't do it, you know, the hammer was too big, but I was trying as hard as I could. You left me up there for a while and then you took me down. I was so mad. And what I remember, I'll never forget, when we were going home and I asked you why those stupid niggers lived there, you told me I sounded ignorant talking like that, and you refused to live with an ignorant person in your house. Do you remember that?" His father doesn't say anything or make a sign, but Mike can tell he's remembering. "And I said they stink, and you said that none of us smell too good at the end of a long day. And I said they were lazy and you said there's a little lazy everywhere. No matter what I said you wouldn't let me hate them. But I hated them until I got old enough to be ashamed. You did that. You made sure."

Clayton's still looking out down the road, where the Dickerson truck has long since disapeared, and Mike realizes his father's hands are shaking too.

"Just tell me honestly," Mike says. "Tell me that you can imagine Blue or B.D. ever saying that to their sons. No matter how much luck or land they ever had. Tell me they didn't treat those migrants like shit. That they're any good."

"Who knows if the circumstances were moved around," his father says. "We got to have peace. To leave the past alone. And move on."

"But can you hear them ever saying that?"

"Maybe I can," Clayton says. "It's hard to know everything about everybody. I can hear something. Now let's go inside." He starts up the porch stairs. "Things do change, I know that," he says as he opens the door. "You know that, don't you, Michael."

And Mike passes through the front door of his childhood and climbs the stairs to his old room, where he does not sleep but does not move either in his bed. He tries to think but nothing in his head will stay still long enough for him to recognize it until, finally, the only thing he can hold is a time hunting with Harvey, walking next to each other in the woods in the quiet and then the sudden chaos when they saw a squirrel and shot. They were nine, maybe. They both hit it in the head. When they got up to the remains there wasn't much of a head left, and they argued over who hit it first. "It's yours," Harvey said finally. "Who wants a damn squirrel without a head."

He wakes up when the light begins to come up outside. He gets out of bed and puts on his pants, his shirt, and even before the sun has crested the trees to the east, Mike is at the edge of his father's fields, head down, his feet flying over the tractor ruts in the dry earth. He runs as fast as he can, but when he gets to the migrant camp, they are already gone.

BEACH

SHE SMOOTHS HER skirt down over her hips and thighs, swings the huge door open, and slides into the car. She takes the enormous steering wheel in her hands, gauging its weight and size, and then reaches underneath to the key and turns. The key moves smoothly past the angle of resistance, breaking the surface and submerging itself in the thick, viscous power of the engine, which booms and then murmurs way deep down on the register, like a great quantity of water passing through an enormous drain. She touches a small black button on the dash and the roof moves above her and retracts, folding neatly into a tidy accordion in the back, and the bright sun begins to heat the right side of her face, her nape, her neck. It's a clean, sharp heat, a Mexican heat. She loves it. She puts the car into gear and slowly, so slowly that the car seems to protest, she carves a wide circle in the clearing and rolls down the slight incline of the ruddy dirt track through the fields.

She reaches the main road, this straight black line that heads through the small town or off into nothing. Depending how she turns, this road can take her almost anywhere, and she is about to make up her mind when she sees him. He grows as he approaches, until he is almost full-size, running, his head thrown back, his arms loose, his stride long, let out as far as it can go, and she wonders why he doesn't run for her more. He is a beautiful runner. He looks taller, then, and lean, he looks healthy at a full gallop. He runs erotically. He has spotted her now but his pace remains the same, fast and even. He grows.

She can't help but smile. She waves to him, and then takes her foot off the brake and turns the car to the right, away from the town, and begins to drive slowly down the road, watching him in her rearview mirror. She laughs. She calls to him over her shoulder, hooks an arm back, waves. He's close now. He can almost touch the car. When she looks in the rearview mirror, she can see his eyes, very big, very blue.

When she checks again, the eyes are gone. He is gone, and she feels her breath stop for a moment until she sees him beside her now, keeping pace, running in the lane beside her. The engine hums low and his feet slap against the pavement, whap, whap, whap, like his own personal pistons, and she is very happy with this combination of sounds, and happy to have him close, beside her, running.

They pass his parents' house and more tobacco fields, and then they pass the small shed where the two of them have lain together, alone, and they watch these worlds pass by in unison while the air rushes by them. They begin to pick up speed. She watches him run. The muscles in his arms and legs bulge and then relax, appear and disappear, his shoulders swing forward and then back. She waves at him again.

"I love the way you run for me!" she shouts against the wind and the hum and the pounding of his piston feet.

He can't hear her, shakes his head.

"I love you," she simplifies, at the top of her lungs, not worrying if it's exactly true or not, just yelling.

He points at her, and she can see his lips move. He doesn't have the air for it, but she can see he's agreeing with her.

"Yes!" she shouts, nodding. "Now run, baby, run!" He runs.

It's like that for a while until what they both know is going to happen happens. He starts to slow a little, or she accelerates, it's hard to tell, but the moment it happens, the moment he falls back just a little, he stops cold, vanishes from the space beside her. She turns in her seat. She can see him there behind her, in the middle of the road, his hands on his knees, his head up, breathing hard, watching her away, and she lifts one arm above her head and points, ahead of her and up to the hot Mexican sun moving across the sky. Her foot leans into the accelerator, and in no time at all, he is gone. His absence is sad, but it seems true, anyway.

She drives. The country is unfamiliar to her. There are sections thick with trees, and then fields, and even mountains, where the road winds but there aren't any other cars and she does not need to slow down. She comes out of the mountains onto the flats and there, ahead of her, she can see a structure rising high above the surface of the earth, catching the light. When she gets closer she sees that it's a bridge of gleaming steel and angled girders, standing like a huge frozen horse ankle-deep in the water below, and she crosses it and keeps driving along the last short spit of land until she has to stop but she does not stop. She drives off of the pavement and onto the soft sand, heading towards the edge of the water where the waves crumble into foam, and even then she doesn't stop, smiling to herself as the engine goes silent beneath the water. The car slows and then sinks. She falls with the car, down through the water, down and down until a warm current lifts her from her seat and carries her gently to the surface, where she tilts back her head and breathes enormously. She licks the salt from her lips and smiles. She can feel the blood coming out of her into the water, she looks and cannot see it but she can feel it, and she closes her eyes and accepts the relief. The water is warm around her and the bleeding feels like both an indulgent pleasure and an exchange. A certainty. An end.

She watches the shore and floats and drifts down the coast until she sees an empty beach of sand and brightly colored glass, with a tall thick tree shading a patch of grass dotted by

tiny yellow weeds. Then she strips off her shirt and her blood-
stained pants, watches her clothes sink and drift away, and
reaches out her arms and swims, steadily. She pulls herself
towards the shore with determination, her head up, looking for
her chosen spot where she will lie down and fall asleep in the
warm sun to dream.